He was a quiet high s
gang member. And o

LIZ

Young, blonde, and beautiful, she had a knack for picking the wrong men. But when she fell in love with Bobby Nauss, it was more than a mistake . . .

• • •

THE WARLOCKS

Drug dealing and gang rape were their specialties. They murdered each other, anyone that came between them, and especially young women. Between 1971 and 1975 they were involved in as many as eight killings.

• • •

A SECOND CHANCE

In 1983 Bobby Nauss, serving a sentence for murder, escaped from a maximum security prison. While desperate law enforcement officials scrambled to find him, Bobby began a second life and was known to his friends, family, and neighbors as a decent, generous man. But had he really changed—or was he still a Warlock at heart?

• • •

BORN TO BE WILD

• • •

"Like a disco ball stuffed with dynamite, **BORN TO BE WILD** is an explosive portrait of killer Bobby Nauss and an era when biker gangs hustled for drugs and women while terrifying the towns they called home. Author Bowe has jam-packed his first book with details that signal he investigated the case firsthand—no cut and paste job here."
—**Gregg Olsen, author of *Bitter Almonds***

A main selection of True Crime Book Club™

BARRY BOWE

BORN TO BE WILD

WARNER BOOKS

A Time Warner Company

To My Mother
With Love, Gratitude, and Appreciation

WARNER BOOKS EDITION

Copyright © 1994 by Barry Bowe
All rights reserved.

Cover design by Elaine Groh
Cover photographs by Craig, Urban Archives, Temple University, Philadelphia, Pennsylvania

Warner Books, Inc.
1271 Avenue of the Americas
New York, NY 10020

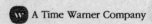 A Time Warner Company

Printed in the United States of America

First Printing: June, 1994

10 9 8 7 6 5 4 3 2 1

ACKNOWLEDGMENTS

A million thanks to Bob Leschoron. Through his efforts, the U.S. Department of Justice and the United States Marshals Service opened all of their unclassified files and investigative information pertinent to this case for my use. The only things withheld were the names of confidential informants. In addition, Ken Briggs, Steve Quinn, and Janet Doyle were made available to interview. My thanks go out to them for their extensive cooperation.

Special thanks to Tom Rapone, who made himself available to me.

Special thanks to Frank Hazel for providing the nuts and bolts of the mammoth undertaking that was the Delaware County Major Crimes Task Force. To George Ellis and Raleigh Witcher. To Tony Truscello and Jimmy Flick. To Joe Washlick at Philly P.D.'s Special Investigations Unit. To Bob Snyder for hooking me up with Witcher. To Karl Lunkenheimer. To Paul Schneider and Bobby Kline. To Jimmy DelBello.

All of these dedicated lawmen possessed an especially vivid recall of the events that took place and had the ability to go on and on. . . .

Special thanks to John Walsh, Jack Breslin, Burk Stone and *America's Most Wanted*.

Special thanks to Eliot Kaplan, Mike Mallowe, and *Philadelphia* magazine.

Special thanks to Peggy Chance and Kim Reynolds at the Delaware County *Daily Times*' library. To the *Daily Times*. To Rose Quinn. To Urban Archives at Temple University. To Gale Kaplan at the Ridley library.

Special thanks to Danielle Dean and the Domestic Relations staff at the Delaware County Courthouse.

Special thanks to Lisa Gamler and Tom Duffy at Cardinal Printing.

Special thanks to John Cappelletti—Heisman Trophy winner, All-American, All-Pro, and classmate of Bobby Nauss—for providing me with insight into the mind-set of male adolescents growing up during the 1960s. To other classmates who filled in vital details. To Dick Rosemblum, Liz Lande's high school biology teacher.

To Luna Pier residents who shall remain nameless.

To others I cannot name.

Special thanks to Connie Clausen, my agent. To Mauro DiPreta, my editor at Warner. To Justine Elias. To Rick Horgan. To Rose Mandelsberg. To Mike DeNoia, my high school English teacher, mentor, and role model. To Larry Hofmeister, my lawyer, who's done everything pro bono—so far.

To the memory of my mother, who encouraged me to undertake this project, read every manuscript from the 700-page first draft to the 400-page final draft—then died a year before she could see the finished product.

Without the contributions of all of these people—and, I'm afraid, several more I've inadvertently omitted—this book would not have been written. Although a minimal number of scenes have been condensed and dramatized to compress time and space, minimize confusion, and ease the flow of words and understanding, this story about Bobby Nauss remains as faithful as possible to the public record of events that actually transpired over more than twenty years.

My heart goes out to the Nauss family, to the Ferrer family, to the Lande family, and to the families of all the victims. They are good people who we'd probably never had read the first word about had it not been for the transgressions of one man.

Something out there is killing them. Something dark and menacing and conspiratorial is damning them, young and beautiful, to shallow graves in the oozing mud of Tinicum marsh. Something profitable enough or powerful enough or perverse enough to have killed five times is still at work and this killing machine, this terribly efficient apparatus of death, is still unknown.

—Mike Mallowe
Philadelphia magazine
May 1976

PART ONE

The Marsh Murders

December 1971–December 1975

CHAPTER

1

Bobby Nauss was making love to his girlfriend at 2:30 in the morning. This was Folcroft, Pennsylvania, two miles outside the Philadelphia city limits, and it was Monday, December 13. The year was 1971. The Age of Aquarius.

A few minutes later, with beads of perspiration still on his forehead, he was standing outside a friend's door, knocking so loud it sounded like a matter of life and death.

Bobby was five months shy of his twentieth birthday, a skinny kid with a boyish face who hadn't begun to fill out yet. He was five feet eight and weighed only 128 pounds. He looked too clean-cut to be a member of a motorcycle gang, but his black leather jacket, black leather boots, and dungarees gave him away.

Sound asleep inside the apartment was one of Bobby's best friends. His name was Bill Standen, although Bobby always called him Stanley.

Standen was twenty-one years old. An eighth-grade dropout, he worked for a door-manufacturing company, preparing doors for the installation of hardware. He was six inches taller than Bobby, but just as skinny, and he was hoping that someday soon Bobby would nominate him for membership in the motorcycle gang.

Bobby succeeded in waking up Standen, but he also woke up Standen's wife, who became upset because someone was knocking on their door in the middle of the night.

"There's nothing wrong," Standen grumbled to her, "just go back to bed." Then he walked down the hall, through the kitchen, and opened the door to let Bobby in.

"Stanley," Bobby said, almost out of breath, "I want to show you something."

"Can't it wait till morning?" Standen asked, hoping to get rid of Bobby fast and get back into his warm bed.

"No, you have to come now," Bobby told him, and the way Bobby said it, Standen knew he meant it.

"Okay."

"Out back in the garage," Bobby specified.

"Okay, I'll be right out."

When Bobby left, Standen crawled back into bed.

Bill Standen and his wife lived in an apartment at 1564 Chester Pike. The pike was the main drag through town and two buildings stood end-to-end on their side of the street. One of the buildings stood four stories tall, the other only two stories, and they housed a string of storefronts and apartments. Aside from the mailman and the paperboy, not many people in town knew the eight or ten families who lived in the apartments above the stores—or paid much attention to their comings and goings.

The pike bustled with traffic during the day. It died at night, forsaken during the midnight hours by the car dealers, gas stations, and a day-care center that checkerboarded the two buildings. A narrow driveway between the buildings led from the pike to a secluded garage another fifty feet behind the apartments, which was where Bobby was waiting for Bill Standen on that mild December night.

As soon as his wife fell asleep, Standen slipped out of bed, got dressed, and went outside. As he walked through the moonless night, he wondered what could be so important to Bobby that it couldn't wait until morning. When he reached the garage, he entered. It was pitch-black inside and the smell of stagnant oil was heavy in the air. Suddenly a tiny flame appeared in the darkness above him.

"Up here," Bobby called out. He was holding a candle and its flickering glimmer highlighted Bobby's face in a spectrum of blacks and yellows. "Come on up."

The stairway leading to the loft was retractable. Standen tugged on a rope and pulled it down. Then he climbed the steps slowly, each tread creaking as his weight shifted from one to the next. By the time he reached the top step, his eyes had adjusted to the darkness.

Bobby was standing a few feet away and the candle was the only illumination upstairs.

"Stanley," Bobby said calmly, "look what I've done here." As Bobby was talking, he took a few steps away from Standen, farther into the shadows. Then Bobby raised the candle so Standen could see what he was talking about.

A nude woman was hanging from the rafters. A rope was around her neck and her head was drooping, tilted downward at a grotesque angle. Long billows of golden hair were hanging down and she was white as a sheet. Her jaw was slack and slobber was drooling out of her mouth. Her toes were dangling two feet above the wooden floor. It was Bobby's girlfriend and it was apparent to Bill Standen that she was dead.

"I killed her," Bobby said smugly. "I hung her. Now she won't bother me anymore."

"I'm getting the hell out of here," Standen said.

"I want you out of here!" Bobby shouted. "Get the fuck out of my sight!"

Standen hurried down the stairs, back to his apartment.

But Bobby just stood there holding the candle. Staring at the body. Grinning.

CHAPTER
2

Elizabeth Lande always went to the beauty parlor on Saturdays. On this particular Saturday, December 11, 1971, shortly before noon, she walked out of the family home with her mother and father.

Elizabeth—usually called Liz or Lizzie—was twenty-one years old and lived with her parents in the Overbrook Park section of Philadelphia. She was completing her first semester as a full-time student at Philadelphia Community College and final exams were starting on Monday.

"Make sure you study over the weekend," her mother told her as they walked. To Liz, it seemed like the millionth time her mother had said the same thing in the past hour. Her parents were leaving for a week's cruise and Liz was going to be on her own for the first time in her life.

"Don't worry," Liz said, raising her voice, "I will."

Liz walked her parents to the car. It was an awkward farewell and there was no kissing. Liz simply waved goodbye as they pulled away, then walked to her noon beauty appointment.

She was five feet tall and weighed 110 pounds, proportioned just so, green eyes with a peachy complexion and pearly teeth, straight and even, a face pretty enough to have competed in a handful of teenage beauty contests. But it was her blond hair that was her trademark, long and luxurious, cascading over her shoulders, wavy at the ends.

After a wash and set, Liz came home and addressed her Christmas cards. She dropped them in a mailbox, then studied for a while. For dinner, she ate a container of strawberry yogurt.

That evening, she invited two friends over and they spent the night talking and watching TV. Liz was wearing a pink nightgown, her hair was up in rollers, and she had cold cream on her face. A creature feature was playing on Channel 10 and Venus, the sickly cat Liz had adopted from an animal shelter and nursed back to health, jumped onto the sofa and settled into Liz's lap.

Around midnight, the phone rang. It was Bobby Nauss and he asked Liz to spend the weekend with him. What the hell, he told Liz, her parents were gone, they couldn't hassle her, and they'd never find out. Besides, Stanley and his wife had taken off for the weekend and they could use Stanley's apartment.

Liz told Bobby she wasn't dressed, he'd have to give her time to get ready.

Because of Bobby's reputation and the late hour, Liz's friends became concerned. They tried to talk her into staying home, but had no luck. So they gave up and went home.

Liz went upstairs, where her quarters occupied most of the second floor, which had been remodeled by her parents into a two-room apartment. One room had a desk and some bookshelves, the other room was a bedroom with teddy bears on the bed and posters of Jimi Hendrix and Janis Joplin on the walls. There was also a private bath and Liz had her own telephone line.

Liz was compulsive about some things. She kept her beauty aids and cosmetics in a neatly organized tray, she ate health foods and took diet pills to maintain her figure, and she was meticulous about her personal habits and appearance. It seemed to take forever whenever she got dressed and that night was no exception.

At 1:50 A.M., a neighbor directly across the street heard a noise outside. He'd been getting ready for bed, but stopped what he was doing, pushed the curtains aside, and looked out the front window. A gold Toronado had pulled up to the curb and was sitting there, its motor running.

The neighbor watched Liz walk out her front door a few moments later. She was wearing a long brown coat, bell-bottom jeans, and platform shoes—the wooden heels clomping like a horse's hooves on the concrete sidewalk. She opened the Toronado's passenger door, got inside, and the car drove away.

By that time, her parents had flown to Miami and were aboard an ocean liner on the turquoise Caribbean Sea, more than a thousand miles from Philadelphia. Their itinerary included some of the most romantic destinations in the northern hemisphere—Puerto Rico, Saint Thomas, Guadeloupe, Barbados, Saint Lucia, Antigua, and Saint Martin.

Frank Lande was fifty-two years old and stood several inches under six feet tall, a stocky, balding man with a confident stride and a bulldog's determination. He worked as a complaint manager at a film processing center in the city, where he solved customers' problems and tried to turn complaints into compliments. Frank was good at his work, a troubleshooter with a knack for getting to the bottom of things.

Frances Lande, at forty-nine, was as dark-haired as her daughter was blond, and she weighed a few more pounds than made her happy. Although not unattractive, she no longer spent hours in front of a mirror primping and preening.

Frank married Frances in 1942, but their marriage was interrupted almost at once. At Uncle Sam's request, Frank went off to fly daredevil missions as a World War II Army Air Corps fighter pilot. A few years later, the Japanese surrendered and Frank returned home. Since they'd never really had a honeymoon, now that Liz was old enough to take care of herself, they were indulging themselves with a luxurious vacation.

For the next six days, beneath a tropical sky, they smeared suntan lotion on their bodies and lounged in deck chairs around the pool. At each port of call, they dressed in bright clothing, left the ship to go on duty-free shopping sprees, and snapped pictures of every tourist attraction they encountered. In the evenings, they fancied up their attire and gambled in the casinos, took in floor shows, and danced in the nightclubs. And at every turn, there was all that sumptuous food, which they ate while swearing oaths to begin dieting just as soon as they returned home.

Frank and Frances Lande arrived home on Saturday, December 18, somewhere between 6 and 7 P.M. They lived at 7651 Overbrook Avenue, in a tree-lined neighborhood of two-story brick row houses, with manicured lawns in front and paved alleyways behind.

Frank unlocked the door, but it resisted when he tried to push it open. He shoved harder until it gave way. Mail was piled behind the door.

As soon as Frank stepped into the living room, Venus ran up and tangled itself between Frank's feet, almost tripping him. The cat was mewing pitifully. To Frank, it sounded as if Venus were starving to death.

At the same time, Frances was stooping down and picking up the mail. What she saw mostly were a lot of unopened Christmas cards addressed to Liz.

Frank and Frances went directly upstairs.

As they stood in Liz's bedroom, giving it the once-over, they thought it looked exactly the same as when they'd left a week earlier. Liz's schoolbooks were on the nightstand, unmoved, her bed was made, and its unruffled covers told them it had not been slept in all week.

Frances inventoried Liz's makeup tray. It was a box with

holes in it and each item had its own place. Everything was there—false eyelashes, mascara, makeup, nail polish. Everything except Liz's lipstick, which, Frances knew, Liz always kept in her pocketbook.

They looked in Liz's bureau drawers and in her closets. Everything seemed to be there. The only items of clothing that were noticeably missing were Liz's favorite pair of platform shoes and an overcoat, which Frances described as a brown cloth maxi with black curly fake lamb's fur around the hem and up the front.

When they went back downstairs, as Frank fed the cat, he realized the house was chilly. He turned up the thermostat, then went into the basement to see if Liz's suitcases were still there. They were.

Meanwhile, Frances picked up the phone and called her mother, who lived a couple of blocks away. Was Liz there? Had she seen her? Then she called Bobby Nauss's mother. Was Liz with Bobby? Had she seen Liz?

In addition to the outgoing calls, Frances answered four or five incoming calls from Liz's friends.

But no one had seen her all week.

Around 11 P.M., Frank and Frances went to bed, but anxiety kept them tossing and turning most of the night.

Liz Lande was a "Baby Boomer." Born in 1950, her recollections of childhood were all pleasant. Her parents loved her. Life was uncomplicated.

All through school, she was an average student. At thirteen, she auditioned for the lead in a repertory theater production of *My Sister Eileen*. She got the part and others followed. While not exactly raves, reviews of her performances were encouraging enough that Liz and her parents began dreaming about her becoming a movie star.

Attractive and popular, she was the kind of girl who got along well with both sexes. All the boys wanted to go out with her and she started dating at fourteen. Her parents trusted her and never once felt the need to limit her contacts with boys.

She avoided any serious relationships until she was seventeen, when she started seeing a boy regularly and fell victim to puppy love. As will happen, he pressured her for sex. Liz resisted until she was afraid of losing him, then she gave in. They had intercourse once and he never called her again. The rejection came as a shock, and Liz was emotionally traumatized. The timing was horrendous.

This was when Martin Luther King was at the peak of his freedom marches across the South. He was sitting-in at lunch counters, riding in the fronts of buses, using rest rooms marked WHITE ONLY, and integrating black youngsters into previously segregated schools. Racial tensions were high. Before long, riots swept through most of the major cities from Los Angeles to Philadelphia and spread into the public school systems.

The kids who lived in Liz's neighborhood attended Overbrook High School in West Philadelphia where seventy percent of the three thousand students were black. Clearly, it was exactly the wrong place for a pretty white face, long blond hair, and a fragile ego. Liz was out of her element and felt threatened. She started coming home with tales of black male students pulling her hair and taunting her. She complained to her father.

"Cut your hair and the *schwartzes* will leave you alone," her father suggested.

"Are you crazy?" she screamed at him. "I'll never cut my hair. Why can't I just go to parochial school?"

"Because you're not Catholic."

"They let Jews in Catholic school nowadays, Daddy," Liz shot back.

"Over my dead body," her father said, and the case was closed.

Liz felt abandoned and started to withdraw. She quit acting. In rebellion, she began associating with a new peer group, teenagers her father described as "troubled kids." She started smoking marijuana and taking pills.

After high school, things got worse. Her only job was at an insurance company and it lasted only three days. Instead of working, Liz stayed home all day and went out with her new friends at night. Her relationship with her mother deteriorated. They argued about anything and everything. Shouting matches. Name calling and threats. Slapping. For the first time in her life, Liz felt completely unloved.

CHAPTER
3

Bobby Nauss's facial features were delicate and his beard was still patchy. His hair was dark and coarse and, like everyone else in the family, he was good-looking.

He lived with his parents in Darby, a mile east of Folcroft. With a population of fifteen thousand, it was a town caught in transition between the city and the suburbs. By city standards, Darby was backyards and barbecues; by suburban standards, it was a roughneck extension of the city. In truth, it was both, just a dot on the map, one of the monotonous blue-collar boroughs that comprised southeastern Delaware County.

With the holidays only a week away, the mood around the Nauss house was festive. The tree was trimmed, the halls were decked with mistletoe and holly, and most of the chitchat was buzzing about which family member wanted what for Christmas. The family's lifestyle was by no means opulent, but nobody wanted for anything. Every year at Christmas, there were plenty of presents under the tree, and the year 1971 would be no different. A favorite among his siblings, Bobby was teased that all he'd find in his stocking would be lumps of coal.

While it was becoming common knowledge that Bobby

13

had joined a motorcycle gang, that topic of conversation went unspoken around the family dinner table. His father had his mind set that Bobby had been raised properly and his mother denied that Bobby would ever dream of doing anything wrong.

But indelible signs of Bobby's new association were his tattoos. In time, there would be a swastika and a naked woman on his left forearm, a huge parrot and wreath on his right upper arm, a skull on his left bicep, and the prophetic epithet BORN TO LOSE scrolled underneath.

The Nausses moved from Philadelphia to Darby around 1950. Bob Nauss, Bobby's father, had married a pretty and smart young woman named Pauline Schladensky a couple of years earlier.

He was a mechanic. Relying on skilled hands, he opened his own business—Bob's Automobile Shop—specializing in transmission repairs. He worked five, six days a week, whatever it took to support his family.

They were good people, Bob and Pauline. The Darby police chief called Bob one of the most respected men in the area, and the neighbors regularly saw them at church.

Robert T. Nauss, Jr., was born in a normal delivery with no complications on May 10, 1952, the third of Bob and Pauline's five girls and three boys. Nancy and Carol came first, Bobby was next, followed by Marianne, Mike, Vinnie, Karen, and Sharon.

For the first nine years of Bobby's life, his family lived on the seamier side of Darby. But by 1961, Bob's business was flourishing. In April of that year, he purchased a house at 1315 Main Street for $24,500—a handsome price at the time. It was a neighborhood of green lawns, mature trees, and well-tended houses that was a far cry from the rest of the borough.

At one end of the block was Fitzgerald Mercy, a hospital run by the Sisters of Mercy, where Pauline attended Sunday afternoon mass in the chapel. At the other end was the Church of the Blessed Virgin Mary, called BVM by its parishioners—gray stone walls, stained-glass windows, a steeple rising majestically in the sky—where Bob usually went to mass on Sunday mornings. Behind the church was the grade school that all the children attended.

Their home was one of the most impressive residences in town, two and a half stories of gray stone and white wooden trim, five to six bedrooms, with a semicircular portico out front and four white columns standing tall. A matching addition extended from one side which, through the years, served as an apartment for one family member or another. To the rear of the property was a triple-wide garage with a loft above.

Bob Nauss was the sole wage earner. That was his job within the family. He came home from work, showered, ate, and watched sports on TV. He drank a beer or two at social functions, but nothing at home. In fact, beer and liquor were rarely, if ever, kept in the house.

Pauline ran the household and raised the children.

All through grammar school, Bobby's classmates described him as a nice guy, someone who'd do anything for a friend. He was well liked and funny, clowning around at times, yet always on the quiet side.

Bobby was a bright boy. He joined the Boy Scouts and played Little League and, as the eldest son, it was assumed he'd take over his father's business one day. At the age of twelve, Bobby started working in the garage after school and on weekends, learning mechanics and getting grease under his fingernails.

By the time he got to high school, Bobby couldn't have cared less about a formal education. He spent his study time at his father's garage or working on his buddies' cars. Yet there was just enough time left over to meet a girl who lived near the shop and start dating. They went to house parties and movies and did all the things normal teenagers do. Before Bobby knew it, he'd fallen in love. In his mind, this was the girl who was going to walk down the aisle beside him in a long white gown, and she was going to be the mother of his children. Three or four would be nice.

By the summer before his senior year, Bobby was an excellent mechanic. He got his hands on a junker of a Grand Prix and tore it apart. He souped it up and started racing it. This was also the summer of 1969, Woodstock summer, when a great many teenagers started experimenting with drugs. Bobby was no exception. He liked to smoke marijuana.

He graduated from Monsignor Bonner High School in 1970. In a class of 609 boys, Bobby was one of the most anonymous members. After four years of high school, there was not one activity listed beneath Bobby's senior picture in the yearbook.

After graduation, he went to work full-time for his father and earned $150–$200 per week. He thought his life was headed in the right direction and then one of the most significant events in his life occurred: His girlfriend broke up with him.

When you're from a small town like Darby and you're only eighteen years old and your girlfriend dumps you for another guy, you feel like your whole world just ended. You think everybody's laughing at you behind your back. You start doubting your manhood. This seemed to be Bobby's state of mind.

For a while, he felt sorry for himself. All he wanted was to love and be loved, get married, raise a family, and live happily ever after. Was that such an impossible dream?

Then he started pointing fingers. He blamed his ex-girlfriend. He blamed his mother because she wore the pants in the family. And he blamed his father because he allowed his mother to wear the pants.

Bobby started drinking heavily and his drug usage progressed from marijuana to methamphetamines. He snorted the meth at first, then began shooting up. He bought a Harley-Davidson motorcycle and he started hanging around with shady characters.

He'd loved and lost. Now Bobby swore it would be a long time before he ever loved or ever trusted another woman.

CHAPTER
4

A year and a half before her disappearance, Liz Lande had an especially emotional quarrel with her parents. It was around 10 P.M. on July 2, 1970, when she locked herself in the bathroom and refused to open the door.

"I'm going to take a whole bottle of pills," Liz yelled through the bathroom door.

When her father heard the water running, he panicked. He ran down to the basement, got a hammer and screwdriver, came back upstairs, and popped the door hinges.

"Ha-ha, I fooled you," Liz said, mocking him. "I was just going to take aspirins."

The very next day, Frank Lande took his daughter to a psychiatrist. Over the next five weeks, Liz was supposed to receive counseling; however, she either arrived late for her appointments or skipped them altogether.

On August 10, describing his daughter as mixed up and troubled and seeing no improvement in her condition, Frank had Liz committed to the Philadelphia Psychiatric Hospital.

Liz's psychiatrist entertained two diagnoses: One, he considered a schizophrenic reaction, paranoid type, in which her personality was split between the reality of adult life and the dependency of childhood. Two, he thought she might be suf-

17

fering from adolescent adjustment reaction. Either way, she
was reverting to childhood.

After extensive consultations, he reached the following
conclusions:

"Every word Elizabeth Lande uttered, every thought she
had, every action she took was directed toward hurting her
parents.

"She would do anything in the world to hurt her mother.

"Elizabeth Lande gets into destructive relationships."

After graduation from high school in 1967, Liz had two
additional sexual relationships. The first lasted about a year,
the second was with a twenty-year-old who was hooked on
heroin. It ended in October 1970 when he went to Florida to
try to kick the habit.

Four months later, in February 1971, Liz met Bobby and
her real problems began.

"I was driving my car through the Sixty-ninth Street area
one night," Bobby later described their encounter, "and I noticed a girl sitting on the curb in front of the Bowlero Bowling Alley. When I stopped, I noticed she was crying. Her
clothes were ripped and she was upset. We talked and she
got in my car. I took her to a gas station and she got fixed up
in the ladies' room. It was about ten o'clock. We went to Kostick's Bar and we drank and talked and left when the bar
closed."

Bobby took her back to his apartment, where they had sex.
Neither one of them was a virgin—she'd had three previous
sexual relationships, Bobby just the one. For Liz, who was
suffering from emotional deprivation, it was love at first
sight. For Bobby, who hadn't gotten over the hurt of his broken romance, Liz was a sex object and nothing more. Liz
spent the night and Bobby dropped her off at home the following morning.

All week long, Liz bragged to her mother about her handsome new boyfriend, how charming he was, and how much

she liked him. The following weekend, they had their first official date.

"I remember the first time he came over the house," Liz's mother said later. "He knocked on the door and I invited him into the living room."

Liz, who was upstairs dressing, ran downstairs.

"Mommy," she said, "this is Bobby." Liz gave him a peck on the cheek, then went back upstairs to finish dressing.

"Hello," Frances said, "have a seat."

Bobby sat down and they spoke briefly.

He seemed okay to Frances.

CHAPTER
5

In the late 1940s in southern California, a group of World War II veterans were having problems adjusting to civilian life. To vent their frustrations, they formed the country's first outlaw motorcycle gang and called themselves the Hell's Angels. By 1967, the Angels had cornered the production and distribution of LSD in the United States and started expanding into Great Britain, the Netherlands, Germany, Denmark, and Australia.

By the 1970s, more than eight hundred outlaw motorcycle gangs had formed in the United States—all patterned after the Hell's Angels: Their illegal activities were conspiratorial, they used violence or threats of violence to achieve their objectives, they insulated their leaders, their primary goal was economic gain, and they used graft to corrupt law enforcement, government agencies, and private individuals. All this translated into criminal activities such as drug and weapons trafficking, prostitution, theft rings, fraud, and assorted racketeering. It also led to the laundering of illegal revenues through investments in legitimate businesses such as motorcycle shops, garages, towing services, security companies, catering firms, adult bookstores, topless lounges, entertainment and escort agencies, and locksmith shops.

* * *

During the summer of 1967, a group of friends were sitting in a Philadelphia coffeehouse. When their conversation got around to motorcycles, somebody suggested forming their own club—bikers always call their groups clubs, never gangs. By that time, nearly every neighborhood in the Philadelphia area had its own motorcycle gang.

Three months later, in October, thirty-seven charter members formed the Warlocks Motorcycle Club, making it the biggest motorcycle gang in the area. They elected a president, vice president, secretary, treasurer, and sergeant-at-arms. They attended weekly meetings and paid weekly dues. They upheld a strict code of silence and formulated rules.

> We are Warlocks and members will follow the Warlocks' way or get out. All members are Brothers and Family. You will not steal your Brothers' possessions, money, women, or honor. If you do, your Brother will do you.

The gang's motto was "One for all and all for one." If a disagreement arose, a fight settled it. Might was right. So the winner was right, the loser wrong. If an outsider, or *citizen* got into a fight with a Warlock, the other gang members turned it into a free-for-all, swarming the outsider like a hungry wolfpack, flooring him, then kicking his head and face—a technique called stomping.

If a member broke the gang's rules, the gang punished him. Penalties ranged from cash fines to beatings to execution.

The Warlocks coat of arms, or colors, consisted of a denim vest with WARLOCKS printed across the top in two-inch red letters. A "1%" insignia and multicolored caricature of a harpy was underneath the lettering. In Greek mythology, a harpy was a winged monster with the head and trunk of a woman and the tail, legs, and talons of a bird. A rapacious and filthy monster, it was seen as a minister of divine vengeance. The 1% symbolized the Warlocks' separation from the other 99% of motorcycle enthusiasts in the country who were considered to be law-abiding citizens.

Colors were to bikers what flags were to countries: sacred. The theft of a gang's colors by a rival gang was a declaration of war.

Members wore German Wehrmacht helmets and iron crosses and christened themselves with exotic or repulsive nicknames. Long hair, bushy sideburns, satanic mustaches, and goatees were common. Three tattoos were mandatory: a swastika, a naked woman, and the words BORN TO LOSE.

The bikers wrapped quarter-inch chains around their bodies, which they used to lock up their motorcycles—unless a fight broke out. Then the chains made excellent weapons with which to flog someone, yet they were not classified as weapons. And they nailed horseshoe cleats to the bottoms of their black leather boots, which inflicted nasty wounds when stomping someone.

Warlocks modified their motorcycles and called them choppers. Riders sat low in the saddle and leaned back against a seat rest, riding in a thronelike posture. The choppers ran without mufflers, which made a single bike sound like rumbling thunder. A pack of Warlocks was a truly intimidating sight and sound.

Membership was by invitation only. Potential members, called prospects, had to be male, between eighteen and thirty-five, own a Harley-Davidson with at least a six-hundred-cubic-centimeter engine, and they were required to commit a felony—a theft, a rape, or a murder.

Not long after Bobby met Liz, the Warlocks invited him to their clubhouse. It was a row house on Woodland Avenue in Southwest Philadelphia, about a mile from his father's garage.

The clubhouse Bobby entered had a pool table in the middle of the room. A desk sat in front of one wall, a bar and a refrigerator in front of another. Chairs were here and there. A swastika flag and crossed sabers were nailed to the wall behind the desk. Blown-up posters of gang members were tacked onto the walls, along with a movie poster from *The Wild One:* Marlon Brando wearing a motorcycle jacket and sitting on a Harley. A huge fishing net was suspended from the ceiling and several dozen empty beer cans had been tossed inside.

To Bobby, this was the realization of a lifetime of fantasies from Robin Hood to Bonnie and Clyde to James Dean.

That night, Bobby was nominated for membership. His personality changed at once. He began to flirt with danger and he crossed the thin line separating right from wrong.

On either their second or third date, Bobby struck Liz. They were sitting in a bar with a group of friends. She had given Bobby little or no provocation, but it didn't matter. Bobby was "wired" out of his mind on methamphetamine and felt like acting out. So he punched Liz and knocked her down.

"I'm sorry," she said to him as she picked herself up off the floor, holding back her tears.

Bobby bent his elbow and cocked a second blow. When Liz flinched, he laughed. Instead of hitting her, he bought everyone another round of drinks.

At 3 A.M., Bobby and Liz were in bed making love.

And that was their relationship.

Bobby and Liz saw each other regularly. They were boyfriend and girlfriend. Liz loved Bobby and absorbed all of his abuses. He liked to be seen with her, and he used her for sex. Every once in a while, she would tell him she'd had enough of him and break off the relationship. But a few hours later, or the next day, she'd call Bobby, say she was sorry, and the cycle would continue.

As a prospect for membership with the Warlocks, Bobby attended meetings all spring and summer. He went on runs, which were long motorcycle rides cruising through the small towns of upstate Pennsylvania, down to the Jersey shore, and into the rural areas of the neighboring states of Delaware and New York. It was a bonding process and a feeling-out process: the Warlocks seeing if they liked Bobby and testing his loyalty and mettle.

The gang approved him in the middle of September and scheduled his initiation. This was a sacred ritual symbolizing the cutting of Bobby's ties with mainstream society and establishing his new identity. Bobby took the nickname "Mattress," and later added a second, "Mumford." But he rarely used either.

The first part of his initiation took place in the clubhouse and consisted of other members punching him and kicking him, spitting in Bobby's face, and urinating on him. If rival gang members are to be believed, Bobby was also obliged to perform homosexual acts on other members.

Once the first part was done, one more remained.

To Warlocks, women were chattel. They believed a female's sole purpose was to provide sexual gratification, and they demanded that a member's first allegiance was to the gang, not to his woman. Therefore, to prove his ultimate loyalty to the gang, a prospect had to deliver his wife or girlfriend for a practice called training.

That night, Bobby picked Liz up at home and drove her to a secluded portion of the Tinicum Marsh behind Philadelphia's International Airport. He fed her a handful of barbiturates on the way over and she was woozy by the time they arrived.

As soon as Bobby turned off the motor, he unbuttoned her blouse and unzipped her jeans. He helped her unsnap her bra and slip out of her panties. An instant later, flat on her back, Liz felt a hardness penetrate her. She was in no condition to resist or to count the number of Warlocks who violated her over the next two hours.

At first, Liz wouldn't tell anyone about the gang rape. But instinctively, her father knew something was bothering her. When he asked her what was wrong, she broke down and cried, eventually pouring out all of the sordid details.

Once again, her parents sought professional help. They found a new psychiatrist and he began treating Liz. This time, Liz showed up for her appointments and seemed to be making progress with every maladjustment except one: She continued seeing Bobby.

CHAPTER
6

Frank Lande was lying in bed on Sunday morning, the day after he and his wife returned from their cruise, the day after they discovered Liz was missing. He wasn't sure what time it was, but the sun had not come up yet. His head was throbbing and his chest was pounding.

It had been a miserable night, hardly any sleep, what with the alarm clock ticking in his ear and his imagination torturing him. For half the night, he'd stared at the ceiling and tried to recall the good times with Liz, of which there had been many through the years—watching her grow up, taking her to the movies, having her friends over to the house, playing parlor games. For the other half, he worried. Where was she? What had happened to her? Was she still alive?

At 6:30, he couldn't take it any longer. He got out of bed and put on the morning coffee. Before the percolator started bubbling, his wife joined him. It had not been an easy night for Frances, either. Wearing their bathrobes, they sat in the living room sipping coffee, saying very little to each other, and trying to stare the hours off the clock.

Around ten o'clock Frank dressed and left the house. He went to the police station at Sixty-first and Thompson streets to report Liz missing.

A sergeant listened to Frank's story, but told him teenagers were running away from home every day and heading for California to become hippies. Maybe that's where his daughter was. San Francisco.

The policeman asked Frank: Did your daughter leave home to avoid parental discipline? To avoid domestic turmoil? To become self-supporting? Because of financial or personal problems? To evade arrest or legal process?

"No," Frank said, "Liz would never run away from home. All of her clothes are still in her bedroom and she isn't in any sort of trouble."

"What sort of evidence do you have that foul play exists?"

Other than a father's gut instinct, Frank was forced to admit he had nothing.

"Sorry," the sergeant told him, "without evidence of foul play, there's nothing we can do. Your daughter's over twenty-one and free to come and go as she pleases."

By the time Frank returned home, his wife was calling all of Liz's acquaintances, trying to see if anyone knew where she was—without success. In fact, the only thing they learned all day was that someone had picked up Liz in a gold Toronado. As a result, both parents spent another restless night.

On his way to work Monday morning, Frank stopped at Philadelphia Community College in center city. He checked with the dean of students and learned that Liz had not taken her final exams, which meant she'd disappeared between the time the Toronado picked her up around 2 A.M. on the night he and Frances had left for their cruise, and Monday morning, when her exams were scheduled to begin.

Two weeks passed. The Christmas holidays came and went without much celebration in the Lande home. A new year, 1972, had begun. By then, all of Liz's friends were calling the house asking if Frank and Frances had heard from Liz. All of her friends, that is, except one.

It took Frank a while to pick up on it. Prior to Liz's disappearance, Bobby Nauss called Liz once or twice a day.

Sometimes more often. Since she disappeared, not once. Why? Because, Frank told himself, Bobby knew Liz wasn't ever coming home.

Frank knew Bobby lived in Darby, so he went to the Darby Police Station. It was the third week in January by then and three officers were standing in a group, talking and laughing, when Frank walked in. He asked them, "Do any of you know Bobby Nauss?"

One of the officers asked why.

"He put a bullet through my daughter's bedroom window." Frank said the incident had taken place the previous summer. In July. He said he and his wife were sitting in the living room watching TV and Liz was in her bedroom on the second floor in the rear of the house. It was somewhere after 10 P.M. They heard Liz's phone ring upstairs, which wasn't unusual. She was popular and got a lot of calls.

"Five or ten minutes later," Frank said, "she ran down the steps screaming, 'Bobby tried to shoot me! He tried to kill me!'"

He raced up to her room, Frank continued, and saw a bullet hole in the screen. Later, he found the bullet lodged in the ceiling.

"Why did you wait so long to register a complaint?"

"She wouldn't let us," Frank said, throwing up his arms. "She said she owed it to Bobby not to press charges."

"So why the sudden change?"

"My daughter's missing, and I think Bobby Nauss is responsible."

"Look," the officer said, "even if you had proof, there's nothing we can do. If the incident took place in Philadelphia, that's where you have to register your complaint."

The next day, Frank felt desperate enough to drive into center city and pay a visit to the FBI office. For the third time, he told the story about Liz's disappearance.

"Can you help me?" he asked hopefully.

A special agent shook his head. The way he saw it, there was no evidence of a kidnapping, no evidence of any federal laws having been broken. "In fact," the special agent said, "there's no evidence of any foul play whatsoever."

He told Frank his best bet was to go to the Philadelphia police headquarters and he gave Frank the name of a specific captain to see. As Frank drove to Eighth and Race streets, he couldn't shake the feeling that he was riding a giant merry-go-round, in one door, out the other, one station house after the next. But unless he wanted to search for Liz himself, he had no other alternatives.

Inside police headquarters, Frank talked to the captain and something in Frank's voice convinced him that foul play might have occurred. The captain made a phone call, then told Frank to go to Fifty-fifth and Pine streets in West Philadelphia. A detective at the West Detective Division would take on the case.

Raleigh Witcher was twenty-eight years old, a black seven-year cop who'd been promoted to detective two years earlier.

"My daughter's missing," Frank said. "She has no bank accounts, no credit cards, and she had only twenty-five dollars in cash when we left."

According to her habits and pattern of life, Frank explained, Liz would never leave the house without saying where she was going. She called four or five times a day regardless of where she was. Frank said his wife almost lost her job because Liz called her so often at work. About nothing. Just to talk. Figuratively speaking, she'd never severed the umbilical cord with her mother.

"Liz could never go for days without contacting her mother," Frank said. "Not if she were still alive."

Raleigh Witcher had his first talk with Bobby on January 30, 1972, at the Nauss home.

He looked like a choirboy, was Witcher's first impression.

Bobby was wearing slacks and a sports shirt. He was neat and clean. His hair was short and he was clean-shaven.

"It was a very nice house, very nice people," Witcher said later. "His mother and father and a sister were also present. He was polite and mannerly in every way."

Bobby told Witcher he'd tell him what he knew. The last time he'd seen Liz was three months earlier, at the end of October, no later than the middle of November. He'd only picked her up at her house twice. The first time was last winter, almost a year in the past, when he took her to a nightclub on MacDade Boulevard. The other time was last summer, to take her to the Warlocks' clubhouse.

Witcher asked Bobby specifically if he'd called Liz the previous December 11, the night she disappeared.

Bobby said he'd never called her in December, but he had received a Christmas card from her, somewhere around December 18. He wasn't aware of any family problems Liz might have had and he had no idea where she was.

Witcher was impressed by how calm Bobby was and that no one in the family seemed the least bit skittish or jittery.

That same night, back at West Detectives, Raleigh Witcher was filling out reports of his interview with Bobby when Frank Lande walked up to his desk.

"What happened?" Frank asked.

"Bottom line," Witcher told him, "he said he had no knowledge of your daughter's whereabouts."

"That's bullshit," Frank said, and he slammed his fist on the policeman's desk.

Phil Formicola grew up in South Philadelphia and he always wanted to be a cop. He joined the Philadelphia Police Department in 1962 and was promoted to detective six years later.

Formicola worked steady day shift at West Detectives. His

job was to follow up cases which had been assigned to detectives on the night shifts. Liz Lande was one of those cases.

First he reviewed Raleigh Witcher's reports. Next he checked the teletype, looking for young Jane Does that had recently turned up out of town. Then he interviewed Frank and Frances Lande.

Liz's parents told him about the shooting incident, then Frank mentioned something he'd withheld from Witcher. It was difficult, but Frank got it out: Liz had been gang-raped by the Warlocks just three months before she disappeared, and Bobby Nauss had instigated it.

"From that point on," Formicola would say later, "personally, I believed foul play had occurred."

He teletyped Liz's description to all fifty states. He printed a thousand missing-persons fliers with Liz's picture, sent them to every police agency in the greater Philadelphia area, and posted them in every business establishment in the neighborhoods Liz was known to frequent. Then he sat down and tried to figure out what might have happened. He came up with three scenarios.

First, she might be dead, the victim of an accidental drug overdose, suicide, or murder. Second, he considered the possibility she was working as a topless dancer or prostitute for Bobby Nauss. And third, Bobby might be holding Liz captive.

"In all three examples," Formicola explained, "I believed Nauss had the information that could help us find out what happened."

Formicola hit the streets to test his theories. He went to center city and checked every bar and restaurant, thinking Liz might be working as a go-go dancer, hooker, or waitress. He talked to the owners, employees, and patrons. Showed them Liz's picture.

When he drew nothing but blanks in center city, he expanded his search to encompass South Philadelphia, West Philadelphia, and Southwest Philadelphia.

Frank Lande dropped by West Detectives on March 15 and demanded to know what progress had been made. He was struck by what seemed to him to be a lack of development in the case after six weeks. How could he put any faith in the police when nothing was happening?

He expected them to solve the case. Already he was impatient. Why didn't they just arrest Bobby Nauss?

Raleigh Witcher told him to stop back around nine o'clock. They were going to interview Bobby once again.

"By then," Witcher would explain later, "we'd done a little background and we all felt Bobby Nauss was responsible." On the street, Witcher had been hearing a great deal about Bobby, very little of it consistent with the image Bobby had presented during their first conversation. He'd been told Bobby was into drugs and carried a gun. Bobby was also known to have a mean streak.

"We began to interview members of the Warlocks," he recalled. "Sometimes they spoke to us, reluctantly, and sometimes they just plain refused. So I contacted the head of the Warlocks, explained the situation, and asked him to bring Bobby Nauss into the station."

Shortly after 9 P.M., Bobby arrived at West Detectives. Phil Formicola, who'd had no prior face-to-face contact with Bobby, stayed after his shift ended. He took Bobby into one of the interview rooms.

Frank Lande and Raleigh Witcher watched via a see-through mirror in the adjacent room. The first time Witcher had seen him, Bobby looked and acted like a choirboy. Not this time. His hair was longer and his attitude was cocky.

"Do you know where Elizabeth Lande is right now?" Formicola asked Bobby, his tone businesslike.

"No."

"Do you have Elizabeth Lande working for you as a prostitute in center city?"

"No way."

"On December eleventh of last year, did you place a phone call to Elizabeth Lande's residence and speak to her?"

"No," Bobby said, and he looked past Formicola.

"Pick her up at her residence?"

"Un-uh."

"Wait outside for her in a vehicle?"

"Nah."

"Did Elizabeth Lande exit her residence and get into a car with you?"

"No way."

"Do you own a gold Oldsmobile Toronado?"

"No," Bobby said, looking at Formicola, seeming to be bored, "I don't."

"Have access to a gold Toronado?"

Bobby shook his head and said no.

"Any place where you can borrow one?"

"Nah."

"Do you own a gold Buick Riviera?"

"All I own is a '56 Harley," Bobby said defiantly, "and it's blue."

"Is Elizabeth Lande a junkie?"

"She does take pills," Bobby replied, "but I don't know what all she does."

"Did you, on one occasion in the past, fire a gunshot into her place of residence?"

"I heard about it, but I don't know anything about it."

"Did you ever engage in sexual intercourse with her, along with several other males?"

Bobby said no.

"You never trained Elizabeth Lande?"

"Nobody ever trained Liz," Bobby said, and he smirked, "because she was easy. If you ever wanted any, all you had to do was ask."

When Phil Formicola terminated the interview, Frank Lande was already in the hallway. He stepped in front of Bobby and blocked his path.

"Bobby," Frank said, his tone confrontational, "I know you're lying. I dare you to take a lie-detector test."

"See my lawyer," Bobby said. Then he laughed in Frank's face and walked out of the police station.

* * *

"Even if we wanted to forget this case," Raleigh Witcher explained, "Frank Lande was so overwhelmingly determined to find his daughter, or find out what happened to her, he would not let us. Every time I came to work, he was at the door with new information, or he had some private detective calling, or he was calling me on the phone—he'd learned this, he'd learned that.

"In a case like this, when we get to a point where there's nothing more to run on, we have other priorities. We leave it alone until we get another tidbit. Then we run that next tidbit as far as we can. When we run into a brick wall, we back off until we find something else.

"So it's understandable why Frank Lande might have gotten the impression that we walked away from the case. But as far as the Philadelphia Police Department was concerned, it was never forgotten.

"But like I said, Frank Lande would not let you forget. And because we never found his daughter, he wasn't satisfied with anything we did."

"All along," Frank Lande would say later, "I knew I'd have to track Liz down myself."

At the end of March, he placed newspaper ads and printed reward posters. Initially, he offered $1,000 for information leading to his daughter's whereabouts, but he soon raised it to $2,000.

In the vicinity of the Warlocks' clubhouse in Southwest Philadelphia, Frank nailed the posters to telephone poles, taped them to the windows of storefronts, and slipped them underneath the windshield wipers of vehicles parked on Woodland Avenue. He also dropped off some posters at the Darby Police Station. And right from the beginning, he logged every step he took in a little black notebook.

He couldn't sleep at night, so he started roaming the streets, trying to trace Liz's movements. He desperately wanted to find out where she was and locate anyone who'd seen her. Everywhere he went, he passed out the reward posters.

His travels took him to the go-go bars on Locust Street in Philadelphia, to the taprooms in Delaware County, and to the topless lounges across the river on Admiral Wilson Boulevard in Camden, New Jersey. For the most part, he focused on biker hangouts.

"Everybody said they could help," he recalled, "and everybody figured me for an easy mark. It was always the same: I'd flash her picture and ask if anybody knew anything about her. The bartender would swear he'd seen her in there. A couple minutes later, he'd call me over to a side table, insist he knew where her body was, then put a price tag on the whole thing. At first I paid everybody. Then I realized how pointless it was. They didn't know any more than I did.

"Sometimes I didn't know what I was doing out there. Who was I looking for? What could I do that the cops couldn't do? But I just thought, if I could only find her body, I could prove to my wife that Liz was really dead. My wife still won't accept it. But I think I'd be satisfied just knowing she had a proper burial.

"So I hired a private detective. I didn't have the money, but I hired him anyway. I think he asked for a hundred dollars a day, plus expenses, and he said he was certain he could find Liz.

"Around that time, I decided to work through the Warlocks. One day, I went to their clubhouse with the private detective. All I wanted to do was talk to them and leave some reward posters. We were parked across the street, just sitting there, trying to work up enough courage to go in. Pretty soon, they came over and surrounded the car. The next thing I knew, this tough-guy detective takes off like a jet down Woodland Avenue, scared to death.

"That was the last time I hired a private eye."

Frank Lande went back to the Warlocks' clubhouse a few minutes later and barged through the door like a maniac. The

Warlocks were so shocked, they just sat there and listened to him.

"I told them I was Liz Lande's father and I was offering a reward. I figured they knew Bobby Nauss killed my daughter and for a two-thousand-dollar reward, somebody was bound to turn him in. I don't know what it is, but they don't operate that way. You can't turn them. I don't think they would have cooperated for two million dollars.

"But I'll never forget how Bobby Nauss laughed at me when I asked him to help me find Liz."

CHAPTER
7

"Bobby never really had a strong male role model," a family member would say later in strictest confidence, "and he lacked self-esteem. He felt he wasn't a man and there was a certain macho image he was always trying to attain. But he was lazy, he was always looking for a way to beat the system, and he was always looking for someone to make him something he wasn't."

During adolescence, Bobby leaned on his girlfriend. When she rebuffed him, his self-esteem hit rock bottom and a huge void was created. That was where the Warlocks fit in. The gang became his crutch.

As soon as Bobby joined the gang, he became a career criminal. Car thefts were among his earliest crimes and he usually teamed up with Bill Standen, who was trying to work his way into the gang.

"A lot of people watched the eleven o'clock news, then walked their dogs," Bobby would explain later, "so we waited until the news was over. Then we'd go out and cut over to West Philly, cover the City Line area, then up the expressway to some areas that Stanley was more familiar with than me. We went up to an area in Bucks County, the Neshaminy area—we used to get a lot of cars up there—then we came back down I-95, over Delaware Avenue, and hit South Philly.

"Sometimes, if we were looking for a particular car, if it was a difficult car to find, we'd put out the word: If anybody saw this type of car, get its tag number. Then we'd look it up and find out where the owner lived. I'd park in the vicinity where I could observe the car. Stanley would get out and remove the door lock and bring it back to me.

"I carried a key-making machine. I'd take the code numbers off the side of the lock and look it up in a book that gave me a certain number to punch to make the key. Then I'd make the key for the car. Stanley would go back and get in and drive away as if it were his own car.

"I could only make keys for cars that had locking steering columns, primarily General Motors cars. With older cars, we used a slide hammer to remove the ignition. After the engine started, you took the screwdriver out and drove it off.

"Then we'd take the cars apart and sell the parts."

The Lansdowne Police Department caught Bobby in the act on May 1, 1972. He was charged with larceny of an automobile, fraudulent concealment of stolen property, and obtaining a motor vehicle by fraudulent means.

At that time in Delaware County, politicians were especially corruptible. A bribe was paid and Bobby's case was dismissed before it came to trial. But getting arrested was a powerful stimulus to prod Bobby's ingenuity toward finding a better way to make easy money while at the same time assuming fewer risks.

During this period, four motorcycle gangs were controlling nearly fifty percent of all the dangerous drugs manufactured, sold, and consumed in the United States. The gangs focused on five illegal drugs: LSD, PCP, methaqualone, amphetamine, and methamphetamine.

Years earlier, the Hell's Angels had staked a claim on the West Coast. The remainder of the country was partitioned off by three other gangs:

• The Outlaws formed in Chicago in the late 1950s and owned the reputation as the "baddest" of the outlaw gangs. After monopolizing the Great Lakes states, the Outlaws moved into adjoining states in a southward direction all the way to Florida. Membership reached three thousand.

The bulk of the Outlaws' income came from trafficking LSD, meth, cocaine, and diazepan (Valium), but the Outlaws were also active in prostitution, car thefts, extortion, the trafficking of illegal weapons and explosives, and contract murder.

• The Bandidos started in Texas in 1966, then expanded into the south-central and central states until nearly three hundred Bandidos comprised thirty-three chapters. Meth was the gang's most profitable drug. The Bandidos also trafficked in cocaine and heroin and engaged in prostitution, arson, extortion, fencing stolen property and weapons, welfare and bank fraud, and contract killings.

• The Pagans started in 1959 in Washington, D. C., and expanded into Maryland, Delaware, Virginia, New Jersey, New York, the New England states, and Pennsylvania. With nearly six hundred members, the Pagans controlled the flow of meth, PCP, and amphetamine throughout the northeastern corridor of the U.S. The Pagans also dealt cocaine and hashish and were grossing more than $15 million per year from drug trafficking. In addition to drugs, the Pagans were involved in prostitution, arson, and contract killings.

The M.O. of all four gangs was similar. They bought the necessary chemicals and shipped them to secret laboratories, usually in some remote farm area, desert, or mountainous region. There, chemists, or cookers, transformed the raw ingredients into finished products.

Once cooked, the illegal drugs passed through tight-knit biker pipelines, changing hands several times along the way. By the time the drugs reached the street, they'd been diluted up to five hundred percent, and their price had been inflated up to one thousand percent. Because of the strict code of silence within the gangs, the operations were extremely secure.

By contrast, during this same time, the Warlocks had fewer than a hundred members and were far less sophisticated. The average Warlock was a user more than he was a dealer. He usually purchased small quantities of meth for his own consumption, concealed them under the battery case of his motorcycle, then roared off into the sunset to get high.

The gang had earned a reputation for beatings and rapes, car thefts and murders. But the Warlocks had not established a drug manufacturing and distribution network—which left a void for enterprising freelancers.

Six months after Liz Lande's disappearance, Bobby Nauss came to a turning point in his life. If he bought more meth than he consumed, he asked himself, could he resell the remainder at a great enough profit to support his own habit?

By midsummer, when he bought himself a brand-new Cadillac, Bobby had the answer: Drugs were his destiny.

At the same time, he decided to align himself with three other Warlocks who shared the same goal. Swearing death oaths to each other, they formed a gang within the gang and, through trial and error, they set out to build an empire.

The others were:

Eric "Rick" Martinson, twenty-two, who'd grown up a mile from Bobby in Drexel Hill. He seemed to be the least flamboyant of the four, yet was the unofficial president of the gang for more than a decade. In time, he became a millionaire.

Bobby Marconi, at twenty-nine, was the oldest. He was a Casanova with dark, curly hair and swarthy good looks. Although only medium in height, he had bulging biceps and the kind of body that tight clothes flattered. His wardrobe was stylish and he always wore sunglasses. His tastes were lavish and included a white Rolls-Royce and good-looking women.

Steve DeMarco, short and barrel-chested, had a craving for underage girls. Although only twenty-one, his rap sheet already listed motorcycle and car thefts, drug possessions, corrupting the morals of a minor, and assaults with firearms and without firearms. A court-appointed psychiatrist classified him as the "antisocial type" and gang members called him a "needle freak." By his own admission, he aspired to become the meth king of Delaware County.

For the typical young white male from the Philadelphia area, a rite of passage is spending time at the Jersey shore during the summer months. He lies on the beach during the day, working on his tan and watching the bikini-clad women walking along the edge of the surf. At night, he parties in bars and nightclubs and tries to pick up girls. If he hasn't made a connection by closing time, he goes to the after-hours clubs and keeps trying. It's a ritual that's been reenacted each and every summer from Memorial Day to Labor Day for as long as anyone can remember. And it will continue as long as there are sun and sand, the ocean, boys and girls.

In that regard, Bobby Nauss was no different. He loved the shore. It was during June 1972 in Margate, New Jersey, that Bobby met the next significant woman in his life.

She called herself Cookie and she was seventeen. Her full name was Mary Ciglinsky and she'd grown up a few blocks from the Warlocks' clubhouse in St. Barabas parish in Southwest Philadelphia. She graduated from West Catholic Girls High and, like Bobby, came from a large family: four brothers and two sisters. Although red hair ran in her family, Cookie was an attractive blue-eyed blond, five feet five inches tall.

"Cookie was a bleached blond," was the way one Nauss family member described her, "thin, well-built, with a nice set. But she was hard-looking, like she belonged on the back of a Harley. She wore tube tops and skin-tight jeans, and she was more in love with the biker scene than Bobby was."

Bobby and Cookie started dating. In Jersey shore parlance, that meant they engaged in frequent sex.

* * *

On a sultry July night in 1972, in a Darby taproom not far from home, Bobby got into an argument with another biker over his colors. To settle the fight, Bobby drew his gun and shot twice. One bullet tore into the other man's liver, the second punctured a lung. As soon as the wounded biker hit the floor, Bobby aimed at his head and squeezed the trigger. But the gun jammed.

Moving quickly, Bobby and two other Warlocks carried the bleeding man outside and threw him into the back of a van. They figured he was going to die, so they sped off toward the Tinicum Marsh to dispose of the body. In their haste, they drove the wrong way down a one-way street and a police officer flagged them down.

The officer found the shooting victim in the back of the van—he was still alive, but barely. The officer also found a .25-caliber automatic and a .32 revolver. He confiscated the guns and called for an ambulance.

"At the time of the arrest," Darby police officer Tom Salerno later explained, "I could recall when Mr. Lande came to the station with some kind of circulars indicating there was a reward for his daughter."

The policeman had no inkling that foul play had occurred in the disappearance of Liz Lande, but he decided to seize the opportunity in an attempt to find out.

"Do you know Elizabeth Lande?" he asked Bobby.

"Yes, I do," Bobby replied.

"Do you know where she is?"

"I have no idea," Bobby said in an annoyed tone. "As far as I know, nothing happened to her. Believe me, she's walking around somewhere."

Bobby was charged with aggravated assault and battery with the intent to kill, criminal conspiracy, and violations of the uniform firearms act.

*   *   *

Frank Lande heard about the shooting through his police contacts. The next day, he drove to the hospital.

"He was in Fitzgerald Mercy," Frank recalled, "in what was supposed to be a heavily guarded room. I took a box of candy with me and there was one cop outside. I told him I was a relative and he let me go right in. I didn't know this guy and had no idea how to approach him. But I figured, if he were that shot-up, he couldn't do anything to me in the room and maybe he would help me."

Inside the room, the wounded biker was pale. One tube stuck out of his chest keeping his collapsed lung pumped up, another was in his arm supplying him with IV fluids, and a third was in his other arm transfusing his blood. His eyes were glossy from sedation.

Frank introduced himself and showed him Liz's picture.

"Never seen her," the biker said, and his voice was so soft Frank had to strain to hear.

"She's my daughter," Frank said. "Her name's Liz."

"Never heard of her."

"She was Bobby Nauss's girlfriend, and I think he murdered her."

The mention of Bobby's name made the biker's eyes smolder. His voice grew stronger at once. One time, he told Frank, Bobby bragged about shooting his little blond girlfriend. They were watching TV. Fooling around. She kicked him in the ass and he got pissed off. So he chased her, but she locked herself in the bathroom.

He said Bobby told him he'd shot five bullets through the bathroom door and two hit his girlfriend. So he rolled her up inside an old rug and dumped her in the usual place. Tinicum Marsh. But he wasn't sure where the shooting took place. An apartment somewhere in Delaware County was all he knew.

"Will you swear to this?" Frank asked. "To the cops?"

"No fucking way," he said, laughing. "The Warlocks would kill me if I ratted Bobby out. But I'll make you a deal. Smuggle a gun in to me and when I get stronger, I'll sneak out of here one night, shoot the motherfucker, and get even for both of us."

"Please," Frank begged him, "you've got to go to the police with me and tell them what you know."

The biker shook his head slowly, then drifted off.

A few nights later, the day before doctors were scheduled to remove the two bullets that were still inside him, the biker sneaked out of the hospital. Soon after he disappeared, the charges against Bobby were dropped.

From that point on, Frank Lande was proceeding under the premise that Bobby had shot Liz. And he began channeling his energies toward finding the mystery apartment.

Five weeks later, on August 17, 1972, Bobby got wrecked on drugs and pulled out his gun once more. It was shortly after 2 A.M. in the parking lot of the Anvil Inn, a rock 'n' roll bar thirty miles out on Baltimore Pike in Chester County.

He robbed two patrons at gunpoint as they were walking to their car. The victims were a Chester County public defender and his girlfriend.

Bobby didn't get far. He was arrested and charged with robbery, possession of marijuana, possession of firearms, possession of offensive weapons, possession of a rifle, larceny, and pointing a deadly weapon.

He posted bail but couldn't find anyone in the Chester County judicial system willing to take a bribe. So Bobby jumped bail and fled to New Jersey to avoid prosecution. He moved into the Summit Ridge Apartments in Glassboro, a college town twenty minutes on the Jersey side of the Walt Whitman Bridge. His roommate was Steve DeMarco, who'd rented the apartment under a fictitious name.

By then, Bobby Marconi had established some connections with suppliers of marijuana and methamphetamine. In addition, the Warlocks had opened a chapter in South Jersey. So, for the next six weeks, Bobby Nauss and Steve DeMarco concentrated on opening a drug pipeline between Delaware County and South Jersey.

By this point in time, Bobby was a suspect in the disappearance of Liz Lande, he'd shot and nearly killed a rival biker, he'd stolen dozens of cars, he'd pulled an armed robbery, and he'd trafficked in drugs. For all of those transgressions, he'd been arrested a total of three times. He had no convictions, he'd served no time in jail, and no one had come after him for jumping bail in Chester County. He was starting to believe he was above the law.

During the daylight hours of October 14, 1972, narcotics officers established a stakeout of apartment H-114 at Summit Ridge—which was Bobby's apartment. For the previous two weeks, complaints had been coming in about biker types coming and going at all hours.

The officers observed a 1972 Cadillac with Pennsylvania plates parked outside the target apartment. They ran the tags and learned it was registered to a Robert T. Nauss. They then contacted the Pennsylvania State Police to see if any outstanding warrants existed against the owner.

An hour later, a teletype arrived at the Glassboro Police Station. Robert T. Nauss was wanted for armed robbery in Chester County.

Two hours later, one of the officers approached the apartment. The front door was open and the only thing separating him from Bobby Nauss was a screen. Bobby was sitting on a sofa in the living room, doing something with his hands. The officer drew his service revolver.

"Police officer!" he yelled as he flung open the screen door. "On the floor! Facedown! Hands up!"

As Bobby did what he was told, the officer observed a plastic envelope on the floor. Two baggies were inside. To him, it looked like meth. Another officer entered and handcuffed Bobby, then both policemen searched the apartment.

The smell of marijuana hit them as soon as they opened the first bedroom door. Several plastic packets and a large white scale were sitting on the night table. Tiny brown flakes were visible on top of the scale, and a small box of Glad bags sat alongside. Sitting on a bookshelf was an eighteen-inch length of PVC tubing which had been made into a pipe. Traces of marijuana were stuck to the bowl. A billy club was hanging from a nail and its shaft had been hollowed out to form a pipe. One of the officers sniffed it.

"Definitely marijuana," he said.

In the other bedroom, a holster was hanging from a bedpost. A loaded revolver was inside. There was also a loaded carbine in the closet and a green trash bag containing what looked like marijuana.

Bobby was booked on suspicion of possession. Afterward, he waived extradition and was returned to Chester County. This time, he was released in his parents' custody to await trial for his armed robbery charges. At the same time, the evidence seized from Bobby's Glassboro apartment was sent to the New Jersey state lab for testing.

The lab report came back two days later, positive to the tune of 289 grams of marijuana and 4.5 grams of methamphetamine. Sheriff's deputies from New Jersey arrested Bobby a day later on a Gloucester County grand jury indictment charging him with possession of a controlled substance. Bail was set at $15,000.

The Hell's Angels had long since devised a three-pronged system for dealing with the judicial system, which the Warlocks copied. It consisted of retaining lawyers who were adept at stretching the legal system to its limits, creating a pool of funds to bail members out of jail, and making sure the defendant got a shave and a haircut and was wearing a suit if he appeared in court.

That said, Bobby Nauss remained in the Gloucester County Jail for fifty-five days without posting bail. The reasoning was convoluted. Suffice it to say, he was trying to beat the drug charges. To do so, it was necessary to create the illusion that he was not affiliated with the Warlocks. So Bobby bided his time behind bars while his attorney worked the system.

On December 8, 1972, bail was reduced to $2,000. Bobby posted ten percent and went home. A few days later, right around the first anniversary of Liz Lande's disappearance, Cookie Ciglinsky told Bobby she was pregnant.

On February 15, 1973, three months before his twenty-first birthday, Bobby married Cookie and the newlyweds moved into the apartment in the Nauss family home on Main Street.

"There was a bizarre relationship between Cookie and the rest of the family," a family member would later confide. "She was scum. Nobody in the family liked her, but we had to listen to all of her bullshit and we had to pretend we cared about her. Our mother said we had to accept Cookie, we had to be nice to her. It was like Cookie had something on Bobby.

"But all Cookie was ever looking for was her next drunk, her next high, her next piece of ass.

"I never saw Bobby abuse Cookie. I never saw him loud or aggressive toward her. But did he love her? Let's just say we were Catholic and at that time, he needed her."

Called Tommy, Robert Thomas Nauss III would be born at Fitzgerald Mercy Hospital on April 6, 1973. To someone trying to beat drug charges, this was a significant development. And so was going back to work for his father.

For eight months, Frank Lande was combing Delaware County for the apartment where he believed Bobby Nauss had shot his daughter to death. In March 1973, a month after Bobby and Cookie's wedding, he found it.

"I got the tip from a shopkeeper," Frank explained. "I'd been hitting every town, going from door to door on the commercial blocks, showing pictures of Lizzie and asking about any apartments where bikers may have congregated. The shopkeeper told me there was one place where the Warlocks used to ride their motorcycles through the hallways."

Frank held his breath as he entered the building. Scared to death, he found a deserted apartment and inspected the bathroom. He couldn't believe his luck: The bathroom door was full of holes.

Frank got in his car and drove to Media, the county seat, to report his discovery to the county's Criminal Investigation Division (CID).

CHAPTER
8

Four hundred thousand people attended a Rolling Stones concert at the Altamont Speedway near San Francisco, California, on December 9, 1969.

"Hey, people," Mick Jagger pleaded into the microphone, "who's fighting, and what for? We don't have to fight."

All the while, berserk members of the Hell's Angels motorcycle gang—armed with lead pipes, tire irons, knives, chains, and lead-weighted, sawed-off pool cues—randomly, wantonly, and viciously were attacking defenseless spectators near the edge of the stage, close enough that blood almost squirted on Jagger's boots.

"Like—we've got to stop this right now," Jagger stammered, "you know—we can't—there's no point."

By the time a helicopter whisked Jagger and the rest of the Stones away to safety, hundreds of fans had been savagely beaten and four dead bodies lay on the ground below: one drowned in a drainage ditch, two run over, and one stabbed and stomped to death.

Millions of television viewers across the country watched the highlights of that ugly, brutal, and bloody night and came away with a single message: Bikers were scary as hell. But three thousand miles to the east, to the half million people who lived in Delaware County, things like that might happen in California, but they could never happen in Pennsylvania. To the local police, the Warlocks were neighborhood punks, nothing like the Hell's Angels, and certainly not a threat to law and order.

Each municipality in Delaware County had its own small police force. Officers wrote tickets for running stop signs and red lights, handled traffic accidents, responded to bar-room brawls, investigated break-ins, and sorted out domestic disputes. If anything major occurred, such as a homicide, it was turned over to the county CID.

In those days, the county detectives were political appointees, recipients of patronage jobs doled out for helping politicians get reelected in a staunchly Republican, perennially corrupt county. Experience in law enforcement was not a requisite. As a result, behind its back, CID was described as "a bunch of shoe salesmen and ice-cream vendors masquerading as detectives." The lone exception seemed to be CID's chief.

Rocco "Rocky" Urella was in his mid-fifties, six feet tall, white-haired, and a former high school wrestling coach. A throwback to Elliot Ness, he'd joined the state police way back in 1937 and earned a reputation as a fearless lawman who'd once busted down a door with his gun drawn to arrest a cop killer.

Governor Milton Shapp appointed Urella state police commissioner in 1971. But by then, Urella was frustrated by a newfangled system that was suddenly more concerned with legal technicalities and an accused's rights than with the fact the accused was guilty. He became distrustful of lawyers and started bugging the state attorney general's phone. But he got caught late in 1972. When the news of his bungled wiretap hit the presses, politicians from Philadelphia to Pittsburgh were screaming for Urella's scalp.

On New Year's night in 1973, on his way home from Penn State's 14–0 Sugar Bowl loss to Oklahoma, the governor fired Urella. Two days later, the Delaware County district attorney hired him to head up CID.

Two months later, Frank Lande was sitting across the desk from Rocky Urella, telling his story. To Urella, the father sounded convincing. The information he'd alphabetized and cross-indexed in his little black book added up. So Urella assigned a detective to the case.

"Cowboy Lou" D'Iorio interviewed Frank Lande, then drove to Folcroft, to a flat-roofed, three-story, red brick building at 1528 Elmwood Avenue. Ironically, it was a block away from the Folcroft Police Station.

D'Iorio, who'd gotten his nickname because he wore cowboy boots, entered the building. The first thing that caught his eye was the trail of black skid marks up and down the halls. And they led him to the vacant apartment Frank Lande had described. D'Iorio went inside.

Who in hell had lived there? The place was a pigsty. Grease stains all over the carpet. Grimy handprints everywhere. Holes punched into the walls. And the bathroom door! It looked like Swiss cheese. It must have been used for target practice. There were dart holes and bow-and-arrow holes and knife holes. But bullet holes? He couldn't really tell, but he doubted it.

That was the one part of Frank Lande's story he'd found hard to believe. It was inconceivable that five gunshots could have been fired in a quiet apartment building in a peaceful residential neighborhood just one block from the police station—and gone unreported. Then again, it was hard to believe a biker enclave existed there.

He left the apartment and started knocking on doors.

One neighbor asked for ID before she allowed him to enter. Nervously, she identified a photo of Liz Lande. The neighbor told D'Iorio that the cute little blond had been a frequent visitor to the apartment but suddenly stopped coming around. When? Right around Christmas—not this past Christmas—two Christmases ago, 1971.

Steve DeMarco, she told D'Iorio, was who'd been renting the apartment back then. He was a scary guy. Drunk, high, and loud most of the time. Always throwing noisy parties. But nobody complained. Everybody was too afraid of reprisal from the Warlocks. So they looked the other way and prayed for the day he'd move out. A few bikers still lived in the building, but they were nothing like DeMarco and his crowd.

On his way back to headquarters, Lou D'Iorio began to formulate his own theory: Steve DeMarco—not Bobby Nauss—had killed the Lande girl, and she'd been stabbed or strangled—not shot.

But there was no evidence, no body. So he lost interest in the case.

While law enforcement was in a state of denial concerning the growing menace of motorcycle gangs in Delaware County, battle lines were being drawn.

On one side were the Pagans, who had moved their national headquarters, or Mother Chapter, to the tiny borough of Marcus Hook four years earlier. The geography was much better for controlling the gang's $15 million per year drug empire in the northeast quadrant of the United States.

On the other side were the Warlocks, who had been opening new chapters and growing in strength to nearly two hundred members. The Warlocks were now armed with AK-1 automatic rifles, sawed-off M-1 carbines, sawed-off shotguns, Thompson submachine guns, hand grenades, pipe bombs, and plastic explosives.

Objectively, the Pagans were still much stronger and more unified. According to a confidential police memo out of New York, the Pagans were tied to organized crime:

Suffolk County Police Department

May 1973

In recent months, information has been received that outlaw cyclists have been employed by certain crime families to drive hijacked trucks from New York City to Long Island. They have also been utilized by these crime families to act as enforcers or "musclemen" for shylock operations.

It has been reported that they are used because they are close-mouthed and will not talk to police if apprehended, thereby lessening the chance of police agencies getting any closer to arresting members of organized crime.

In addition, the Pagans kept an assassination squad in Marcus Hook and contracted out for mob hits. The link between the Mafia and the Pagans had been traced to a Pagan who was the nephew of the reputed Mafia don of Pittsburgh.

As the summer of 1973 began, while law enforcement kept its head buried in the sand, the Pagans and Warlocks were moving closer and closer to declaring a territorial war.

Bobby Nauss's father was suffering from ill-health—a recurring heart condition—which contributed to Bobby's obtaining a hardship deferment from the draft. As a result, Bobby never served in the military.

Most bikers, however, were armed forces veterans—Army and Marine Corps grunts who'd survived Hitler, Hirohito, Korea, and Vietnam—and they had a macho mind-set. They wanted the world to perceive them as superpatriots and misunderstood individuals who just happened to love riding motorcycles. Let them alone to do their own thing and they would let you alone. But the truth was, they were racists, somewhere between the Ku Klux Klan and skinheads. They were neo-Nazis on wheels with little, if any, morality. They were thugs who singled out the weak and ganged up on the strong.

A motorcycle gang was an environment in which violence was not only tolerated, it was encouraged and rewarded. It was an atmosphere in which women were mistreated, abused, and used for emotionless sex. At the time, it was the perfect medium for Bobby.

In this world, he changed from the meek, mild, rosy-cheeked kid next door to a hooligan no one ever wanted to meet in a dark alley. He affected a cocked-shoulder swagger that sent the message he was carrying a chip on his shoulder and daring anyone to knock it off. He snapped out often and for no apparent reason, and he always carried a gun. As often as not, a second was strapped to his leg.

On the night of June 28, 1973, a half-dozen Warlocks went to the Mohawk Bar on MacDade Boulevard to drink beer and pass the time. When they left at closing time, they walked right into an ambush.

From the Esso station across the street, shots rang out and three Warlocks were wounded. Although the gunmen remained anonymous, the Warlocks suspected the Pagans and tension mounted all summer.

At the time, Bobby belonged to the Warlocks' vigilante squad. Called the Inner Circle, it was a select group whose purpose was to right wrongs within the gang and to seek revenge against outsiders. Killing was within its scope.

Members of the Inner Circle walked into the Palace Bar on Chester Pike on September 10. A Pagan was inside, seated at the bar, and one word led to another. Shooting started and the Pagan was wounded.

As far as the Warlocks were concerned, the score was now even. But the fact was, a couple of independent bikers had been responsible for the prior shooting. Instead of settling accounts, the Warlocks had launched an unprovoked attack. It was now the Pagans' turn to retaliate.

Eleven days later, on September 21, a Warlock left the

MacDade Mall at 9 P.M. As he walked toward his car, an automatic weapon opened fire. The Warlock was hit in the chest, abdomen, and arm. An ambulance rushed him to the hospital, but he died on the operating table.

Two nights later, Bobby Nauss was one of fifty Warlocks attending the viewing at the McCausland-Bathhurst Funeral Home on Chester Pike. Afterward, they went straight to the Palace Bar.

Inside, two Pagans were sitting at the bar drinking beer. The Warlocks walked in and surrounded the Pagans. One of the Warlocks threw a drink in one of the Pagans' faces and punches were thrown. Beer bottles were hurled. Chains and metal pipes were swung. Shots were fired. When the smoke cleared, the two Pagans lay on the floor, bloodied and beaten.

Police officers responded, followed by a pair of ambulances, a number of Pagans, and one newspaper reporter.

"I promise you," a Pagan leader told the reporter, "there will be swift and bloody retaliation."

Less than an hour later, at 11 P.M., Bobby Nauss was standing on the sidewalk outside the Warlocks' clubhouse with two or three gang members. Cars were routinely passing on Woodland Avenue. Suddenly a car full of Pagans stopped at point-blank range and opened fire. Bobby hit the deck and returned fire. One of the Warlocks caught a bullet in the thigh.

At the same time, twenty miles west of the clubhouse, a Warlock was watching television at his girlfriend's house. It was hot and the windows were open. Suddenly he heard footsteps on the gravel driveway. Looking through the screen, he saw three dark forms outside approaching the house. He grabbed a shotgun and went outside to see who it was.

Exactly three steps outside the front door, the first blast of machine gun fire hit him. He went down, but fired his shotgun at his attackers. By then, he noticed he was losing a lot of blood and drove himself to the hospital. Police officers arrested him at the emergency room an hour later. A police search of his girlfriend's home uncovered a cache of weapons, and a significant amount of stolen property. But the night was far from over.

At 4 A.M., midway between the first two incidents geographically, an explosion destroyed a motorcycle shop belonging to a Warlocks' chapter president.

The skirmishes continued in the days that followed. Warlocks gunned down a Pagan in a broad daylight drive-by shooting. An early morning blast at an apartment complex claimed a Pagan's car. An afternoon shootout at a roadside hot dog stand wounded members of both gangs.

On October 8, Rocky Urella called a press conference.

"We are taking emergency measures," he announced, "because these guys have declared open warfare. Our main concern is to confiscate as many weapons as possible." Which was exactly what was happening. The police would respond to the shootings, arrest the survivors, search their vehicles and residences, and confiscate weapons and ammunition.

A day later, leaders from both gangs met at the Ridley Township Police Station to hold their own press conference.

"Both sides are winning nothing," the Pagans' spokesman said. "The only ones winning are the police."

"Whether it's the country that goes to war or something like this," the Warlocks' representative said, "the most important consideration is the expense. Last week, we had to raise seventy-five thousand dollars to bail out three Warlocks who were arrested."

A truce was signed later that same day, and it was none too soon to meet Bobby Nauss's needs. His criminal cases were about to go to court.

Bobby was convicted of armed robbery in Chester County, but he appealed his decision and remained free on bail pending the outcome of his appeal. At the same time, the second anniversary of Liz Lande's disappearance passed without any developments, and another year ended.

On January 3, 1974, Bobby's lawyer sent a letter to the
Gloucester County Prosecutor's Office. In part, it read:

> As I expressed to you, Mr. Nauss is in the peculiar
> situation of needing a conditional dismissal of the
> narcotics complaint against him, by reason of the
> fact that he is presently the sole operator of his fa-
> ther's auto repair business and, thusly, the sole sup-
> port of his father's family, consisting of a wife and
> seven children living at home, as well as the defen-
> dant's own family, consisting of a wife and an in-
> fant.

Five months later on June 24, Bobby presented his side of
the story at a plea bargaining session. Clean-shaven, his hair
cut to a short length, Bobby was wearing a coat and tie when
he addressed the prosecuting attorney.

"A few months before this happened," Bobby said in a hum-
ble manner, "I was riding through Glassboro and my motorcycle broke down. These guys came by on motorcycles—I'd
never seen them before—and they stopped to give me a hand.
They got my bike running and invited me back to their apartment. That was when I found out they belonged to the Warlocks Motorcycle Club.

"From time to time, I came back to see them and got to
know them and that's how I came to be in the apartment on
the night it got raided."

Bobby admitted to having possessed both marijuana and
methamphetamine that night, then his lawyer took over.

"The defendant," the lawyer told the prosecutor, "has
made remarkable advancements in maturity in the nearly two
years since the incident happened. His manner is more responsible, and he's become more polite and more cooperative.

"By his own admission, the defendant associated with the
motorcycle club two years earlier. But, in retrospect, he was
displeased that he was forced to alter his behavior and be-

come involved with drugs. Apparently, the two months the defendant spent in jail afforded him ample opportunity to evaluate his life and redirect its course."

He said Bobby deserved a break.

After the hearing, the prosecutor concluded:

> Apparently, an accidental set of circumstances found the defendant in Glassboro, where he became entangled with companions suspected of being involved in illegal drug trafficking.

In exchange for pleading guilty, Bobby received a six-month suspended sentence and was fined $500. Bobby paid $250 on the spot and walked out of court a free man. Over the next five months, he made five $50 installments to fulfill his sentence.

Months passed.

No one in the law enforcement community was even thinking about Liz Lande anymore, let alone working on the case. Her disappearance seemed destined to remain an unsolved mystery. In fact, Frank Lande was the only person trying to prove that Bobby Nauss had kidnapped his daughter and shot her to death. But as one agonizing month flowed into the next, another year, 1974, was almost history. Liz had been missing for three years and, other than locating the apartment where he believed the shooting had taken place, Frank had no more clues than he had on the day he started. And the chase was taking a toll on him physically.

Frank's life had deteriorated into a treadmill of going to work, searching for clues after work and on weekends, and lying awake most nights for hours, worrying. His nerves were shot and his blood pressure and cholesterol levels were elevated.

"It's been a torture," he told a reporter who was writing a

human interest story. "Liz's mother began to withdraw and I've continued to pursue it, really, just to save her sanity.

"My kid was one of that generation suddenly in rebellion. Her downfall was that she was so exceptionally good-looking, and I have no doubt at all that Liz is dead.

"I've known for three years that Bobby Nauss and the Warlocks were involved. All along, I've been warning the police that other young girls are going to be killed, and they laugh at me."

But Frank Lande's warning was an accurate prediction and 1975 would become an open season for murdering young women in Delaware County.

CHAPTER
9

Around 6:30 P.M. on Holy Thursday evening, March 27, 1975, Mary Ann Lees, fifteen, and Layne Spicer, sixteen, went out for the evening.

Called inseparable friends, they lived across the street from one another on Clinton Road in the Stonehurst Hills section of Upper Darby. (Darby, Upper Darby, and Darby Township are three separate municipalities in Delaware County.) Both were attractive, with long dark hair.

Mary Ann Lees and Layne Spicer stopped for a pizza that night, then hitched a ride to a boyfriend's house about two miles away. They listened to David Bowie albums in the basement rec room, then left around 11:15. But they never returned home.

At 7:30 the next morning, both girls' mothers reported their daughters missing.

Easter weekend passed without a trace of either girl.

On Monday morning, March 31, Frank Lande increased the reward for his missing daughter to $5,000.

"I guess I should say, for information leading to her present location—living or dead," he told a reporter. "I've put so much into this already, I can't actually lay my hands on that much money. But if anybody can tell me where Lizzie is buried, I'll sell the house."

On April 1, the headline in Delaware County's *Daily Times* said 2 COUNTY GIRLS SHOT; BODIES FOUND IN RIVER. The story said the bodies of Mary Ann Lees and Layne Spicer were seen in the Schuylkill River around 2:30 P.M. on Monday by a man repairing the roof of Jerry's Corner Market, near Sixty-first and Passyunk in Southwest Philadelphia.

One body had been recovered by the harbor patrol on the western edge of the river, the other by fireboat crewmen.

The medical examiner indicated that Layne Spicer had been shot three times in the head and neck, Mary Ann Lees twice in the head and back. All five bullets had been fired from the same .32-caliber handgun. The estimated time of death was twenty-four to forty-eight hours prior to the discovery of the bodies.

A combined unit of twenty officers from Philadelphia, Upper Darby, and CID joined hands on the investigation. The investigators theorized that the girls were probably hitchhiking, someone picked them up, raped them, then killed them. But the investigators failed to uncover a single clue and the investigation ground to a halt two weeks later.

Frustrated by the lack of progress, Frank "Sonny" Lees, Mary Ann's father, tore a page out of Frank Lande's book by starting his own search for his daughter's killer.

Perhaps it was the discovery of the bodies of the two Upper Darby teenagers that prodded Cowboy Lou D'Iorio back into action. In early April, after more than a year of virtual inactivity on the Elizabeth Lande case, he returned to the apartment building on Elmwood Avenue in Folcroft.

Taking his time, he wandered from one room to the next in Steve DeMarco's old apartment. It had been renovated and rented but, once again, was unoccupied.

Something kept drawing D'Iorio into the bathroom. He

couldn't put his finger on it, but something was wrong. Then it hit him. Compared to the rest of the fixtures, the medicine cabinet looked new. Why?

He pulled the cabinet out of the wall. Inside the hollow space between the walls, he saw two splotches of patching plaster. Carefully, he chipped away the plaster. Underneath were two slugs. These could have been the missed shots, he reasoned, from Frank Lande's story. But how in hell could shots have been fired and not been reported?

Cowboy Lou drew his .25 automatic and aimed it at the inner wall. He pulled the trigger and fired two shots. Then he waited for a commotion. But none came. No one knocked on the door. And no curious onlookers gathered in the hall when he exited moments later.

D'Iorio drove back to CID headquarters, then phoned the Folcroft Police Station. Had anyone reported gunshots in the vicinity of Elmwood Avenue? No?

The people in that apartment building, he concluded, were still too frightened of the Warlocks to get involved. But it *was* possible that someone could have fired five shots and killed Liz Lande in that very apartment.

Sensing he was on to something, he called the Darby Police Department and requested that the .25 automatic and the .32 revolver which had been confiscated from Bobby Nauss in July 1972 be sent to the ATF (Federal Bureau of Alcohol, Tobacco, and Firearms) ballistics testing lab in Philadelphia. Maybe Frank Lande was right after all.

The .25 arrived safe and sound, but the ID tag from the .32 was attached to it. And somewhere between the Darby Police Station and the ATF offices, the .32 had disappeared. To Cowboy Lou D'Iorio, something smelled rotten, so he went to Rocky Urella and convinced him to bring in Steve De-Marco for questioning.

Yeah, DeMarco told the CID chief, he'd known Liz Lande. So what? Yeah, he'd heard she'd been killed. Once he'd been at a Warlocks' party and overheard a conversation about someone killing Liz—but no names—and the way he'd heard it, the killer buried her in the Jersey pine barrens with her legs spread and her knees sticking up above the ground.

Urella asked, *Was Bobby Nauss there?* Where? *At the party?* What party? *The party you just told me about.*

DeMarco said he couldn't remember, it was a long time ago. Besides, he barely knew Liz Lande or Bobby Nauss.

Once again, the search for Liz Lande had hit a dead end.

Fifteen-year-old Sharon Jones* never came home from school on May 3. She lived on South Fifth Street in Colwyn, a tiny borough right next to Darby, about four blocks from where Bobby Nauss worked.

Three days passed without a trace of her.

At 1:50 P.M. on May 7, the phone rang at the Marcus Hook police station. The caller had just seen a girl stumble while she was walking along the Penn Central railroad tracks underneath the Market Street Bridge.

A few minutes later, officers found Sharon Jones. She was battered and unconscious, lying beside the tracks. A plastic cord was tied around her neck.

Later that night, CID detectives questioned her in the hospital.

She said she'd gone to the MacDade Mall on the night she disappeared. She was on her way home, waiting for a bus, when a car pulled up and two men asked her if she needed a ride. She said yes and got in the car. Instead of taking her home, they drove in the opposite direction. She had no idea where they took her. But she did remember being beaten, injected with methamphetamine, and raped. After that, she passed out.

Sharon Jones told the detectives she couldn't remember anything else and she couldn't identify her attackers.

*Name has been changed to protect her privacy.

* * *

On May 10, neighbors watched Denise Seaman arguing with her boyfriend on the porch of her family's twin home. She lived in Colwyn, on South Fifth Street, just a few doors away from Sharon Jones.

The boyfriend was yelling that he was going out alone, and Denise was pleading with him to take her along. He got into his pickup truck by himself and pulled away.

Denise Seaman was five feet two and 105 pounds, good-looking, with olive-hued skin, big brown eyes, and long dark hair. She was seventeen and she'd dropped out of Upper Darby High School a week earlier to take a job as a fast-food waitress.

That night, as her boyfriend pulled away, she chased him up the street to the stop sign. When he stopped, he let her in and they drove away together.

Denise Seaman never made it back home that night.

Her mother called the police the next morning. For two days, Colwyn police officers talked to Denise Seaman's friends, neighbors, and schoolmates, but came up blank. So they called CID for help on the case.

Denise Seaman's mother told the CID detectives she'd heard the horror stories about Sharon Jones—the abduction, the rape, the attempted murder—and she feared the worst had also happened to her daughter. They'd only lived in Colwyn for a year and a half and Sharon and Denise were friends. And what was worse, prior to moving to Colwyn, they'd lived in the Stonehurst Hills section of Upper Darby, about a block away from where Mary Ann Lees and Layne Spicer had lived before they were murdered. The three of them were best friends. Even after moving to Colwyn, Denise kept in touch with Mary Ann and Layne. They went to the same places and shared the same friends. Now, the mother said, she was afraid something awful had happened to Denise.

The detectives believed she was right, but kept their opinions to themselves. Instead, they asked Denise's mother for the name, address, and phone number of her daughter's boyfriend.

They'd gone to the MacDade House, the boyfriend told the detectives, got there around 6:30 that night. They'd been fighting and Denise was still upset, so he left her outside in the pickup by herself. He'd gone inside to have a few beers with some of his buddies.

After a while, the boyfriend continued, Denise came inside and told him it was time to leave. He told her to "fuck off," and she left in a huff, saying she was going to the MacDade Mall. Around nine o'clock, he left the bar and went to the mall to look for Denise. But he never found her, so he went home.

"There is reason to believe Denise Seaman may have been abducted," a CID spokesman told the press. To his fellow officers, he shared a more candid view: "I figure if she ran away, she'll be back by the end of the summer. If she fails to return by then, her body will turn up once the hunters hit the fields next hunting season."

Around 6:30 P.M. on May 28, Sonny Lees was driving east on Powell Road in Springfield. The word around town was that Sonny was making better progress than the police and he was getting close to finding out who killed his daughter.

Suddenly his van appeared to swerve. It sideswiped an oncoming vehicle and veered off the road, wedging itself between a tree and a telephone pole. An instant later, a series of explosions rocked the van. It burst into flames with Sonny Lees pinned behind the wheel.

By the time the firemen arrived and extinguished the flames, he'd suffered third-degree burns over eighty percent of his lower body. Am ambulance sped him to the burn treatment center at Crozer-Chester Medical Center in extremely critical condition.

Sonny Lees' condition worsened overnight. In an attempt to save his life, surgeons amputated both of his legs.

Sonny Lees died at 5:45 A.M. four days later.

His wife buried him in a plot at Saints Peter and Paul Cemetery, right next to their daughter's grave.

At 11 A.M. on Saturday, August 17, the phone rang at the Collingdale Police Station. It was a distraught mother calling.

The officer began the same way he handled every missing persons report. He opened the three-ring binder that was crammed with reports of missing young girls, more than fifty in a town with a population of only ten thousand, and he said, "Name?"

When the *Daily Times* came out Sunday morning, the page-one headline announced, COLLINGDALE WOMAN, 20, VANISHES. Beneath the headline was a picture of a smiling Debbie Delozier.

The story quoted Rocky Urella as saying the missing girl had last been seen by a girlfriend a few minutes after midnight on Saturday when she went home to finish packing for an anticipated flight to Nashville the next morning to vacation with relatives. "She was seen a block from home," Urella said, "but she failed to arrive home, and she did not use her airline ticket the following morning."

Urella described Debbie Delozier as being five-two, 115 pounds, with shoulder-length dark-brown hair. And he indicated that CID detectives were questioning her neighbors and acquaintances.

The next day, an anonymous letter arrived in the Deloziers' mailbox. No return address. Philadelphia postmark. Inside, a single sheet of paper. Single-spaced:

Dear Mr. and Mrs. Delozier:

Debra Jean won't be coming home. She knew too much about things that could have caused trouble for a lot of people. We'll tell you where to find the body so you can give her a decent burial.

It's too bad it had to be this way. She was so incredibly beautiful.

Debbie's parents turned the letter over to CID. Her mother believed the letter was authentic, but Rocky Urella thought it was a prank.

The next day, an anonymous caller told the Collingdale police that Debbie Delozier's body had been dumped in the Tinicum Marsh. Helicopters conducted a two-hour aerial search but found nothing.

A police officer was on a routine motor patrol in Darby Township during the early morning hours of September 13 when he observed two cars parked in the middle of the street. One of them was a Cadillac limousine. The officer stopped to see if some sort of problem existed.

Approaching on foot, he was halfway to the limo when he saw the driver's window go down and a .45 aim in his general direction. He ducked for cover just as a shot rang out, then both vehicles sped away.

The policeman radioed for backup as he pursued the fleeing limousine, and for a good twenty minutes, a wild high-speed chase ensued, zigging and zagging across Delaware County, picking up a half dozen police cars along the way.

Eventually, when the limo reached an affluent neighborhood on the outskirts of Media, the limo pulled into a driveway and skidded to a halt in front of an eerie-looking mansion.

The driver never hesitated. Dodging a volley of bullets, he ran toward the mansion. On the porch, he found an open window and disappeared inside.

All but two of the officers fanned out and surrounded the mansion. The other two approached the limo, where they found two underage girls sitting inside. The officers radioed headquarters with instructions to contact the girls' parents, then they searched the limo. They found no weapons, no drugs, but they found a photograph of the missing Debbie Delozier on the front seat. The back of the photo was stamped: CID CONFIDENTIAL FILE.

Quickly, the officers checked the limo's tags with the Bureau of Motor Vehicles (BMV) and came up with the name of Robert Marconi as the registered owner. The name was familiar to the policemen. Bobby Marconi was earning a colorful reputation as a fence for stolen property, an up-and-coming drug dealer, and a womanizer; and this was his home. The officer approached the mansion's front door and knocked.

It was an hour when most people in the Eastern Time Zone were sound asleep, but Bobby Marconi came to the door fully dressed. Wide awake. Although it was dark and the porch light was not lit, the officers took one good look at Marconi and knew at once he wasn't the limo driver.

Bobby Marconi stood in front of the doorway. He wasn't about to let the officers enter his home—not yet, anyway.

"Listen," the original officer said to him, "I chased somebody all the way from Darby Township to here, and he just climbed through your window. We'd like to come inside and look for him."

"Got a warrant?" Marconi asked.

The officer shook his head, then explained he didn't need one because probable cause existed.

Bobby Marconi acted as if he were familiar with the legalities of the search and seizure statutes but wanted to stall them for as long as possible. Finally he stepped aside.

Three officers searched the residence while the original officer asked Marconi a few questions.

Limo? Yeah, he owned a couple of limos—a Rolls-Royce, too—he operated a limo service. But he hadn't rented any limos that night and he, personally, had not left home all night—and he had witnesses to prove it. If one of his limos had been involved in any sort of incident, someone must have ripped it off and taken it for a joyride.

Debbie Delozier? No, he knew no one by that name. Wait

a minute. Wasn't that the name of the girl from Collingdale who'd run away from home? Her picture? No, he had no idea how her picture could have gotten into his limo, or who could have put it there. By the way, he told the officer, if there were any more questions, could they wait until he phoned his lawyer?

The officer said that wouldn't be necessary.

The search failed to find the suspect. Under the circumstances, there was little the officers could do except impound the limo to conduct a more thorough search and issue a John Doe warrant for the driver.

This was not the first time police officers had visited Bobby Marconi's residence on Plush Mill Road.

Known as the "Castle," it was a forty-room Gothic mansion constructed out of granite. Two years earlier, Marconi had purchased it for $80,000 cash. Ironically, at the time of the purchase, he was collecting welfare.

The Castle was an Agatha Christie dream come true. Built by a wealthy Philadelphia family around the turn of the century, it contained secret passageways, trapdoors, revolving bookcases, and an underground escape tunnel. Marconi had customized it since he'd moved in. For entertainment, he'd added a pool table, a shuffle-bowling machine, and assorted pinball machines to the game room. Out back, he'd installed a heated, in-ground swimming pool.

Bobby Nauss was a frequent visitor at the Castle, Steve DeMarco lived there, and young girls came and went at all hours of the day and night.

This was an exclusive neighborhood and residents called the police on a regular basis to complain about hearing women's screams and gunshots in the middle of the night. In addition, acting on tips, police officers had raided the Castle on two other occasions.

A little before sunrise on Friday, October 17, a small boat landed on the west bank of the Delaware River. Three hunters stepped ashore. This was their favorite spot, a swampy area of fallen trees, tall reeds, and backwater ponds in the Tinicum Marsh, perfect for duck hunting. It was directly beneath the landing pattern of Philadelphia International, just south of the airport.

The air was cool and crisp. They sat and waited. They watched the sun come up—a dazzling burst of yellow and orange rising above the Jersey flatlands on the opposite side of the river. When a flock of ducks took wing shortly after sunrise, a barrage of shotgun blasts filled the air and several ducks fell from the sky.

It was seven o'clock when the hunters went to retrieve their catch. One of the hunters was beating the bush a good 50 to 75 feet from the river and 150 feet away from the closest footpath. When he stumbled over a pile of weather-beaten rags, he pulled the weeds apart and kicked at an old red shirt. That was when he saw the leg bones sticking out.

The *Daily Times* carried the front-page story: DETECTIVE'S GRISLY PREDICTION COMES TRUE: ONCE THE HUNTERS HIT THE FIELDS, WE'LL GET SOMETHING. Beneath the headline, to the left of the story, was a photo of two CID detectives examining the high school ring which provided the preliminary identification of the skeletal remains. To the right of the story was a picture of a smiling Denise Seaman, who'd been missing for five months.

The story quoted Rocco Urella as saying that CID investigators had established a pattern in the disappearances of Denise Seaman and Debbie Delozier, the abduction of Sharon Jones, and the murders of Mary Ann Lees and Layne Spicer. But he refused comment about the pattern.

At the site where the hunters had discovered Denise Seaman's remains, Urella instructed his forensic people to excavate the entire section of ground surrounding the skeleton. He told them to dig down six to eight inches, bring everything back to headquarters, and sift it for evidence.

The next day, an autopsy specified the cause of death as either one of two .22-caliber slugs which had been embedded in the victim's skull. In addition, the medical examiner noted that her right jaw had been fractured prior to her death.

After the autopsy, Urella called another press conference.

"This is another piece in the puzzle," he told the reporters. "There is a drug-related problem linking all of these girls. A number of their common acquaintances are very much drug-oriented and the girls were all involved with a local motorcycle group.

"I'm not saying that one perpetrator is responsible for all of these, but because of the places the girls visited, many of the same people turned up in all of the investigations. We feel there's a strong relationship.

"In addition, the disappearance of Elizabeth Lande, who was last seen in Folcroft in December of 1971, might also be linked to the same group."

This was an election year. One of the offices up for reelection was district attorney.

Ever since the bodies of Mary Ann Lees and Layne Spicer had been discovered floating in the Schuylkill River six months earlier, the newspapers kept running updates on the missing girls—and the lack of progress in the ongoing investigations. Residents around the county were becoming uneasy, especially the parents of teenage girls.

With the election just a couple of weeks away, the outcry for increased law and order was growing quite loud. The candidates were campaigning, trying to woo voters and making the usual promises.

What the voters wanted were results.

On the day after the election, November 5, early in the evening, CID detectives were interviewing Sharon Jones for what seemed like the hundredth time. In essence, she was the only survivor of what Rocco Urella believed were all related attacks, and he felt she knew more than she was telling.

That night, she told the detectives that Steve DeMarco had

been one of the men who'd abducted her six months earlier, the previous May. The reason she'd been abducted, she said, was because she'd witnessed the murders of Mary Ann Lees and Layne Spicer. She told the detectives that DeMarco wanted to shut her up.

Rocco Urella established a protective surveillance around the teenager and dispatched two teams of detectives to look for DeMarco.

They searched for three days without finding him. At the same time, other detectives kept reviewing Sharon Jones's statement with her. But with each telling, her story changed. Which moved Rocco Urella to ask her parents for permission to administer a lie-detector test.

She failed her polygraph on Friday, November 8. Rocco Urella then called off the search for Steve DeMarco and canceled the net of protection around Sharon Jones.

The following Monday, Sharon Jones did not come home from school.

Detectives spotted Steve DeMarco, accompanied by a young girl, shopping at a shoe store in the MacDade Mall. They brought him into CID headquarters for questioning.

No, he told the detectives, he had nothing to do with Sharon Jones's disappearances—either one of them. He didn't even know the girl. With no grounds on which to be held, DeMarco was free to go.

At 7:20 the next morning, Sharon Jones's body was found in a parking lot near Marcus Hook. She was lying underneath a tractor-trailer on a bed of gravel. A rope had been twisted around her neck three times.

"She was almost dead," said the policeman who found her. "I broke the cord and immediately gave her oxygen."

Sharon Jones survived the attack. However, after she recovered, she refused to answer any more questions from the CID detectives.

As 1975 drew to a close, the police blotter showed: three young girls abducted and murdered; one young girl abducted, raped, and almost murdered on two separate occasions; one automobile accident claiming the life of the father of one of the murder victims; and one young girl still missing after four months and presumed dead—not to mention Liz Lande, whose disappearance and apparent homicide remained a mystery after four years.

Clearly, there was a killer or killers who were going about their work, murdering young girls in a cold-hearted, cold-blooded fashion. Worse, this pattern gave every indication the killings would continue.

In the new year ahead, Frank Hazel, who'd won the election for district attorney of Delaware County, had his work cut out for him.

PART TWO

The Chase

January 1976–December 1979

CHAPTER
10

When he took office, District Attorney Frank Hazel faced three major problems: the widespread allegations of political and governmental corruption in Delaware County, the motorcycle gangs, and the unsolved murders. There was also a backlog of thirty-two hundred untried criminal cases that had to be adjudicated within 270 days of the original complaint—or they would be dismissed.

He knew nothing about being a cop or conducting an investigation. All he knew was that the Warlocks problem, the Pagans problem, and the murders were interlocked and that little, if any, cooperation existed between the local, county, and state law enforcement agencies. All of those preexisting conditions conspired to thrust him into the most frustrating, most exciting period of his life.

At thirty-four, with close-cropped dark hair and a dapper flair, he moved with the fluid confidence of the Catholic Youth Organization all-star football receiver he was before a knee injury ended his career in high school. Ironically, he graduated from Bobby Nauss's alma mater, Monsignor Bonner, although he graduated ten years ahead of Bobby.

Integrity defined his character. After nine years of building a successful private law practice, he was one of the most respected criminal lawyers in Delaware County, someone who knew his way around the court system. Yet the word used most often to describe him was *clean*. The Republican party, which was suffering from a tarnished image at the time, handpicked him to run for district attorney because his reputation brought instant credibility to the party. Plus, he kept his fingers on the pulse of the community where he'd grown up and still lived.

"The solution of these murders and disappearances is my top priority," he said at his swearing-in ceremony on January 5, 1976.

Saturday morning, January 17, dawned sunny.

A pair of rabbit hunters were sloshing through the thawing muck and mire of the Tinicum Marsh near Cargo City, just south of the airport. Ankle deep in mud, they spotted bones protruding above the water.

The bones were picked so clean, the coroner who was called to the scene didn't even bother to put on a pair of rubber gloves to handle them. Instead, he reached into the icy water and fished around with his bare hands, speaking into his tape recorder as he worked:

"Body submerged and completely hidden. Water level receded . . . irregular, frozen topsoil with matted vegetation . . . rodent tunnels under the body . . . jeans, brassiere, and sweatshirt—no panties . . . three rings, crucifix on a chain— no socks, no shoes, shirt pulled up over her head."

Working carefully, he freed the bones from the mud below, retrieving a complete skeleton. It was obvious to him that rodents had eaten away the flesh.

The *Daily Times* played it up big, front-page headlines: DELOZIER GIRL'S BODY FOUND IN MARSH; BULLET STUDIED FOR LINK IN KILLINGS. Below was a photo of Rocco Urella and two detectives standing in a jungle of tall reeds, searching for clues. The story said dental records were needed to make a positive identification.

The autopsy cited the cause of death as a .22-caliber gunshot wound to the back of the head, left rear side. In addition, the medical examiner noted blunt trauma injuries to the head and face, including a fracture of the right cheekbone. In his opinion, the victim had lived for several hours after being beaten and shot. He estimated her time of death as sometime during the previous summer, which was consistent with the facts in the case—Debbie Delozier had disappeared the previous August 16.

At a press conference the next day, Rocco Urella said, "It is rather clear that the deaths of Denise Seaman and Debbie Delozier were carried out by the same person. They were found a mile apart, both died from .22-caliber bullets to the head, both had broken jaws, they lived in neighboring communities, and they shared common acquaintances who were members of a local motorcycle group."

In addition, Urella reconfirmed the direction of the investigation: CID believed the same person or group was also responsible for the slayings of Mary Ann Lees and Layne Spicer, the two abductions of Sharon Jones, and the disappearance of Liz Lande.

By then, Bobby Nauss had quit working at his father's garage. He and Cookie and little Tommy had moved out of the Nauss family home and into a two-bedroom apartment in Brookhaven, a community farther out in the suburbs, about six miles west of Darby.

At the age of twenty-three, Bobby had reached the point in his life where holding down a mundane job conflicted with his master plan of gaining fortune and fame. Plus, he needed more privacy to go about his business. He and his closest associates had established a direct link with a meth-cooking lab and were buying direct. They bought pure meth, doubled the price, then resold it to street-level "pushers"—people like Billy "Feathers" Turner.

Billy Turner had known Bobby for nearly five years, from back when Turner had been a prospect for the Warlocks. In fact, he'd purchased meth from Bobby as far back as four

years earlier, in 1972. But that was when Turner got himself
arrested for stealing a motorcycle and fled to New York State
to avoid prosecution. Turner then didn't see Bobby until he
returned to Delaware County two years later.

When Turner returned, he ran into Bobby on the street one
day. Needing a place to stay, he asked and Bobby offered
and Billy Turner wound up moving in with Bobby, Cookie,
and the baby in the apartment which was attached to the
Nauss home in Darby. Turner stayed until he saved enough
money to get his own place.

At that point, Bobby lost the appeals on his armed robbery
conviction and served nearly a year in the Chester County
prison. With his source of meth behind bars, Billy Turner
began buying his drugs elsewhere. But just as soon as Bobby
was released and dealing again, Turner sought him out.

For Bobby Nauss, the timing was perfect. He was just
reestablishing himself and looking for pushers. Since Bobby
had always trusted him, he cut Billy Turner a special deal.

"Nauss would give it to me up front," Turner admitted
later, "and I'd pay him for it later."

Turner said he passed the "crank" down the line to a
bunch of Warlocks and their girlfriends. In no time at all, he
was making daily buys from Bobby and moving a lot of
"product," anything from $15 bags, called quarter-Ts (quar-
ter-grams), to full ounces. More importantly for Bobby, Billy
Turner was putting Bobby in touch with additional pushers.

For instance, a few months after Turner started buying
meth from Bobby again, he introduced Bobby to a friend of
his named Norm Hansell. Like Billy Turner, Hansell was
low on cash. So Hansell asked Bobby if he would front him
the crank as well. If so, they'd already worked it out: Billy
would sell larger quantities, Hansell would sell smaller
amounts.

Bobby said yes, but told them no one else was getting a
free ride.

Norm Hansell called Bobby whenever he needed meth. He
usually ordered twenty quarter-Ts at a time. A quarter-T cost

Bobby $5. He charged Hansell $10 per bag, and Hansell
resold each bag for $15. As soon as Hansell sold all twenty
bags, he would call Bobby to reorder. When Hansell picked
up his new order, he paid Bobby the $200 he owed from the
previous transaction. Bobby pocketed $100 profit and the
cycle began again. In this fashion, Norm Hansell made two
to three buys per week.

Whenever Hansell called, Bobby usually had the twenty
quarter-Ts all bagged and ready to go. Bobby would deliver
them to Hansell's apartment or they'd meet at a neutral site
to make the exchange. But every once in a while, the meth
wasn't ready when Hansell called. On those occasions, Norm
Hansell would drive over to Bobby's apartment and sit in the
bedroom while Bobby finished weighing and bagging the
meth from a large brick Bobby kept in a plastic trash bag.

Billy Turner also introduced Bobby to another friend of
his. At the time of the introduction, Gary "Weasel" Warrington was buying $25 and $50 bags of meth from Turner. But
Warrington wanted to go into business for himself. So Warrington asked Bobby, could he buy direct?

When Warrington told Bobby he had cash up front, the
deal was made.

"I'd call Nauss and tell him what I wanted in code," Gary
Warrington later explained, "and he'd meet me somewhere
and deliver it." Warrington averaged one buy per week, usually quarter-ounces, which cost him $375 each and earned
Bobby Nauss nearly $200 in profit.

In similar fashion, Bobby established a network of drug
pushers. Business was soon booming and the cash was
rolling in. On one hand, he was pleased with his success. On
the other hand, he felt he was still missing an opportunity to
maximize his profits. If only he knew how to manufacture
the meth himself . . .

Once District Attorney Frank Hazel observed CID in action, he thought: For one reason or another, nothing is getting done. Everyone looks busy, but they aren't

accomplishing anything. A lot of the leads, most of which had existed right from the beginning of each case, had gotten cold because nobody was working them.

Specifically, he blamed CID chief Rocco Urella for the lack of progress and shoddy police work. Frank Hazel met with Urella, but the two men failed to reach an accord.

"At that point," Hazel later explained, "I decided to revamp CID to get it back up to snuff. I realized just how ill-equipped law enforcement was to deal with the Warlocks and the Pagans. You can do all the talking you want, but unless you have the vehicle to perform the investigations, you go nowhere. And we did not have that vehicle."

It was Frank Hazel's conclusion that the only way to effectively address the outlaw biker problem and the unsolved murders was to create a multidimensional task force. From his experience as a criminal lawyer, he'd gotten to know several local lawmen whom he considered to be excellent investigators and whose characters were beyond reproach. He openly coveted those men for his special squad.

First, he contacted the state police and persuaded the commissioner to assign two troopers to CID on a full-time basis—George Ellis from the Lima Barracks outside of Media and Bill Davis from Philadelphia's Belmont Barracks. Next, he obtained federal grant money and started talking to some of the local police departments around the county, offering to pick up the salaries of the officers he wanted. His first success was convincing Upper Darby to assign Paul Schneider to the task force.

One by one, Hazel handpicked six men—Troopers Ellis and Davis, Paul Schneider and another local policeman, one officer from the Philadelphia Police Department, and one CID detective. Hazel then charged his men with the investigation and prosecution of what he called "Organized Crime"—the Pagans and the Warlocks—and he gave his Major Crimes Task Force two directives only: to stem the wave of biker crimes and to solve the Marsh Murders.

"We looked at it as good versus evil," Frank Hazel later

recalled, "a death struggle, the galvanization of law enforcement against the forces who were breaching the peace of the people of Delaware County."

At the time, very little information existed within the traditional law enforcement establishment regarding the Pagan-Warlock organizations. No one knew exactly what the gangs did or how they did it and, with few exceptions, most of the gang members still remained nameless.

"The initial stage was to identify the enemy," Frank Hazel continued to explain. "All we had was this amorphous Pagan-Warlock group. Who the hell were we talking about?

"We had to figure out who was Warlock, who was Pagan, who was Warlock-related, who was Pagan-related, and what relationships were there, if any, among all of these people."

He believed the only way to accomplish his objective was to "turn" gang members, get them to become informers. To do this, he needed a "hammer," some sort of leverage to elicit their cooperation in giving up the vital information.

To the officers in his task force, Frank Hazel put out the word that all Warlocks, Pagans, and their associates were to be arrested for any wrongdoing—no matter how insignificant. It made no difference—simple assaults, passing bad checks, running stop signs, whatever—anything to get them off the street in an attempt to work on them to develop some information.

To all of the prosecutors in the District Attorney's Office, he issued the instructions that those cases were not to be plea-bargained. In fact, no deals were to be made without his consent. The bikers would be prosecuted to the maximum legal limits. And with the cooperation of the county judges, as much jail time as possible would be handed out—unless, that is, the defendants were willing to trade significant information in exchange for a degree of leniency.

CHAPTER
11

Although he was new to criminology, Frank Hazel understood that physical evidence was essential to the solution of any criminal investigation. Yet, in all of the unsolved murders combined, the CID evidence files contained virtually nothing.

Less than a month after taking office, on January 31, Frank Hazel snubbed Rocco Urella by putting John Reilly in charge of the task force. Reilly was Hazel's first-deputy district attorney. Twenty years older than his boss, John Reilly was Hazel's physical clone—with gray hair. His demeanor around the courthouse reminded co-workers of a friendly parish priest and he was known as a deductive thinker. He had Hazel's trust.

Frank Hazel sent John Reilly directly to the CID files and told him to get acquainted with the players, to put every file under the microscope. "Look for patterns," Hazel said. "Draw conclusions. And see if anything's been overlooked."

Right off, Reilly noticed certain themes that kept repeating—the MacDade Mall, the Castle, drugs, fear, violence, rape, and murder—and certain names that kept repeating—Bobby Nauss, Bobby Marconi, and Steve DeMarco.

When John Reilly looked at Debbie Delozier's file, he

read the anonymous letter which had been sent to Debbie's parents shortly after her disappearance.

"It says she knew too much," he said out loud to the investigators helping him that day. "Look, Liz Lande was a crime of passion, the others were executions. Maybe they all knew too much. But too much about what?"

It was a good question—too good, because none of the investigators could answer it. Instead, they resorted to conjecture.

One of the investigators mentioned that the Warlocks liked to go partying on weekends. Which, he explained, meant getting into a van with lots of beer and rotgut wine and drugs, then cruising the streets looking for young female hitchhikers. Once they succeeded in getting a couple of girls inside the van, the Warlocks drove to the middle of nowhere and explained to the girls that everyone was going to get naked and fuck—the Warlocks called it training, he explained to Reilly. If the girls resisted, the Warlocks stood them in front of a tree and threw knives all around them—just like in the circus—or they lined them up in front of a big rock, took out their guns, and shot all around them. And if the girls ultimately refused to give in to their demands, murder was a distinct possibility.

Take the Lees and Spicer girls, for instance. They were known to hitchhike. In fact, they planned to hitchhike home on the night they disappeared. They could have gotten into a van with some Warlocks—for the sake of argument, Bobby Nauss and Steve DeMarco—and wound up getting killed.

Another investigator mentioned that he'd heard Steve DeMarco was dating Debbie Delozier right around the time she disappeared. That certainly would have given DeMarco the opportunity to kill her. But what about motive?

One of the investigators decided to run Steve DeMarco's name through the Records & Information and BMV computers. He found out DeMarco was currently on parole from a prior stolen car conviction. In addition, his driver's license had been suspended.

"Pass the word to all the locals," John Reilly told the task force officers, "first chance they get, lock the son of a bitch up."

A few weeks later, on the night of March 3, Steve De-Marco pulled into a gas station on Chester Pike. Before he was able to drive away, police officers arrested him. Frank Hazel then pulled a few strings around the courthouse and succeeded in revoking DeMarco's parole—he would serve the two years remaining on his sentence.

With Steve DeMarco out of the way, the task force officers moved along to the next name on their list: Bobby Marconi. They brought him into CID headquarters and asked him: How was it that Debbie Delozier's picture was found on the front seat of his limo? And what did he know about her disappearance?

Afterward, outside the courthouse, newspaper reporters swarmed Bobby Marconi. But he refused to comment. Instead, his attorney spoke to the press.

"Rocco gave the picture to Bobby Marconi to pass around to people he knew," the lawyer said, "to find out if anybody saw her. There's nothing there. It's all an excuse. They have absolutely no evidence at all. It's all an effort to make things look as if they're doing something."

A month later, Frank Hazel was sipping coffee as he paced the floor of the task force office.

What was happening was amazing. In addition to creating the task force and revamping CID, Hazel was reorganizing the District Attorney's Office itself, transforming a staff of part-time prosecutors into full-timers. He was also juggling the new prosecutions that were coming in every day with the tremendous backlog of cases that had to be tried as expeditiously as possible—and he was getting convictions.

The prosecutors worked on the main floor of the courthouse in an orthodox office environment. Sunshine streamed through huge windows and fluorescent lights glowed overhead. In contrast, the task force office was located in the basement of the courthouse annex. Dark and mysterious, it came to be known as the "Bat Cave."

To the task force officers, who were coming and going at all hours, their subterranean sanctum was more a beehive than a bat cave. In addition to digging into the five unsolved murders, the officers were trying to gather information on the Pagans and Warlocks. This sometimes meant cultivating informants and trying to convince the bikers they'd already arrested into giving up some information. At the same time, they were guarding the witnesses who were willing to testify against the Warlocks, protecting them by moving them from one motel to another along the turnpike between Philadelphia and Harrisburg.

CHAPTER
12

On a hot, humid afternoon late in June 1976, Bobby Nauss was lifting weights in air-conditioned comfort at Don's Gym on Chester Pike in Glenolden. He was an inch taller and forty pounds heavier than the night he'd hanged Liz Lande to death more than four years earlier. Half of it had resulted from the normal boy-to-man growth changes, but the other half was solid muscle.

He was just adding a pair of twenty-five-pound plates to the bench press when Billy Turner and Gary Warrington walked through the door. They were perspiring from the heat outside. Earlier, Turner had called Bobby at home to order some meth. Bobby lay down on the bench and pumped out a few reps. Then he walked outside with Turner and Warrington.

Bobby felt a blast of heat as soon as he stepped into the parking lot. Sweat was dribbling down his back by the time he reached his car. He looked around in every direction. When he was certain no one was watching, he popped the trunk of his new Cadillac. Billy Turner's meth was inside.

At this point in time, Frank Hazel had been in office for nearly six months without coming up with any reason to bring Bobby Nauss into headquarters for questioning. In fact, inadvertently, Hazel had become Bobby's benefactor. The way the arrests were falling, Hazel was locking up many of the Warlocks who were pushing drugs, which meant an increased demand came Bobby's way. As a result, his business took off.

Before summer ended, Bobby and Cookie were able to buy a three-bedroom split-level home on a quarter-acre lot on Merionville Road in Aston. The area was sub-suburban and a bit farther west of their former apartment in Brookhaven, not far from the Delaware state line. It had a brick front, asbestos siding, a detached garage, and cost Bobby $41,500. He put down $11,500 in cash and spent another $7,500 on a heated, in-ground swimming pool right after his family moved in.

In addition to the new Cadillac, Bobby had also purchased a new $5,000 Harley. Cookie drove a five-year-old Chevelle.

The summer of 1976 was difficult for Frank Lande. His daughter had been missing for four and a half years and he'd long since given up hope she was still alive. But he was still driven to find her killer.

One hot, humid day, he had a stroke and nearly died. It left him with partial paralysis and forced him to take an early retirement from his job.

For Frank Hazel, however, the summer of 1976 was especially fruitful. Like a string of stacked dominoes, the Warlocks started falling—more than a dozen arrested by his task force officers.

Then, after successfully prosecuting each and every one of them, Frank Hazel made a bold move, a move that would indirectly give him the firepower he needed to go after Bobby Nauss.

"Right from the beginning," Hazel explained, "I tried, without success, to get the feds involved in our investigations. We didn't have investigating grand juries, we didn't have electronic surveillance and wiretaps, and we did not have the power to grant immunity or to offer witness protection.

"The feds had it all, and we needed it all to be effective. So that became another goal: to get the feds into the fight with us."

As a result of the summer's arrests and prosecutions, the task force had accumulated a significant amount of intelligence information about the Warlocks and the Pagans: who they were, what they did, how they did it, and exactly how long their tentacles reached. But a major problem still existed.

The Pagans had established their national headquarters in Marcus Hook and were virtually paralyzing the tiny town through intimidation tactics. So Frank Hazel's next priority became breaking the Pagans' stranglehold on Marcus Hook.

Near the end of the summer, in a predawn raid, task force officers stormed the Pagans' clubhouse. In the process, they seized motorcycles, weapons, charts, documents, recent photographs of gang members, and stolen property.

"We now had more information about motorcycle gangs," Frank Hazel recalled, "than any other law enforcement agency in the country. And we now had the information the feds needed. So they contacted us and made a deal."

The U.S. attorney for the Philadelphia District made the formal announcement on September 12:

"Local law enforcement officials alone cannot cope with the motorcycle gang problem. Published reports have made it clear that drug dealing, illegal weapons, and interstate sales of stolen goods are routine activities of the motorcycle gangs. These are all federal crimes and I intend to enlist all appropriate federal agencies to fight these crimes."

From that moment on, the DEA, ATF, FBI, and IRS were instructed to assist all state, county, and local law enforcement agencies whenever possible.

* * *

Disco was king in 1976.

His friends say Bobby Nauss loved disco and wasn't about to let marriage and fatherhood come between himself and the good times. He was turned on by the fancy high-tech lighting, high-decibel sound systems, and the bevies of whirling, swirling young women in fancy attire. He indulged himself by becoming a regular on the county's nightclub circuit.

In addition, the Warlocks regularly threw parties at their clubhouse, in private homes, and in rented motel rooms. These affairs tended to be wild in nature and featured an abundance of alcohol, drugs, young women, and sex. There was one particular incident that came to be legend in the Warlocks' circle, still bragged about by those who'd taken part, when a sixteen-year-old girl engaged in oral sex with so many Warlocks she had to be rushed to the hospital to have their semen pumped from her stomach.

Despite having the time of his life and making more money than he ever thought possible, Bobby continued to have problems. He could not stop abusing alcohol and drugs. He tended to drink until he was drunk, at which time he would "speed" the alcohol out of his system with meth—all of which gave him a different kind of high, a rush of omnipotent power. Then he'd start drinking to level off and the roller coaster ride would begin all over again.

In those states of mind, Bobby was manic and hyper: up for anything in the name of fun and games, acting on impulses, and always on the verge of losing control.

For several years, Bobby Nauss and the Warlocks had a good thing going.

"Actually, the Warlocks turned the heat up on themselves," Paul Schneider, one of the task force officers, later reflected. "Young girls started disappearing around the county and turning up dead—floating in the Tinicum Marsh—victims of the Warlocks.

"The press made a federal case out of it and, for the first

time, a concentrated task force was put together to deal with them.

"When I first started working on the case, for the first three days I went home every day with a headache . . . just from reading about what they were doing. I would have never believed people could do such things to each other.

"The Warlocks were made up of individuals. Some were good, some were bad, and others were worse. Did you ever hear the word amoral?"

CHAPTER
13

When the doorbell rang at an apartment at 408 West State Street in Media just after 4:30 P.M. on October 30, 1976, Catherine Ingram* was taking a shower. Her roommate answered the door and let the callers in—Billy Turner, Norm Hansell, and Bobby Nauss. They sat and waited while Catherine got dressed.

Fifteen minutes later, Catherine walked into the living room. She recognized Turner and Hansell—the three of them had attended a drug rehab program together at Haverford State Hospital—but she'd never seen Bobby before. In a soft voice, she said, "What's going on?"

"How ya doing?" Turner replied.

"Okay." She looked at Bobby, as if waiting to be introduced, but neither Turner nor Hansell bothered to introduce them. Bobby never said a word.

Catherine was wearing jeans and a body shirt. She was twenty-one years old, about five-three, and slender. She had light brown hair and a pale complexion.

"Is there a State Store around here?" Turner asked.

"Right up the street."

*Name has been changed to protect her privacy.

Billy Turner said they weren't familiar with Media. If they promised to drop her off right after they bought some liquor, would she show them the way?

They drove down State Street in Bobby's Cadillac, Catherine sitting in front in between Bobby and Norm Hansell, Billy Turner in back. It was a short ride to the State Store, where Bobby and Turner bought two quart bottles of Orange Driver, a premixed concoction of vodka and orange juice.

Next, they stopped at a fast-food restaurant to pick up some paper cups, and they bought a bag of ice at a gas station. With the essentials for mixing the drinks now in hand, the three men poured themselves a round—Catherine said she didn't want one—and they started drinking. But instead of taking Catherine back to her apartment, Bobby headed out of town.

"Hey," she said, "I have to be back to baby-sit."

"We have to go somewhere first," Turner told her. "Then we'll drop you off."

The night bartender at Maximillian's Bar in Chichester Township, eight miles outside of Media, started his shift that night at seven o'clock.

He'd been working about half an hour when Turner, Hansell, Bobby, and Catherine entered the bar. He'd never seen her before, but he knew the three men. His brother was married to one of Bobby's sisters.

The three men sat there at the bar drinking beers for a good forty-five minutes, while Catherine drank nothing. Then, without saying a word, she went outside.

Moments later, Norm Hansell followed her.

It was around 8:30 when Billy Turner called the bartender over. "Can we use your apartment?" Turner asked him.

"What for?"

"To party with the chick. Norm and I partied with her before, and she's really wild. We'll save you some."

* * *

Catherine thought they were taking her home. Instead, Bobby drove farther into the country, onto dark, secluded roads. She had no idea where they were.

The three men snorted some meth.

"Get in back," Turner said to her.

"What for?"

"You know."

"Look," she said, "I've got to get back to baby-sit."

"Get the fuck back here," Turner said, and he grabbed her by the shirt and pulled her over the seat. Then he held a knife against her throat and threatened, "Now take your clothes off or I'll slice your fucking throat."

Catherine stripped.

Billy Turner mounted her and initiated intercourse with her. When he couldn't hold out any longer, he withdrew his penis from her vagina, inserted it in her mouth, and ejaculated.

"Now get back up front," he told her.

Catherine crawled over the seat and sat between Bobby and Norm Hansell.

While he continued to steer the car with his left hand, Bobby put his right hand behind Catherine's head. When he pulled her face into his lap, she performed oral sex on him. And when she finished with Bobby, she did the same thing for Norm Hansell.

By then, Bobby had pulled off the road. He and Hansell then pushed Catherine onto the seat, spread her legs apart, and the two of them took turns performing cunnilingus on her. When they were through with her, they passed Catherine back to Billy Turner.

He leaned back into the corner of the seat. She stooped over him on all fours, trying to bring him to an orgasm orally. Suddenly she felt the coldest sensation she'd ever felt and let out a shriek.

Bobby was laughing and trying to push another ice cube into Catherine's rectum.

"Finish Billy!" Bobby shouted at her. Then he waited for her to turn around and watched while she started back in on Turner. Then Bobby picked up one of the liquor bottles, leaned over the seat, and inserted its neck into her vagina.

Catherine screamed in pain.

"Stop it! What's wrong with you?"

"Shut the fuck up!" Bobby shouted. And he snapped. He started punching her thighs. Her buttocks. "Just do what the fuck you're told or I'll kill you!"

Bobby parked the Cadillac in front of the E Building at the Trimble Run Apartments in Brookhaven. His mood was somewhat mellower than before, but his lust was far from satisfied.

They led Catherine into apartment E-11. Straight into the bedroom. Billy Turner told her to get undressed and get in bed.

The three men snorted some more meth.

Bobby took off his pants and lay on the bed on his back. When he told Catherine he wanted another blow job, she complied. But Bobby was having difficulty sustaining his erection. So he withdrew his penis from her mouth and rolled onto his stomach.

"I'm having trouble getting off," Bobby told her. "Lick my asshole until I get another hard-on."

Once again, Catherine did what she was told. But it didn't help.

"She's lousy," Bobby complained. "Hit her. Make her do it better."

Billy Turner took off his belt and whipped Catherine across her bare buttocks.

"Do it better!" he yelled.

But it was too late for Bobby. He rolled off the bed and stormed out of the bedroom.

Billy Turner pushed Catherine off the bed and shoved her into the hallway, which was where Bobby was standing. Bobby's pants were still off.

"Get down on your knees," Turner told Catherine. "Suck him off and do it right this time."

Bobby's limp penis was back in her mouth and she was trying her best to arouse him. Just get this over, she told herself, and everything will be all right.

"She's still lousy!" Bobby yelled a few moments later, and Billy Turner whipped her with his belt a few more times. But nothing seemed to help Bobby. So he pulled his penis out of Catherine's mouth and walked into the living room. There he snorted some more meth.

Meanwhile, Billy Turner and Norm Hansell led Catherine back into the bedroom, where they took turns on her once again. Turner went first, alternating intercourse with oral sex. And while she was bringing him to another orgasm orally, Norm Hansell inserted a vibrator into her vagina.

When she finished with Billy Turner, Norm Hansell withdrew the vibrator, lay down on the bed, and spread his legs. He told Catherine to massage his testicles with the vibrator while she performed oral sex on him—which she did. When he ejaculated in her mouth, she told herself, finally, it was over.

Wrong.

Bobby Nauss came back into the bedroom with an erection. He rolled Catherine over, pushed her face down on the bed, and sodomized her. After he achieved orgasm, Bobby went back out to the living room. He then phoned his brother-in-law and told him to come over.

Meanwhile, Billy Turner and Norm Hansell were taking another turn with Catherine in the bedroom.

The doorbell rang sometime after midnight. Norm Hansell answered the door. It was Bobby's brother-in-law.

"Come on in," Norm Hansell told him. "Billy wanted to surprise you. Go take a look in the bedroom."

The brother-in-law walked into the bedroom. Billy Turner and Catherine were still in bed—both naked.

"He's a friend of mine," Turner told Catherine. "Take care of him."

While he undressed, the brother-in-law mentioned to Catherine that his name was Bob. Then he got in bed and had oral and genital sex with her.

A little after 2 A.M., Bobby Nauss, the brother-in-law, and Norm Hansell went home.

Catherine was sleeping in the bedroom.

After the others left, Billy Turner woke her up. He took her into the living room and had sex with her on the couch. Afterward, she passed out.

The next time she opened her eyes, it was light out and the bartender from Maximillian's was standing over her. As soon as she saw him, she started crying.

"Relax," he said, "I'm tired and just want to go to bed. Do you need a ride somewhere?"

It was eight o'clock in the morning, October 31, when Catherine Ingram walked back into her own apartment. At 8:10, she took a shower. By 8:30, she was sitting on the living room sofa, sobbing.

Her roommate came out and asked, "What's wrong?"

Venting her pent-up emotions, Catherine recounted the events of the previous fourteen hours.

"Come on," her roommate said, and she took Catherine's hand.

"Where?"

"I'm taking you to the police."

"No way." Catherine forced a nervous laugh and pulled her hand back. "I'm just glad I'm still alive."

She got up and walked into her bedroom and lay on the bed. But she couldn't sleep and the morning hours dragged by. All the while, slowly, her indignation began to simmer.

At ten minutes before noon, Catherine Ingram walked into the Media Police Station and said she'd been gang-raped by four men. She identified Billy Turner and Norm Hansell as two of her attackers, but she couldn't identify the other two—nor did she know that Bobby Nauss was a member of the Warlocks motorcycle gang.

As a result, when the sergeant from Media P.D. called the county CID, the complaint passed through normal channels. The Major Crimes Task Force was not notified.

In the early afternoon, four arrest warrants were issued: one each for Billy Turner and Norm Hansell, and two John Does.

At three o'clock that afternoon, while a CID detective waited in the lobby of the emergency room at Crozer Hospital, a resident physician examined Catherine Ingram.

After the exam, the detective spoke with the doctor.

There was only the slightest trace of sperm in the victim's vagina, the doctor informed the detective, and none was detected in her anus.

"Shit," the detective said. In almost every rape case, the first thing the victim does is take a shower, to psychologically cleanse herself. And this case was no different. Catherine Ingram had washed the evidence down the drain immediately after returning home.

And, the doctor continued, there were no lacerations on the young lady's vagina, and none on her anus.

To the detective, the way the case looked, there were only two chances of getting a conviction: Find an eyewitness or get somebody to confess.

By nightfall, regular CID detectives began searching for Billy Turner and Norm Hansell.

They were not successful.

Turner and Hansell had packed their bags and were already driving south on I-95 to stay with Turner's brother until the heat died down. The brother lived several hundred miles away, in Savannah, Georgia.

CHAPTER
14

Bobby Nauss made a quick trip to Savannah in early February 1977—nearly four months after the rape of Catherine Ingram.

Billy Turner's brother had moved back to Delaware County, leaving Billy and Norm Hansell hiding out in Georgia by themselves. But he'd left his motorcycle behind and he asked Bobby if he could borrow Bobby's pickup truck to drive down to Savannah to get his bike. Bobby said sure. In fact, he'd go with him to give him a hand.

The trip took three days, down and back, and was uneventful. But while Bobby was on his way back, the rape case started to break.

The task force officers had been buttonholing their informants, trying to build some sort of case against Bobby. That's when they heard, for the first time, that he'd participated in the rape of Catherine Ingram. So they squeezed their informants a little harder and learned the intimate details of the rape, and they found out where Billy Turner and Norm Hansell were hiding. If the information was reliable, they had Bobby Nauss on a silver platter.

Bill Davis and George Ellis arrived in Savannah on February 17.

Ellis was tall, around six-two, and good-looking in a raw-boned way. In his customary shirt and tie, sport jacket, slacks, and sunglasses, he looked like the Marlboro man on his way to a wedding. At thirty-three, he'd been with the state police for six years, and his superiors and colleagues held him in the highest esteem.

Davis, age thirty-two, was a nine-year state police veteran. He was dark and ruggedly handsome. He and George Ellis were perfect foils for each other. Whereas Ellis was reserved and came across as fatherly and sympathetic, Bill Davis was a needler, talkative, and a master of sarcasm.

Davis didn't beat around the bush with Turner and Hansell. He came right out and asked them why they'd raped Catherine Ingram.

They played dumb. Rape? What rape?

And now I bet you're going to try to tell me you don't even know the girl, right?

Of course they knew her, they admitted. So okay, they'd had sex with her. They'd had sex with her lots of times. But always because she wanted to. She was a nympho.

Bill Davis kept pressing.

"Who was with you when you picked her up?"

No answer.

To Turner: "Why'd you threaten her with a knife?"

"Hey, man, a knife. No way. In my whole life, I've never ever even carried a knife."

"Let's go back to that day. October thirtieth. Right before Halloween. Three guys pick her up at her apartment in Media and drive her to Maximillian's. Two of those guys are you two. Whose car were you using? It was a Cadillac, wasn't it? Whose Cadillac? Bobby Nauss's Cadillac?"

"I don't know what you're talking about."

"Oh, really? Then let's change the subject. Let's talk about drugs."

"I don't know nothing about drugs."

"Bullshit. You've been buying meth from Bobby Nauss

for the past year. Want me to give you the names and dates
of the people you sell to?"

Silence.

"You fucking assholes. You have no idea, do you? We
know you beat her up. I can tell you where it happened and I
can tell you Bobby's brother-in-law came over and fucked
her, too. Do you have any idea how many years you're staring at?" Davis threw the warrants on the table. "Clue them
in, George."

Ellis unfolded the warrants and explained that they were
being arrested for simple assault, indecent assault, involuntary sexual intercourse, conspiracy, rape, and kidnapping.

Bill Davis and George Ellis let them stew awhile. Then
Davis stepped outside the front door and Ellis offered cigarettes to Turner and Hansell.

"Between you and me," Ellis said in his most paternal
tones, "nobody gives a shit about you two." Then he paused
to let it sink in. "Frank Hazel's got a hard-on for Bobby
Nauss. That's who we're after. Not you.

"Look, I know you're scared. I would be, too, if I were in
your shoes. But I promise you, if you cooperate, if you give
us Nauss on the rape case *and* on the drug case, you're both
off the hook. We won't prosecute you for the rape and we
won't prosecute you for the drugs. We'll get you new identities and we'll relocate you somewhere else at the federal
government's expense."

At this point, Billy Turner, who'd been staring at his
boots, looked up at Hansell. Then he looked at Ellis.

"Okay," he said, "I'll do it."

George Ellis looked at Hansell.

Norm Hansell nodded his agreement.

Turner and Hansell were thus slated for the Witness Protection Program.

"By this point," George Ellis explained, "we also knew
that Nauss killed the Lande girl, but we lacked the evidence.
But we knew Nauss was in the drug business and we knew if

we worked long enough and hard enough, focusing on Nauss the whole time, taking it one step at a time, infiltrating further and further into the Warlocks, we had a chance to break the murder case."

Strategically, Turner and Hansell were sequestered. For the previous year, the U.S. Attorney's Office had been conducting a massive sting operation in which Bobby Nauss and Steve DeMarco had been identified as central figures in a drug conspiracy. The U.S. attorney was close to making a move, but not quite ready. Arresting Bobby Nauss at that time would have jeopardized the entire investigation and negated a tremendous amount of time and effort. Besides, he wanted to make his case against Bobby just a little bit tighter. So the arrest warrants for Bobby Nauss and his brother-in-law were sealed.

Nearly a month later, on March 13, a confidential informant called the ATF office in Philadelphia. He'd been working with Special Agent Gil Amoroso for nearly a year and he told Amoroso he'd just purchased some meth from Bobby Nauss at Bobby's home in Aston.

"I need a favor," Amoroso told his informant.

"Name it."

"Can you set up another buy from Nauss?"

"No problem. When I was leaving, he told me anytime I needed meth, just come over, he always kept it in the house."

Two days later, the informant called back and said the deal was set.

Three days after that, on March 18, the ATF agent sat in his car half a block away from Bobby's house while his informant walked in Bobby's front door.

Inside, the informant and Bobby sat around for a while. They made small talk and snorted a few lines of meth. Then they made a deal.

Half an hour later, Gil Amoroso watched his informant leave Bobby's house. Amoroso pulled away and met his informant at a prearranged location. As soon as the informant handed over his "buy," the agent drove directly to the ATF office.

Gil Amoroso weighed the buy: 40.2 grams.

He tested it: pure meth.

For nearly a month, task force officers were trying to locate Catherine Ingram to see if she could positively identify Bobby Nauss as one of the men who'd raped her. But she no longer lived at the apartment in Media and she'd left no forwarding address.

Finally, on March 20, they located her in Cape May, New Jersey.

The next day, she picked Bobby's photo out of an array that was presented to her.

Six weeks later, at 4 A.M. on May 4, a combined force of 135 federal agents, state troopers, local policemen, and task force officers assembled at the state police barracks outside of Media. In a synchronized action some twelve hundred miles to the south, another dozen agents were gathering in Miami, Florida.

At five o'clock, Bill Davis led a team of five men to Bobby Nauss's home in Aston.

Inside, Bobby and Cookie were sleeping in an upstairs bedroom in the rear of the house. Four-year-old Tommy slept in another bedroom.

The officers were in position by 5:20.

"Police, open up!" Bill Davis yelled as he knocked on the front door.

Standing to the right of the door, his back pressed against the wall, was George Ellis. Paul Schneider stood to the left of the door. Gil Amoroso and an Aston police officer were watching the rear of the house.

Bill Davis waited exactly one minute. When he failed to hear any sounds coming from inside, he smashed a sledgehammer against the door. It was textbook procedure which generally knocked doors down clean and fast. But not this time. What he didn't know was that Bobby had replaced the original with a three-inch-thick oak door and he'd secured it with three heavy-duty hinges on one side and three steel bolts on the other.

Davis kept slamming away, but the door didn't budge.

"You don't have to break it down," Bobby yelled from inside in a sleepy, irritated voice.

As soon as Bobby opened the door, the officers stormed inside. They cocked their shotguns and screamed: *"Police. . . . Don't move. . . . Put your fucking hands up. . . . You're under arrest."*

They handcuffed Bobby and advised him of his rights. Two officers ushered him outside, put him in the backseat of an unmarked car, and transported him straight to the state police barracks.

At the same time, similar scenes were taking place throughout Delaware County and in Florida.

In Miami, the agents made six arrests, seizing six pounds of Colombian cocaine and two hundred pounds of South American marijuana.

Locally, the strike force arrested forty-one Warlock and Pagan members, former members, and associates. Included in that batch were Steve DeMarco, who was already serving time in jail, and Billy Turner and Norm Hansell. It wasn't that law enforcement was reneging on its promise to them. Simply put, it might seem fishy if Turner and Hansell were not arrested with the others. Such an oversight would surely expose them to danger and could possibly terminate them as witnesses against Bobby Nauss.

The local raids also confiscated large quantities of meth, PCP, and cocaine, along with seven shotguns, eleven sawed-off shotguns, twenty-nine pipe bombs, forty-one blasting caps, fourteen handguns, nine rifles, four pen guns, six silencers, and another thirty assorted weapons.

* * *

It was barely 6 A.M. when the officers started searching Bobby's home, which from a point of law was a mistake. The search warrant had not yet arrived.

Cookie Nauss was sitting in the living room with little Tommy. She was an emotional wreck.

Upstairs, two officers found a loaded Remington 1100 shotgun in a corner of Bobby and Cookie's bedroom. A gray briefcase was underneath the bed and a ledger book was hidden between the box springs and mattress. The entries appeared to be records of drug transactions.

The officers also found a Sears & Roebuck Model 21 shotgun in another bedroom. Moving downstairs, in the recreation room, they found a motorcycle jacket with a set of Warlocks' colors attached to its back. In the kitchen, they found a triple-beam scale under the sink and a plastic bag with marijuana residue in the trash can. But they failed to find either a sizable stash of drugs or a large amount of cash.

At eight o'clock, when the search warrant finally arrived, Cookie asked Bill Davis why Bobby had been arrested.

He told her there were a couple of reasons. There was the matter of the violations of the federal Controlled Substance, Drug, Device, and Cosmetics Act Number 64, and there was the matter of the violations of the Federal Firearms Act. By the way, there was also the matter of the rape.

Rape? What rape?

Last Halloween.

Impossible, Cookie said, Bobby didn't have sex with anyone but her. And rape? That was ridiculous!

Bill Davis told her he didn't want to pry into their personal lives, but the rape victim had vividly described a birthmark or wart or something on Bobby's penis. Personally, Davis said, tongue in cheek, he thought she was lying, but he was anxious to see Bobby's penis for himself, to find out whether or not she was telling the truth.

"That was when Nauss's wife dropped the evidence to Bill Davis," George Ellis would later explain. "I think you could say they were having some sort of domestic problem at the time.

"So she gave us Bill Standen's name and the address of the apartment he'd rented on Chester Pike in Folcroft where Liz Lande was murdered."

Finally, they'd learned the name of a good source who would be able to connect Bobby Nauss with Elizabeth Lande's disappearance and apparent murder.

Meanwhile, at the state police barracks, Bobby was finding out he was not only being charged in a drug-trafficking conspiracy, but he was also being charged for raping Catherine Ingram.

He was arraigned that afternoon, remanded to the Delaware County prison, and held without bail.

A week later, on May 11, Catherine Ingram arrived to testify at Bobby's preliminary hearing. In the interim, she'd received threatening phone calls. She appeared to be upset and confused.

The prosecutor asked for a one-week's continuance.

On May 15, she returned to the courtroom. This time, much more composed, she testified and Bobby was bound over for trial.

Bail was set at $100,000 on the rape charges—his bail on the drug charges had already been set at $15,000. Bobby posted both bonds and was released. The drug trial was slated to begin in July, the rape in August.

Discovering that Bill Standen had long since vacated the apartment on Chester Pike, the task force officers began staking out Standen's mother's house in Philadelphia. But Standen, they did not know, had moved to the Florida Keys shortly after Liz Lande's apparent murder in 1971.

The rest of May passed, and June, as police officers performed regular drive-bys, with no results. Then, sometime after midnight on July 2, they got a break when a vehicle with Florida license plates was parked outside.

"Bill Standen was inside," George Ellis said later. "We woke him up and brought him in and found out he was wanted on an outstanding bench warrant for an old shooting charge."

If nothing else, they now had a reason to hold Standen and try to break him down.

George Ellis told Standen his choice was simple: He could stand trial along with Bobby Nauss and spend the rest of his life in jail, or he could turn state's evidence and be granted immunity from prosecution.

Objectively, it was a simple call. Subjectively, the decision was agonizing—and not just from a sense of friendship or a vow to uphold the time-honored adage of loyalty among thieves.

Some of the outlaw bikers were more like the characters in *The Godfather* than the fictional Godfather himself. They not only believed in killing witnesses to the crimes, they also believed in killing people who might be witnesses. Some of them were quite capable of putting out a contract on someone's life with no compunctions whatsoever. And among his peers, Bobby Nauss had that reputation.

Bill Standen considered his choices carefully.

"He gave up the case," George Ellis said later. "He gave us everything."

What Frank Hazel now needed to ensure a successful homicide prosecution against Bobby Nauss was Liz Lande's body.

On July 12, Bill Standen directed George Ellis and a search party to a location in the New Jersey pine barrens where he said he'd helped Bobby bury Liz Lande. It was an area outside of Williamstown, sixteen miles to the southeast of Philadelphia. At the time of the murder, the area had been pine trees and wilderness. At the time of the search, nearly six years later, it had been transformed into housing subdivisions.

Nothing looked the same to Bill Standen.

For the better part of the daylight hours, he pointed out one spot after another. The officers dug and dug, but they failed to find Liz Lande's body.

"We had to make a choice," Frank Hazel would later explain. "We either had to try the homicide case with what we had, or we had to abandon it altogether."

He called a meeting of the task force members.

"One group," he recalled, "believed we should continue to investigate with a view toward recovering the body, or parts of it. But without a corpus delicti in a first-degree murder case, our chances of success were minimal—especially when one considers the nature of our witnesses, all of whom had a checkered career and were Warlocks associates, and none of whom would ever be invited to have tea with the bishop of Boston.

"Another group believed we weren't ever going to be successful finding the body and if we didn't proceed right away, we never would because we couldn't hold the people we'd turned very much longer. For two reasons. Reason one, our hammer would be gone. Reason two, our witnesses might recant their testimonies or be terrorized to the extent we could no longer rely on them.

"And the third group believed we had as strong a circumstantial case as we were ever going to get and we weren't ever going to find the body. Even if we did, we'd be so far down the road, we would compromise our own witnesses—all of whom we were holding at various locations."

After the meeting, Frank Hazel went home to mull over the options.

CHAPTER
15

Shortly after 6 P.M. on Friday, July 15, Bill Davis arrested Bobby Nauss at a convenience store near Bobby's home.

At 7:15, Bobby was charged in district court with criminal homicide and murder. Bail was denied and Bobby was sent to Delaware County Prison.

"We have evidence," Frank Hazel announced at a press conference the following Monday, "that Miss Lande was hanged by the neck and her body disposed of in the state of New Jersey."

"Did you find the body?" a reporter shot at Hazel, but the district attorney declined to comment.

The headline in the Philadelphia *Bulletin* said, WARLOCK IS CHARGED IN DEATH OF WOMAN. Below Liz Lande's picture, the story referred to Bobby as the gang's vice president.

The next day's newspaper story quoted members of the Warlocks as saying they'd learned that two witnesses had been found. One was going to say he'd seen the hanging itself, and the other was going to say he'd seen the dead body after it had been cut down. But Frank Hazel refused to confirm or deny those rumors, and he remained close-lipped about whether or not he'd recovered the body.

However, one reporter went to New Jersey to do some

digging on his own. The following day's headline in the Philadelphia *Inquirer* read SEARCH IN N.J. FOR DELCO GIRL'S BODY WAS FRUITLESS, DETECTIVE SAYS. Citing a Gloucester County detective who'd assisted in the search as his source, the reporter said detectives from Delaware County had searched a site in Monroe Township earlier in the month without success, and they had not been back since.

In each succeeding story during the week and on almost every television broadcast of the day's news, Bobby Nauss was being called a Warlock, a drug dealer, a rapist, and a murderer.

District court in the Tinicum Township Municipal Building was a small room with wood paneling, a tile floor, and folding chairs.

Ordinarily, a preliminary hearing in a murder case is a rubber-stamp procedure. Sheriff's deputies deliver the defendant to court, the prosecutor calls witnesses and presents a few pieces of evidence, and the district justice sends the case along to court to allow a judge and jury to decide the fate of the accused. As a rule, every murder case has a corpus delicti—that's what makes it a murder case.

Frank Hazel knew, without a body, this was one preliminary hearing in which no one would be just going through the motions. This was one time when the case just might be thrown out before it ever got to court.

On this particular Friday, July 22, 1977, the district justice called the proceedings to order at 10 A.M. His name was Tony Truscello and he was exactly the type of law-and-order magistrate that Frank Hazel, given his choice, would have selected to determine whether or not his case was strong enough to try Bobby Nauss for murder.

"I try to cut through the bullshit," is the way Truscello describes his style, "and stick to the facts." He was forty years old and he lived in Folcroft. He had a teenage son and daughter and a sensitivity to the community he called home.

It was an emotional scene. Jammed close together, the

families watched. Frank and Frances Lande came to see the murderer of their only child finally stand accused of his crime. They sat in the front row. Bobby's mother and wife and a large number of family members showed up to support Bobby because they believed he was innocent. They sat farther back. Mixed in between were the reporters who'd been following the unsolved murders for better than a year.

Bobby was sitting at a table no more than ten feet from the witness stand, showing no emotion, seemingly oblivious to what was happening all around him. Next to Bobby sat Malcolm Berkowitz, his attorney, considered by colleagues to be capable but not overly impressive. But to the Warlocks, he was a superstar. Early on, he'd successfully defended several cases involving gang members. As a result, when a biker found himself in trouble, his name was one of the first that came to mind.

In regard to Bobby, Malcolm Berkowitz was prepared to represent him in all three cases, but he was more concerned about the drug and the rape charges than he was about the homicide. What prosecutor in his right mind would take a murder case to court without a body? And expect to win?

Thousand of man-hours had gone into the pursuit and apprehension of Bobby Nauss, and this was one of the highest-profile cases to ever hit the county. Although Frank Hazel believed Bobby was guilty, the decision to try him without a corpse had been difficult. Another delicate decision had been the choice of the prosecuting attorney.

"Being downstairs from the rest of the office," Hazel would explain later, "the task force people were unique. They were a part of us, but they weren't. They didn't report to anybody from their original jurisdictions and they didn't report to the chief of CID. They reported to me, and that was it. So there was some feeling—the type of feeling you get internally in any organization—that these guys had access to the boss that nobody else had.

"Nobody knows the effort they put into this. It wasn't a

job, it was a crusade. So a good relationship between the task
force people and the prosecuting attorney was of paramount
importance. He had to have the respect of the task force
members—and something more. He had to be immune from
the threats and intimidation that were part and parcel of Warlock prosecutions.

"We all sat down and picked Jim DelBello because he had
the exact temperament for the job. And he had the guts."

Sitting in the witness chair, Frank Lande showed none of
the ill effects of the stroke he'd suffered the previous summer. His speech was unimpaired.

All the while Frank Lande testified, Bobby Nauss avoided
making eye contact with him. Bobby sat there and listened
passively as Liz's father described the circumstances of her
disappearance and her relationship with Bobby.

Through the prison grapevine, Bobby had heard that Bill
Standen had been located and that he was going to testify
against him. Still, when Bobby saw his buddy Stanley raise
his right hand and swear to tell the whole truth and nothing
but the truth, Bobby was livid.

In a straightforward monologue, Bill Standen told the
court how Bobby had awakened him in the middle of the
night, how he'd gone out to the garage and up into the loft,
how he'd seen Liz Lande's nude body hanging by the neck,
and how he'd helped Bobby bury her the following morning
in the Jersey pine barrens.

After two witnesses, Jim DelBello rested his case.

Malcolm Berkowitz stood and approached Bill Standen.

"It's incredible," Berkowitz began, his tone confrontational, "that a person could be burdened down with this
knowledge for all these years and not make it public—then
suddenly come forward."

He inched forward and fired questions at Standen in rapid
succession: "Why aren't you being charged for murder?
What sort of deal have you made with the district attorney?

Are you collecting the reward money by volunteering this information? Isn't it a fact that you couldn't find the body?"

This was the question everyone in the courtroom had been
waiting to hear. Everyone thought they knew the answer, but
they weren't sure. Just maybe Frank Hazel *had* found the
body and was holding it as his trump card for this very moment.

But Bill Standen just sat there without blurting out the answer. He'd been forewarned to expect this question and he'd
been instructed not to answer it.

"Objection," Jim DelBello said.

District Justice Truscello sustained the objection.

Malcolm Berkowitz wheeled to face the judge.

"A criminal homicide of any degree," he fumed, "requires
proof that someone has been killed by unlawful means.
There has been no such evidence presented here. You have a
body hanging, but you have nothing to indicate that Mr.
Nauss had anything to do with the body being hung.

"The fact that he and Mr. Standen disposed of the body by
burying it in no way indicates that Mr. Nauss was involved
in any killing.

"The criminal complaint says Mr. Nauss took a rope and
hung a woman, but there is nothing here that says that. There
is no credible evidence before the court which would indicate Mr. Nauss participated in a killing—if in fact there was
one."

It was now Jim DelBello's turn to address the judge.
"Your Honor," he said firmly, "the witness testified that
when he went up into the loft, he saw Elizabeth Lande's
body hanging. Nauss was grinning, saying he did it.

"Based on the case of the Commonwealth versus Burns,
which is 409 Pennsylvania 619, decided in 1963, and a very
able opinion by Mr. Justice O'Brien in considering a case
similar to this, where a body was not produced, nor was any
part of a body produced, I submit to the court that such evidence right now is not only sufficient for a finding of a prima

facie case, but also sufficient for a finding of guilty beyond a
reasonable doubt."

Tony Truscello had discussed the case with Frank Hazel
earlier in the week.

"Where's the body?" he'd asked the district attorney.

"We don't need a body," Hazel replied, mentioning the
Burns decision as his legal precedent, which sent Truscello
to his library to research the case.

What he learned from the Burns decision was that the female victim and one of her girlfriends had been walking
home together from a bar. The victim entered a house in
which she cohabited with her boyfriend, and her friend continued on her way home. But suddenly the girlfriend heard a
disturbance coming from inside the house. So she went back
and knocked on the front door. She was allowed to enter—at
which time she saw the victim lying on the floor with blood
on her forehead. The girlfriend left and phoned the police.
But by the time the officers responded, the body was gone.
Never to be seen again.

The defendant was tried and convicted based on the girlfriend's testimony. The conviction was appealed and went all
the way to the Pennsylvania Supreme Court, where it was
upheld.

It was 11:30 A.M. District Justice Truscello had heard both
sides of the argument and was ready to make a ruling.

"The elements that were required in the Commonwealth
versus Burns," he said dispassionately, "have been produced
by the Commonwealth and sufficient evidence has been produced to hold the defendant over for the next term of court."

Bail was set at $1 million.

A sheriff's deputy snapped handcuffs onto Bobby's wrists.
As family members watched the deputy lead Bobby out the
back door, Frank Lande looked at their faces and recognized

their pain. He already knew what it was like to lose a loved one and he felt nothing but compassion for Bobby's family.

Although Bobby's bail would be reduced to $750,000 later the same day, he was nearly cashed out, facing staggering legal fees, and no one from the Warlocks came forward to bail him out.

Three days later, it was time for what the newspapers were calling the "Warlock Drug Trial" to begin.

Malcolm Berkowitz arrived at the federal courthouse in Philadelphia on July 25 armed with newspaper articles, transcripts of radio broadcasts, and videotapes of television newscasts. He moved for dismissal of the drug charges due to the "overwhelming prejudicial publicity."

Judge Alfred Luongo denied the request.

Bobby's lawyer then requested a change of venue.

Although the judge openly chastised Frank Hazel's timing of the homicide arrest because it was in such close proximity to the beginning of the drug trial, he refused to move the trial out of the city.

Berkowitz next moved to suppress the evidence that had been seized from Bobby's home on the day of the raid, pointing out that the actual search had taken place an hour and a half before the warrant was issued. Judge Luongo denied this motion as well.

Finally, Malcolm Berkowitz requested a cooling off period of thirty days be granted prior to jury selection. The judge gave him a week.

Frank Hazel did not want to go to court without a body.

"We decided," he explained later, "to keep digging up various portions of the pinelands to find it."

On July 28, Bill Standen led George Ellis and another search party back to New Jersey. This time, Ellis took heavy equipment with him.

"I can remember being on vacation down the Jersey

shore," Frank Hazel recalled, "and getting a call from some official who wanted to know why these front-end loaders from Delaware County, Pennsylvania, were digging up the pinelands.

"We had gotten all of the permits, but it was a Sunday morning and this guy didn't know anything about it. He was ready to arrest about eight of our guys."

After the phone call, the digging continued.

George Ellis and his crew concentrated on the same area they'd searched three weeks earlier. But this time, he tripled the size of the excavation.

"We leveled two acres," he said later, "and we tried everything to find the body. We even used bulldozers, but the results were still negative."

The search resumed the following day, July 29.

"We borrowed a special dog from the New York State Police," Ellis continued, "a dog trained to sniff out dead meat that was buried. The dog worked that entire railroad bed off of Lakedale Road—in particular, the area we had bulldozed the day before. The dog found a lot of dead meat, but not what we wanted."

"We just couldn't locate the body," Frank Hazel explained. "Our belief was that the body, essentially, had been dismembered, scattered over the terrain, and we just couldn't come up with it.

"To us, not having a body wasn't something the jury was going to worry about. But it was a legal problem. Would it hold up in court?"

CHAPTER
16

Bobby's only federal offense was the drug case. The trial, a relatively cut-and-dried affair, began on August 1.

Rather than risk contaminating the case, the U.S. attorney did not introduce any evidence which had been seized from Bobby's home under the "tainted" search warrant. Instead, he based his case on the eyewitness testimonies of Billy Turner, Norm Hansell, and Gary Warrington, and he supported it with evidence which had been gathered by various ATF and DEA agents and the task force officers.

The evidence showed that between May 1972 and February 1977, Bobby Nauss and Steve DeMarco had supplied methamphetamine to Turner, Hansell, and Warrington. They, in turn, delivered it to other individuals.

It took the jury just three hours to convict Bobby and Steve DeMarco.

Bobby's conviction carried a maximum jail term of five years and a fine of up to $15,000. Sentencing was deferred to a later date.

Malcolm Berkowitz appealed the verdict to the U.S. Third Circuit Court of Appeals.

CHAPTER
17

Eight days later, on August 12, sheriff's deputies escorted Bobby into the Delaware County Courthouse for his homicide arraignment.

Although he would continue to represent Bobby in the rape case and the drug appeals, Malcolm Berkowitz was standing at Bobby's side for the last time in the murder proceedings. At this time, Bobby informed the judge he could no longer afford a lawyer. The court now had to appoint a public defender to represent him.

The judge granted a one-week continuance to make the necessary arrangements.

"I was six years out of law school," says Jim Flick, "and I'd been with the PD's [Public Defender's] Office for three years."

Ironically, he'd grown up in the 1500 block of Glen Avenue in Folcroft, less than two blocks from where Bobby had hanged Liz Lande. Jim Flick was a graduate of Penn State and Temple Law School and a pretty sharp up-and-coming attorney.

"Face it," he explains, "I was in because I was free. But obviously, this was a high-profile case of greatest notoriety and the PD's Office didn't want a raw recruit to handle it. A guy or a gal right out of law school would have shit their pants on this case. Nauss would have eaten them alive."

On August 19, Bobby was formally arraigned and officially charged on docket #3770-A for "feloniously, willfully, and of malice aforethought (making) an assault on and upon the body of Elizabeth Lande . . . (and) feloniously, willfully, and of malice aforethought, (killing and murdering) the said Elizabeth Lande."

Bobby entered a plea of not guilty.

The trial was scheduled for September 29.

CHAPTER
18

Malcolm Berkowitz asked for a continuance in the rape trial. He told the judge he'd been defending his client against drug charges in a separate case and had not had sufficient time to prepare his defense in this matter.

Berkowitz wanted to know the reason for the delay between the alleged rape back in October 1976 and his client's arrest the following May. When did the investigation focus on his client? And why?

The judge moved the trial to September 19.

Convicting Bobby Nauss had become a vendetta and Frank Hazel was not about to risk losing either the rape case or the murder case due to a lack of preparation or by spreading his resources too thinly. Thus, he assigned another prosecutor to the rape case. Whereas Jim DelBello was the perfect choice to prosecute the homicide, Ed Weiss was perfect for the rape.

Ed Weiss was an honest man, highly religious and righteous. He'd graduated at the top of his high school class, attended the University of Pennsylvania on an academic scholarship, and graduated from NYU Law School. He was fluent in Hebrew and he knew the law inside and out.

Seated across the desk from Frank Hazel, Ed Weiss was explaining what kind of plaintiff Catherine Ingram would make. He'd read her medical records and researched her personal history and background. Clearly, there were potential problems.

Face-to-face, she was hard-looking and came across cold. She'd dropped out of school in the tenth grade, gotten married, had a baby, and divorced. She gave her baby to her parents so that she could move into an apartment with a girlfriend. Twice she'd been convicted of burglary and was facing charges of committing a third. She'd been hospitalized for drug abuse, alcohol abuse, and sexual promiscuity. When she combined drugs and alcohol, she was prone to severe hallucinations and often lapsed into hypnoticlike trances. When she came out of those stupors, she was often unable to remember what she'd just done.

Her attending physicians categorized her as a compulsive liar, said she was permissive and agreeable to almost anything. She was someone who fantasized about group sexual encounters, spoke openly about her fantasies, and often acted them out in promiscuous fashion.

Several times during her stay at Haverford State Hospital, nurses had caught her in bed having sex—with her boyfriend, with interns, and (here was the worst of it) with Billy Turner and Norm Hansell.

The implications of the latter were weighty. Under Pennsylvania law, evidence of prior sex acts between the plaintiff and the defendant is admissible in court. In this case, if the defense counsel could establish a prior history of consensual sex between Catherine Ingram and any of the four defendants, her credibility would immediately be destroyed and a subsequent conviction would be highly unlikely. Thus, with fornications involving both Billy Turner and Norm Hansell documented by hospital records, Ed Weiss envisioned Malcolm Berkowitz impeaching Catherine and the jury acquitting Bobby Nauss.

Frank Hazel leaned forward and said, "Here's how we handle it. . . . "

As his first ploy, he would separate the defendants. Bobby Nauss and his brother-in-law—charged with criminal conspiracy, kidnapping, simple assault, aggravated assault, indecent assault, reckless endangerment, voluntary and involuntary deviate sexual intercourse, and rape—would stand trial together. They would go first.

Billy Turner and Norm Hansell, facing identical charges, would be scheduled to stand trial together at a later date. Only Frank Hazel, John Reilly, Ed Weiss, Jim DelBello, the task force officers, and Billy Turner and Norm Hansell themselves would know that immunity had been granted to Turner and Hansell and their case would never go to court.

The month of September was sunny and warm. Canadian air masses were creeping down from the north, putting an end to a summer of sultry afternoons. Mornings were cool. The leaves were changing colors.

The rape trial began on September 19.

"I was scared half to death," Catherine Ingram said, her voice meek as she concluded her testimony. "I'd rather have been dead than go through what I did that night."

For a good portion of the three hours she'd been on the witness stand, most of the nine men and three women who comprised the jury squirmed and fidgeted in their seats as Catherine recounted, often tearfully, how she'd been forced to perform twenty-five sex acts on the four defendants. As she graphically described each one, Catherine painted a picture that made the jurors more and more uncomfortable. They were hardworking middle-class Americans and they were horrified by what they were hearing.

Nevertheless, when he stood to cross-examine, Malcolm Berkowitz appeared confident. He'd examined the hospital records and knew about the prior sexual contact between Catherine and Billy Turner and Norm Hansell. His defense

boiled down to getting that evidence admitted into the record
and he anticipated no problems in so doing.

"In the past," he began, "have you ever had sexual relations with either William Turner or Norman Hansell?"

Ed Weiss jumped up, but before he had a chance to object
and stop Catherine Ingram from answering, she blurted out
an answer.

"No," she said.

"Objection," Weiss said.

"I will sustain your objection," Judge Edwin Lippincott
ruled.

Berkowitz requested a sidebar conversation.

"She's lying," Berkowitz hissed at the judge.

The judge told him that might be, but no groundwork had
been laid for such a question. The plaintiff was not on trial
and the question was inappropriate.

Since one of the charges facing his client was conspiracy,
Berkowitz argued, his client was tied directly to Turner and
Hansell. Therefore, his question was relevant and permissi-
ble.

"Your Honor," Ed Weiss said immediately, "the Commonwealth wishes to withdraw the conspiracy charges
against both defendants at this time."

The ploy caught Malcolm Berkowitz off guard.

The only reason the prosecutor was withdrawing the
charges, Berkowitz protested, was to keep out the prior sex
acts between the plaintiff and Turner and Hansell. That sort
of suppression, he argued, was unfair to his client's defense.
Moreover, it was being done in bad faith. Worse yet, the
plaintiff had just perjured herself and Ed Weiss knew it,
which constituted prosecutorial misconduct.

"I don't know what to do," Berkowitz complained to the
judge, "or how to handle the situation of my bringing out the
prior sex acts between the victim, Turner, and Hansell."

That, the judge told him, was his problem. He was sustaining the objection and the conspiracy charges against Mr.
Nauss were being dropped.

Moments later, Catherine Ingram stepped down from the stand and Ed Weiss rested his case.

At that time, the judge ruled that the Commonwealth had failed to produce sufficient evidence to substantiate the kidnapping or aggravated assault charges against both defendants, or the rape charges against Bobby's brother-in-law. Those charges would be dropped.

In addition, Ed Weiss informed the judge that the Commonwealth also wished to drop the endangerment charges against both defendants.

So Bobby Nauss was left to face the following charges: voluntary and involuntary deviate sexual intercourse, simple and indecent assault, and rape.

Only one way remained for Malcolm Berkowitz to get the prior sex acts into the case: He would call Billy Turner and Norm Hansell as defense witnesses.

After court adjourned for the day, Berkowitz approached Turner and Hansell.

No, they told him, they would not willingly testify. What's more, if he subpoenaed them, they had already been instructed by their attorney to invoke the Fifth Amendment rather than risk self-incrimination.

Bobby Nauss took the witness stand a day later.

He admitted to accompanying Billy Turner and Norm Hansell to Catherine Ingram's apartment. But, he said, they'd met her earlier that same day and she'd made a date with the three of them to party.

After they left her apartment, Bobby told the court, they bought some liquor and ice and went for a ride. In the car, she voluntarily performed sex acts on both Turner and Hansell. Since he was driving, Bobby said he didn't participate.

Then they drove to Maximillian's. Bobby said he and Billy Turner sat at the bar and drank beer while Norm

Hansell and the girl went outside and had sex in his car. Then the four of them went to the bartender's apartment because she said she wanted to party some more.

Bobby said he wasn't interested in having sex with her, so he sat in the living room while Turner and Hansell took her into the bedroom. After a while, Billy Turner yelled, "Come see this freak." So he walked into the bedroom. They were all naked and Turner was hitting her with his belt.

"But I never touched the girl," Bobby swore.

Ed Weiss stood to cross-examine. He faced Bobby and launched an all-out offensive. "So there you were," he began, "standing in the bedroom, young and virile, a naked young woman was lying on the bed, and both of your friends were having sex with her. But you refused to indulge?"

"She offered to have sex with me," Bobby said, "and I said I would only go for a blow job. But I never got completely excited. She smelled funny, and she was lousy. She didn't do it very good."

"So you ordered Turner to hit her," Weiss suggested, and it came across as a statement of fact rather than a question.

"No, I just remarked to my friend that she was terrible and he hit her with his belt."

"After Turner hit her," Weiss again suggested, "she did it better, didn't she?"

"No, she was still lousy, and I stopped."

"You asked him to beat her some more, is that right?"

"No."

"You didn't get excited until he beat her, is that right?"

"No, I still couldn't get excited. I never even finished with her."

"She was nothing to you," Ed Weiss said, "so you treated her like nothing, that's why you beat her."

"I didn't beat her."

"And that's why you shoved the bottle up her vagina!"

"I never did that!"

"And the ice cubes!"

"I never did that either!"

"And forced her to perform those other acts!"

"No!"

"None of them are anything to you, are they?"

"Objection!" Malcolm Berkowitz shouted.

The judge sustained the objection, but Bobby's fate had already been decided.

On September 21, the jury deliberated for a little less than five hours. Bobby's brother-in-law was found guilty of voluntary deviate sexual intercourse. Bobby Nauss was convicted of simple and indecent assault, voluntary and involuntary sexual intercourse, and rape. His sentencing was deferred pending the outcome of his murder trial.

CHAPTER
19

On November 2, Bobby changed strategy for his upcoming murder trial.

"I'd met with Nauss," Jim Flick explains, "and was preparing to defend him, planning to use the fact that no body was ever found and constantly harp on that fact. I was going to deny, deny, deny.

"The key was the informant. From a prosecutor's viewpoint, there's always a potential problem when you're using a corrupt source—and this guy was obviously a corrupt source. He was a rat, bad news, and you have a shot with somebody like that.

"I had never met the guy and I had never talked to him, so I didn't know what I could do with him on the stand. But if I could get him to waver or if he came off as a guy just trying to save his own ass because he'd made a deal, I had a shot. Remember, it's proof beyond a reasonable doubt. So what you do is try to insert sufficient doubt to shake the jury.

"But as the trial got nearer, Nauss got nervous. He wanted something different. So the family, or somebody, came up with some money and Nauss hired Ed Savastio and Roy De-Caro to represent him.

"And they took a completely different course."

* * *

At 3:47 P.M. on November 17, the hearing of pretrial motions began in front of Judge Bill Toal, Jr.

Roy DeCaro had a list of pretrial motions. Born and bred in Delaware County, he was twenty-eight years old with short, dark hair, glasses, and an easygoing manner that disappeared once he stepped inside the courtroom. At the top of his list was attacking Justice Truscello's decision at the preliminary hearing.

"If you read the Burns case," DeCaro said to the judge in a polite tone, "it is totally distinguishable from our case. Thus, we say, no corpus delicti, no murder."

"Your Honor," Jim DelBello interrupted, "the purpose of a preliminary hearing is to ascertain whether or not a prima facie case exists. It is not a full trial on the merits of the case. The district justice, in my opinion, ruled correctly on the evidence that was presented."

"I will overrule your motion, Mr. DeCaro," Judge Toal said. Then, one by one, he handled the other motions.

The judge instructed Jim DelBello to hand over his list of witnesses and his list of evidentiary items to the defense attorneys. He interrogated every police officer who'd ever interviewed Bobby Nauss to see if his Constitutional rights had ever been violated. He ruled that all references to motorcycle gangs in general, the Warlocks in particular, Bobby's earlier drug or rape convictions, any part of his criminal history, or any of the unsolved Marsh Murders would be grounds for mistrial.

With those concessions, Roy DeCaro withdrew his motion for a change of venue.

Judge Toal then cleared the courtroom. He had one piece of unfinished business.

"My secretary's name," the judge said, "is Marion Delozier. She is the mother of Debbie Delozier, one of the victims in the unsolved murders. Since Mr. Nauss's name has been mentioned as a possible suspect in the ongoing homi-

cide investigations, I am offering to step down from the case
if either side deems that my objectivity has been impaired.

"Mr. Nauss, I would like to know what position you take
in this matter."

Bobby thought for a moment, then said, "If you think you
can stand fair in this trial, that's good enough for me."

"Is Judge Toal acceptable to you?" Ed Savastio asked
Bobby.

"Yes, he is."

Jury selection began eight days later.

It took a day and a half to sort through a hundred and fifty
prospective jurors. The defense attorneys did not want anyone who lived in Folcroft or Ridley Township, anyone with a
teenage daughter, or any former police officers.

By noon of the second day, fourteen people were selected—eight men and four women to sit on the jury, plus
two female alternates. The jurors ranged in age from their
early twenties to their late fifties and they would be sequestered for the duration of the trial.

CHAPTER
20

Wednesday, November 30, was a dreary day. The trees were leafless and the sky was the color of slate.

Inside the courthouse, Courtroom 3 was packed. It was a large courtroom with high ceilings and marble floors. All of the wooden benches were full of spectators. Bobby's brothers and sisters, some in-laws, his mother, Cookie, and son Tommy, who by then was four years old, sat up front behind the defense table. Lawyers, curious to see how this landmark case unfolded, sat wherever they could find a seat. Frank and Frances Lande sat in the front row behind the prosecutor's table.

Bobby was dressed in a suit and tie, his hair styled, looking much more like a rising junior executive than a convicted drug trafficker and rapist. His face was much thinner than when he was arrested in July and his complexion had taken on a prison pallor. Deputies led him through a back door to the defense table, where he sat down. Bobby kept his head up and tried to look confident.

At 2 P.M., everyone stood. Judge Toal entered the courtroom and instructed the bailiff to call the opening session to order.

After a series of sidebar discussions between the judge and

the lawyers, the jurors filed into the courtroom for the first of many times. For the next two hours, Judge Toal explained the ground rules. As he did, each juror took the opportunity, in his or her own time, to glance at Bobby and begin asking: Could this well-dressed, clean-cut young man commit murder?

When court recessed, reporters rushed into the hallway and got as close to Bobby as the deputies would allow, asking him questions and begging for his comments. But Bobby said nothing at this time, nor at any other time during the duration of the trial. Instead, he disappeared into a small conference room with his lawyers.

Jim DelBello began. A dark, swashbuckling figure, he was wearing a blue three-piece suit, and his flow of words was as smooth as his silk necktie.

"The body has never been found," he said, standing in front of the jury, "but that does not mean a murder has not been committed." As he spoke, he made eye contact with each and every juror and he punctuated his words with a flurry of arm movements that made him look like a bandleader keeping time to march tempo. "Ladies and gentlemen of the jury, I assure you, the Commonwealth will present sufficient evidence to prove beyond a reasonable doubt . . . " and Jim DelBello paused and looked across the courtroom at the defense table; slowly, he raised his right arm and pointed his index finger directly at Bobby and continued, "that Robert Nauss murdered Elizabeth Lande."

Then it was Ed Savastio's turn. He was ten years older than DelBello and less demonstrative. He'd spent a year with the Public Defender's Office, unsuccessfully had run for district attorney, and had pleaded hundreds of criminal cases. He stood at the defense table.

"It was true," he said, "that Elizabeth Lande met her death on December 13, 1971. In fact, she hanged to death."

Ed Savastio's opening statement raised a few eyebrows among the lawyers in the gallery. Here was a landmark case, a homicide trial with no corpus delicti, and the first words out of the defense attorney's mouth were an admission of Liz Lande's death. What was up?

"But you must ask yourself," Savastio continued, "was Mr. Nauss—who weighed only a hundred and twenty-eight pounds at that time—physically capable of hanging a healthy young woman with a history of emotional disturbances and fits of violence?" He paused for dramatic effect, then answered his own question.

"No," he told the jury, "he was not. Elizabeth Lande died on the night of December 13, 1971." He paused again. "But she did not meet her death at the hands of Mr. Nauss." Another pause. "She committed suicide."

Court recessed for dinner.

Frank Lande was the prosecution's first witness after the intermission. To his wife, Frances, the emotion was overwhelming as she watched him move slowly toward the witness stand, dragging his crippled left leg behind him. When he raised his right hand and swore to tell the truth, her eyes filled with tears. For six years, he'd pursued Bobby Nauss and ruined his own health in the process. She'd lost her daughter and she'd nearly lost her husband. What would happen to him, she asked herself, if Bobby Nauss were found innocent?

Frank Lande testified for nearly two hours. When describing how Liz had adopted a sickly cat from an animal shelter and nursed it back to health, he spoke directly to the jury in conversational tones. He told of a loving, lifelong relationship with his daughter. "We had lots of laughs," he said, his eyes aglow in the reverie, "watching TV, going to the movies, and having her friends over."

When he spoke of his daughter's relationship with Bobby, Frank Lande looked at him. He said Bobby had once fired a bullet through her bedroom window. And he said he'd personally investigated her disappearance all these years, and he'd suspected Bobby right from the start.

"His calls stopped abruptly," he said, his voice now heavy, his eyes suddenly sad, aimed at the jury once more, "and he failed to respond to our calls."

Frank Lande finished well after 9 P.M. and court adjourned for the day. This was just the kind of melancholy picture Jim DelBello wanted the jurors to take back to their motel rooms and go to bed with.

Frances Lande was the first one on the witness stand on the trial's second day, a Thursday, December 1. She was wearing a black dress and, sitting there, dwarfed by Judge Toal's huge mahogany bench, she looked tiny. Her hands were folded in her lap.

"Liz had not broken the cord," she said in a voice that threatened to break down at any moment. "If Liz went out, she kept in constant contact with me, day or night. The phone calls were her security blanket."

Frances avoided looking at Bobby as she told the jury that, as close as her relationship was with her daughter, it had its stormy moments as well. She said Liz had angered easily and sometimes struck out at her. "But," she said, "Liz always felt sorry afterward and apologized to me."

"Mrs. Lande," Jim DelBello asked, "when was the last time you saw your daughter?"

"When she came out to the car to say good-bye to us on December 11, 1971."

Terri Leventhal and Juan Pacheco were the next two witnesses.

In turn, they identified themselves as Liz's friends and told identical stories: They'd visited with Liz at the Lande residence on the night of December 11, 1971. They were watching TV when the phone rang and from the sound of their conversation, they knew Liz was talking to Bobby

Nauss. After she hung up, Liz said she was going out. They tried to talk her out of it, but she was adamant. So they went home and neither one ever saw her again.

Raleigh Witcher and Phil Formicola testified next.

They told the jury about the efforts of the Philadelphia Police Department to locate Liz Lande. In addition, both officers said they'd interviewed Bobby Nauss in the past and specifically asked him about her disappearance. Each time, both said, Bobby had denied having any knowledge of her whereabouts.

The next witness Jim DelBello called to the stand was George Foreacre, who described himself as a former acquaintance of Bobby Nauss.

"I direct your attention back to the summer of 1971," DelBello instructed the witness, "and I ask you to look at a photograph which has been marked for identification as Commonwealth Exhibit Three." He handed the photo to the witness. George Foreacre studied it briefly, then DelBello asked, "Could you tell us what that photo represents?"

"It's a picture of a garage."

"Were you ever at that garage in the summer of 1971?"

"Yes."

"With whom were you at that garage?"

"Bobby Nauss and Elizabeth Lande."

"Did you see anything happen with regard to Elizabeth Lande?"

"Bobby and Liz went into the garage," Foreacre said. "Bobby told me to wait outside, and they went in. A couple of minutes later, Liz came out. Blood was on her face. She was crying and she looked upset and she said that Bobby hit her in the face with a padlock from the garage door."

"Did the defendant come out of the garage after that?"

"Yes."

"What, if anything, did the defendant say to you?"

"He stated that he hit her in the face with a padlock. He said you can't treat Liz nice, that you have to push her around and beat on her."

Ed Savastio rose to cross-examine. Just the way he stood and looked at the witness, he radiated confidence. He had purposely restrained himself from tough cross-examinations of Liz Lande's parents and there had really been nothing to challenge in the testimonies of Liz's two friends or the two police officers. But now he stepped forward to salvage what he could from a strong prosecution witness.

"You know what a masochist is?" he began.

"Yes."

"What is your definition of a masochist?"

"It's a person who likes to be treated mean. Rough."

"And he likes it?"

"Right."

"Did Mr. Nauss tell you Liz Lande was a masochist?"

"Yes."

"You mentioned," Ed Savastio said, "that Bobby and Liz went into the garage. Why did they go into the garage?"

"To have sex."

On the way home in the car, Frances Lande turned to her husband and said, "It was awful, just awful, and it made me sick." To her, it seemed as if her daughter, rather than Bobby Nauss, was being put on trial.

"It's going to get worse," Frank warned her.

The third day of prosecution testimony began without Frances Lande in the audience. Frank sat by himself in the front row behind the prosecution table.

The entire day was taken up by the two psychiatrists who had attended Liz during the last year and a half of her life. They presented in-depth looks at her psychological profile and into her case history, and they revealed their psychiatric evaluations of her.

First up was Clancey McKenzie. He said he'd characterized Liz as manipulative and diagnosed her as paranoid schizophrenic.

"Doctor," Jim DelBello asked, "based on your treatment of Miss Lande, what is your opinion, based on medical certainty, as to whether or not she was suicidal?"

"She was not suicidal."

"Cross-examine," DelBello said, having made the point he would try to make time and time again: Liz Lande was not suicidal.

Ed Savastio challenged Dr. McKenzie's opinion. He pointed to the July 1970 episode in which she'd locked herself inside the bathroom and threatened to commit suicide. Wasn't that the very incident which led to her six-week confinement and his professional involvement in the first place?

"That was exactly the point," Dr. McKenzie responded. "Everything she did was aimed at hurting her parents, not herself. If she were going to kill herself, she would kill herself right in front of her parents, where they could find her body. To hurt *them*."

Howard Rosen followed Dr. McKenzie. He had been treating Liz during the final six months of her life. In fact, his last appointment with Liz had taken place just two days before her disappearance.

DelBello asked him to describe Liz Lande's frame of mind during the last few weeks of her life.

"I know she was very eager to establish her own independence from her family," he stated, "and she was very sensitive to any allegations of her being crazy. She was trying to live down that experience.

"Personally, I did not consider her suicidal. If anything, it seemed to me that she was in the phase of her life in which

she was taking, she felt, positive steps. It would have been
out of context for her to have tried to kill herself when things
were finally coming together."

On cross-examination, Ed Savastio tried to get Dr. Rosen
to acknowledge that it was at least possible for Liz Lande to
possess suicidal tendencies. He was not successful.

At 4:20 P.M., Jim DelBello called his star witness.

The moment Bill Standen entered the courtroom, the
drama of the trial reached its highest point so far.

Frank Hazel had kept Standen hidden ever since the preliminary hearing five months earlier. For the trial, he'd gotten Standen a haircut and bought him a suit of clothes. At
six-feet-two and 160 pounds and wearing a white shirt and
tie, Bill Standen cut a clean, upstanding image.

As Standen walked down the center aisle from the courtroom door to the witness stand, Bobby Nauss followed every
step with his eyes. While Standen was being sworn in,
Bobby glared at him. Halfway through the oath, Bill Standen
looked up and caught Bobby's stare. He looked back at
Bobby, his eyes calm. It was an exchange that every juror
observed.

To Jim DelBello, Bill Standen seemed composed. He
hoped Standen would be able to maintain his composure
throughout his testimony.

"What happened when you returned to your apartment on
the night of December 12, 1971?" DelBello asked him.

"My wife and myself came home," Bill Standen responded, "and Bobby and Liz were there, sitting on the
porch. I would say it was ten or eleven in the evening. Liz
was just sitting there, being quiet, not saying much."

Standen said his wife was tired and went straight to bed.
He walked out to the kitchen with Bobby and Bobby told
him Liz had just scared the hell out of him. Bobby said
they'd been out in the loft fighting and he hit her in the head
with a baseball bat. Then they came over to his apartment

and they were still fighting, so he started strangling her. He said he choked her until her eyes closed and she passed out.

Bobby told him she just lay there on the couch for a good fifteen minutes without moving. He thought she was dead. Suddenly she opened her eyes and said something and Bobby was so startled, he actually jumped.

A few times in the past, Bill Standen continued, Bobby had told him about beating Liz up, slapping her around, stuff like that. Two or three times, Bobby had even said she got on his nerves so much, he felt like killing her. But everybody said stuff like that. So he just shook his head. He didn't know if Bobby was telling him the truth or making it all up.

That night, Bill Standen said, he was tired. He said good night and went to bed. He fell right asleep. But a little while later, a racket coming from the living room woke him up, so he went out to see what the noise was all about.

"What's going on?" he'd asked Bobby that night.

"I don't know," Bobby had answered.

"Where the hell's Liz?"

"In the bathroom."

"What's she doing there?"

"Maybe she's killing herself," Bobby told him.

"I want her the fuck out of here," Standen said, and he walked down the hall to the bathroom. When he found the door was locked, he knocked and told Liz to open up. But she refused, so he kicked the door down.

Inside the bathroom, Liz was going through the medicine cabinet, throwing pill bottles into the sink. She could hardly stand up and was bouncing from one wall to the next. So Standen grabbed her shoulders and walked her back into the living room.

"Get her the fuck out of my house," he told Bobby.

Bobby and Liz left.

Bill Standen and his wife, who'd also been awakened by the commotion, straightened up the bathroom, then went back to bed.

But, Standen told the court, Bobby returned in the middle

of the night and woke him up again. This time, Bobby told him to meet him in the garage, which he did.

"When I went upstairs to the loft," he testified, "I saw a nude body hanging from the rafters."

Jim DelBello paused before asking his next question. The courtroom was silent. He glanced at the jury, then said, "Who was it that was hanging?"

"Elizabeth Lande."

"You claimed she was nude, but did you notice anything else concerning her appearance?"

"She was white as a sheet," Bill Standen said, "and her head was, like, off to one side. Rope was around her neck. Her tongue was hanging out and saliva was coming out of her mouth. It was a horrible sight. I was, like, in a daze, but Bobby had, like, a grin on his face. Bobby was smiling and he said, 'Stanley, look what I've done here. I killed her. I hung her. Now she won't bother me anymore.' "

Standen said he then returned to his apartment and paced the floor. He tried sitting in a chair, then lay back down on the bed, but he couldn't fall back asleep because he was so frightened.

"A couple hours went by," he continued, "and that's when I must have dozed off because Bobby was shaking me in bed. It was early in the morning. I don't even remember how he got in, if he knocked or used a spare key or what. I might have even left the door open. Anyway, next thing I know, I'm back in the kitchen with Bobby."

He said Bobby told him to come out to the garage to help him dispose of the body, he couldn't do it himself.

"You're nuts," Standen told him. "I don't want nothing to do with it."

"You call the cops?" Bobby asked him.

"No way."

Then Bobby said, since he didn't call the cops, he was already implicated, an accessory to murder. Now he had no choice, he had to help him get rid of the body.

"No fucking way," Standen said.

"Stanley," Bobby said, "you know the kind of people I hang around with, the kind of people I know. Accidents could happen. Like your car crashing and catching fire. Like your house catching fire in the middle of the night. Like something might happen to your old lady next time she goes shopping at the mall."

Bill Standen had heard enough. He went out front, got into his car, and backed it down the driveway to the garage.

"The body was laying on the floor," he told the jury. "It was just a dirt floor and it was wrapped in a sheet. Her head was covered and just part of her legs and feet were sticking out. I grabbed her feet and Bobby grabbed her head and we picked her up and put her in the trunk. Her legs were stiff and her knees were sticking up. I climbed in the car and Bobby kept slamming the trunk until it shut."

It was sometime after 6 A.M., Standen said, when he pulled his white Bonneville convertible away from the apartment and headed down Chester Pike. From there, they drove to Bobby's parents' house and Bobby ran into the garage and came back out with two shovels. Close to seven, they stopped at Jackie Weir's uncle's garage in Yeadon and got rid of Liz's clothes. Then they got back in the car and left.

Bobby said he wanted to bury her in New Jersey, but he didn't know Jersey very well. So he asked Standen to help him find a place to bury her in Jersey.

Bill Standen took the Walt Whitman Bridge into New Jersey. He drove down 295, then used the White Horse Pike until he reached the Atco area. He said he turned onto the back roads and kept driving until he came to a dirt road that looked as if it'd only been used a few times. He drove into the woods until he found a spot he thought was suitable for a grave. There, both of them got out and started digging.

The ground was soft. It wasn't long before they'd dug a decent-sized hole: four to five feet long, two feet wide, and three feet deep. But suddenly Standen heard car brakes. He looked up and saw a green Jeep sitting on the main road. To him, it looked like a forest ranger. He'd done a lot of hunting in that area and it was the time of year when a forest ranger might think they were poaching deer and burying the carcass.

"We've got to get the hell out of here," he yelled to Bobby.

They threw the shovels in the car and took off. First, he had to drive deeper in the woods to make a U-turn. On the way out, the Jeep was on its way in. The vehicles passed. In the rearview mirror, Standen watched the Jeep stop where they'd been digging. A man got out and started inspecting the hole.

By then, Bill Standen was making a left turn onto the paved road and speeding away. He drove for another ten to fifteen minutes before he slowed down. That was when he saw another dirt road and turned in. This time, he drove a good half-mile into the woods before he stopped.

They got out and dug a shallow hole, dragged the body out of the trunk, and threw it into the hole. While Bobby was covering the body with dirt, Standen was getting back inside the car and turning the key in the ignition.

"Let's get the hell out of here," he yelled.

Bobby threw the shovels in the car and they sped off.

"I really didn't know where I was," he finished his testimony, "until I got back on the main highway. Then I headed back toward Philly."

"Cross-examine," Jim DelBello said.

Judge Toal glanced at his wristwatch. It was after seven and he wanted the jury to hear the cross-examination in its entirety with fresh minds. So he adjourned for the day.

But, he announced, because the jury was being sequestered and Christmas was rapidly approaching, he wanted to minimize the length of time the jurors were separated from their families. Therefore, he was scheduling a rare Saturday session for the following day.

When court resumed the following morning, Bill Standen was back on the witness stand.

Ed Savastio's thrust would be triple-pronged: to paint Standen as an unsavory character, to make it appear as if he were only testifying for self-gain, and to develop inconsistencies in his testimony.

"Let me read you a question," Savastio began—he was wearing a gray suit and regimental tie and his voice was lulling—"that the police asked you on the night you were arrested. Page one, first question on July 22, 1977, at 12:30 A.M. Question: 'How long have you lived in Florida?' Answer: 'Since 1971, near the end of the year.' Now I ask you, was that question asked?"

"Yes, it was," Bill Standen replied flatly.

"Bill, did you respond to the police officers as I have just read?"

"Yes, I did."

"Did you leave for Florida near the end of 1971?"

"No, I didn't."

"No, you didn't," Ed Savastio said, and he acted surprised. He changed his tone. It was no longer benign. "I don't understand. Why did you say that?"

"I got the dates mixed up."

"When *did* you leave for Florida?"

"First couple of months at the beginning of the year."

"What year?"

"1972."

"Have you lived in Florida ever since?"

"Yes, I have."

"You mentioned in your direct examination that part of the consideration you are receiving in return for testifying was some sort of consideration on charges pending in New Jersey. Is that correct?"

"No, it was not put to me like that."

"How was it put to you?" Savastio asked, and he added a hint of sarcasm to his voice.

"They told me I still had some things against me in New Jersey."

"And?"

"And I asked the district attorney if he could find out how I could solve my problem. He said he would look into it for me."

"Would you describe the nature of the problem that was open in New Jersey since 1971?"

"They said I stole a car."

"And with whom did they say you stole a car?"

"Jackie Weir."

"Was there not a warrant out for your arrest in December of 1971 on those charges?"

"That I wouldn't know."

"You wouldn't know?" Ed Savastio's tone now changed from sarcastic to patronizing. "Well, let's talk about that. Were you arrested in New Jersey?"

"Yes, I was."

"Did you go to a preliminary hearing in New Jersey?"

"Yes, I did."

"Was bail set in New Jersey?"

"I think so."

"How much bail?"

"I think it was five hundred dollars."

"Did you ever go back to New Jersey to face those charges?"

Standen didn't respond.

"Are you trying to remember?" Ed Savastio asked.

"Yeah."

"See if you can remember if you ever went back."

"I don't think I did."

"You don't think? Is it a possibility that you went back and you can't remember?"

"No, I don't think so."

Ed Savastio slammed his fist on the defense table.

"You know darn well you weren't there, don't you?"

"I don't think I was there," Bill Standen replied, doing a good job of maintaining his composure in the face of Savastio's needling.

"Now, isn't it true, Mr. Standen, that on December 17,

1971, you were arrested and charged with assault with intent to kill by gunfire in Folcroft?" Savastio asked.

"Yes, I was charged with that."

"And didn't that arise out of a shotgun blast by you at one R. Goldy?"

"Yeah, but it was self-defense."

"Self-defense? When did you face that charge?"

"I didn't."

"You didn't?" Savastio said, acting surprised once again. "You mean it's still hanging open?"

"No, I settled civilly, out of court, with Mr. Goldy.'

Now Ed Savastio was genuinely surprised.

"When?"

"Tuesday."

"This Tuesday?"

"Yes, on Tuesday."

"How much money did you give him?"

"A thousand dollars."

"How convenient," Savastio said, and his tone was patronizing once more. "You testified yesterday about this choking incident, but you didn't tell any of the first three police officers about it. Did you tell the District Attorney's Office about this incident when you were arrested in July?"

"No, I did not."

"And why not?"

"I didn't remember until just last Saturday or Sunday."

"Isn't it true the story you gave to the District Attorney's Office was: 'I remember he said something about a baseball bat?' "

"That's what he told me. The part about the baseball bat is when he told me he hit her when they were in the loft. The reason I remember that was she had just said to him that her head hurt and he thought it was funny."

"But you saw no blood on her, right?"

"No, I didn't see any blood."

For better than two hours, Ed Savastio hammered away at Bill Standen's testimony from the previous day, forward and backward, trying to get him to contradict what he'd already said under oath. Savastio succeeded in getting Standen to admit that some of the dates and exact times were a little hazy, but Standen swore he was telling the truth.

It was close to noon when Bill Standen stepped down. He remained a powerful prosecution witness.

After lunch, Jim DelBello recalled Frank Lande.

"Mr. Lande," he began, "as of the last time you saw Elizabeth, what was her physical health?"

"She was in perfect health at that time."

"Cross-examine," DelBello said.

"Just bear with me," Ed Savastio said as he stood and started shuffling through the notes spread across the top of the defense table. Then he found what he wanted. "Mr. Lande, were you aware of the fact that on December 6, 1971, less than a week before Elizabeth disappeared, she went to Dr. Edward Emanuel and had a culture taken?"

"No, I wasn't aware of that."

"But you were aware of the fact that she went to a gynecologist, is that correct?"

"On a different date, yes. November third."

"Were you aware of the fact that on December 7, 1971, the result of a test taken on your daughter came back as follows: 'Neisseria gonorrhea'? Were you aware of that?"

"No."

"No further questions."

Halbert Fillinger was the next witness for the prosecution. A Heidelberg-trained M.D. with an undergraduate degree from the University of Wisconsin, Dr. Fillinger was the assistant medical examiner for the city of Philadelphia. He was a nationally renowned expert in the field of forensic pathology and a professor of criminology at Temple University.

He was a robust man with white hair and glasses, forty-eight years old, and he spoke in an authoritative manner that made medical terminology almost understandable to the layman. His expertise and more than a hundred expert witness appearances at homicide trials from New York to California made him an imposing witness.

Jim DelBello set the stage for him. Hypothetically speaking, he said to Dr. Fillinger, suppose you were to find a young female's fresh corpse hanging by the neck from a rope, in the nude, white as a sheet, her head tilted down at a weird angle, and saliva coming out of her mouth. What would you conclude?

"All of these factors," Dr. Fillinger stated, "would indicate to me that the cause of death in this deceased is asphyxia by hanging."

"Doctor," Ed Savastio began his cross-examination in a respectful tone, "wouldn't you want to know the subject's mental condition?"

"Well," Dr. Fillinger replied, "the mental condition is not going to make much difference with a rope around the neck. We have seen sane and insane people hanged."

"Wouldn't you like to know the medical history of the individual before you form your opinion?"

"The mental condition doesn't have anything to do with the cause of death, since insanity itself is seldom a cause of death."

"Doctor, in your opinion, given this set of circumstances, isn't it at least possible that Liz Lande might have committed suicide?"

"The thing that speaks most strongly against a suicide," Dr. Fillinger asserted, "is that the deceased is unclothed. Females almost never hang themselves in the nude."

"Doctor, in your opinion, would it be important to know whether or not the deceased was a masochist?"

"Nothing in the description of the appearance of the body has anything to do with female masochism and there are only three known cases in the world's literature in the area of autoerotic female death. But there is not one female masochist's death among them."

"Are these female masochists' deaths generally accidental, by masochists who are engaged in sex by themselves, or with others?"

"Not with others," Dr. Fillinger stated. "If it is with others, then you have sadism-masochism."

"Are those deaths generally accidental or suicidal?"

"They are not suicidal. They may be accidental, or they may be homicidal. When masochist asphyxia occurs in females, it occurs with a much different set of circumstances than have been presented in this hypothesis."

"Well, then," Ed Savastio persisted, "would it be important to know her state of mind in determining whether or not this particular hypothesized case was one that fell into the arena of masochist asphyxia?"

"I wouldn't consider it."

"Even if you knew the person was on medication, had threatened suicide just a few hours before, and had just learned she'd contracted gonorrhea?"

"Counselor," Dr. Fillinger replied, "the circumstances you have posed so far touched nowhere in the field of masochism. We are talking about different things. You are asking about the state of mind and I am giving you the cause of death."

Ed Savastio was almost out of ammunition, and he'd gotten nowhere so far with Fillinger.

"In an asphyxia by hanging, wouldn't the body be purple rather than white?"

"Not necessarily," Dr. Fillinger answered, and he went into a medical explanation about room temperatures and rates of oxygen depletion.

CHAPTER
21

On Monday morning the sun came out for the first time since the trial started. The date was December 5.

The jurors were rested from their day off. Some of them had attended church services on Sunday morning and gone to see *Star Wars* in the afternoon. Others had lounged in their rooms all day watching football games on television.

Jim DelBello stood at the prosecutor's table. He looked down at the handwritten list of witnesses on his yellow legal pad and called out, "The Commonwealth calls John Weir."

Jackie Weir and Bill Standen had been best friends for eleven years. He and Bobby Nauss had been close friends for a shorter length of time. A lean twenty-seven-year-old with dark eyes, he was wearing a suit and Frank Hazel had made sure that his hair had been cut to a presentable length. If he was feeling at all nervous, it didn't show. He entered the courtroom and walked briskly to the witness stand. After swearing his oath, he locked eyes with Bobby and sneered when Bobby tried to stare him down.

"Mr. Weir," DelBello said, approaching his witness, "tell the jury what occurred between Mr. Nauss and Liz Lande in Kostick's Bar in Upper Darby in the early part of 1971."

"It was either the first or second time I met Liz," Jackie

Weir began, looking directly at Bobby. His voice was steady. "They had an argument and Bobby backhanded her. I mean, he knocked her off the stool. Liz flew backward and landed on the floor on her ass."

"Taking your attention now to the summer of 1971, did you have occasion to go to the Lande house in the nighttime along with the defendant?"

Weir nodded.

"Bobby had talked to her on the phone from the Overbrook Shopping Center on City Line Avenue," Jackie Weir replied, "and we proceeded from there."

"Was anyone there at the time, aside from you and the defendant?"

"No."

"By what means did you get to the shopping center?"

"My car. I was driving."

"What occurred when you got to the residence?"

"In the back alley behind the house, Bobby fired a shot out of the passenger window at her bedroom window."

"Do you know what weapon was used by the defendant when he fired the shot?"

"A .32 automatic."

"Did the defendant say anything to explain why he fired that shot?"

"He said he was mad at her."

"Mad at her?" DelBello repeated in a condescending voice; then he pivoted to face the jury. He shrugged his shoulders and turned his palms faceup. Then he turned back to face the witness.

Under DelBello's questioning, Jackie Weir said he'd received a phone call from Bobby late on the afternoon of December 12, 1971. Weir said Bobby told him Liz was spending the weekend with him and asked him to come over. But he'd told Bobby he had other plans.

"Now I'm directing your attention to December 13, 1971," Jim DelBello said, shifting to the morning of the murder. "Did you see the defendant at that time?"

"Yes, I did, around eight-thirty in the morning."

"What happened?"

"Bobby told me he'd hanged Liz Lande the night before," Jackie Weir replied, "and Bobby asked me if I'd get rid of Liz's clothes for him. I said okay and Bobby went back to the car, got the clothes, and brought them back to me."

"How was the clothing contained?"

"In a brown paper shopping bag," he answered, adding that he'd dumped everything—a brown coat with dark brown fur trim, a brown suede pocketbook, a pair of jeans, and a few other articles he could no longer remember—into a fifty-five-gallon drum. He then poured some lacquer into the container and set the clothing on fire with a match. The fire burned for a good two hours until nothing was left but ashes.

Bobby then asked him where he should get rid of the body and he suggested the pine barrens. Bobby asked him to come along, but he said his uncle might get suspicious if he left work.

"What, if anything," Jim DelBello asked, "was told to you by the defendant concerning a Christmas card?"

"A couple of days after that, Bobby came down to the shop again. I went out front to his car and he showed me the card."

"How was it signed?"

"Love, Liz."

"Did the defendant say anything about the card?"

"He said, 'It's kind of weird. Liz is already dead and here I just got a Christmas card from her.' And he laughed."

Ed Savastio had a hundred questions for Jackie Weir. First, he asked him if he'd ever seen the body.

Weir shook his head and said no.

"Did the defendant tell you where the body was?"

"He said it was in the trunk of the car."

"Do you remember the type of car that arrived at your business around eight-thirty?"

"The view of the car was obstructed from where I was by a row of garages."

Weir's answer caught Ed Savastio off guard.

"Would you run that by me again?" he jumped on it. "Does that mean you couldn't see the car?"

"That's correct."

This just might be the opportunity Savastio needed to impeach Jackie Weir's testimony. He started searching through the reams of notes and documents on the defense table. He picked up a copy of a police report and scanned it rapidly. Then he asked, "Do you remember saying, page three, question: 'How did they get to Weir's Garage?' Do you remember that question being asked?"

"Yes, I do."

"Answer: 'Bobby was driving a black Cadillac at that time and that's what he and Stanley drove up in that day. I saw the car from the garage.' Did you state that to the police?"

"Yes, I did."

"Was it a lie?"

"No, it was a wrong assumption on my part."

"You mean you gave the police officers things you assumed?"

"No, his car was parked over there, but it was parked in another section. They were in Stanley's car where I couldn't see it. I just didn't understand. That was six years ago."

"And now you remember something different?" Savastio said sarcastically.

"I don't remember something different," Jackie Weir countered. "It's just clearer now."

"Well, then, how do you know it was Stanley's car that they arrived in, if you didn't see what they arrived in and you were mistaken about the black Cadillac?"

"Later on, Stanley told me they used his car."

"I see," Ed Savastio said, but his tone implied just the opposite. "Was there a rope in the bag?"

"No."

Savastio sat down at the defense table to look at the police report once more.

"I see you suggested they take some lye," he said.

"Yes, I did."

"Did you give them any lye to take?"

"No, I didn't."

"Have you ever buried a body before?"

"Objection," Jim DelBello interrupted, and the judge sustained it.

"What made you say lye?" Ed Savastio continued.

"It decomposes the body."

"How do you know that?"

"I read it," Jackie Weir snapped.

"In accordance with your statement," and Ed Savastio was reading again, "page five, did you tell the District Attorney's Office that Mr. Nauss told you the body was covered with lye?"

"Yes."

"Was that true or false?"

"He's sitting next to you," Weir said flippantly, "ask *him*."

Laughter rippled through the audience, making it necessary for Judge Toal to rap his gavel to restore order.

Ed Savastio glared at Jackie Weir.

"Suppose *you* tell me whether or not," Savastio challenged the witness. "What did he say?"

"He said he put it on her."

Jim DelBello recalled Frank Lande once more and asked him about the bullet he'd removed from Liz's bedroom ceiling.

Frank Lande said he'd placed it inside a brown envelope on which he'd written: "Removed January 30, 1973, from the home of Frank Lande." He said he subsequently gave it to the Darby Township chief of police, who passed it along to the District Attorney's Office. There, a firearms examiner at the CID lab identified it as a .32-caliber slug, which coincided with Jackie Weir's testimony about the type of weapon

Bobby had used to fire a bullet through Liz's bedroom window.

DelBello next called the various police officers who'd handled the bullet and the technician who'd tested it. They verified Frank Lande's statement.

Bill Davis and George Ellis came next.

Davis told the court he'd measured the loft in Folcroft. The most important measurement he'd taken was the seven feet, nine and three-quarter inches from the rafters to the floor. Taking Liz Lande's height, a short length of rope, and Bill Standen's testimony about her toes being a foot and a half to two feet above the floor, it added up.

George Ellis described the futile searches to find Liz Lande's remains in the New Jersey pine barrens.

And then it was time for the last prosecution witness.

Mike Raffa was a Warlock who was serving a fifteen-year sentence in state prison for rape. Just looking at him on the witness stand, dressed like a gentleman, no one would have guessed.

His testimony was about to create the most sensational headlines of the entire trial.

"I want to take your attention back to when the weather became warm in 1972," Jim DelBello began. "Did you have a conversation with Mr. Nauss?"

"Yes."

"Tell the jury about that conversation."

"We pulled in from a run," Raffa began, "and I was parking my bike when Nauss came walking up to me."

"You say you were . . . ?" Judge Toal asked.

"Pulling in from a run," Mike Raffa repeated, "a ride on our motorcycles." The judge nodded and Raffa continued. "I was taking the kickstand down on my bike and Nauss came walking up to me and said, 'Mike, I killed Liz.' And I said, 'Liz who?' "

Bobby Nauss's graduation photo, Monsignor Bonner High School, Class of 1970.

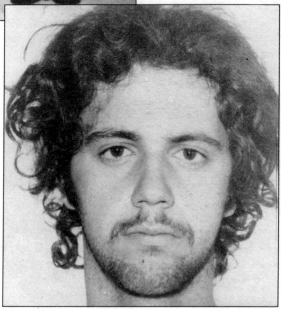

Bobby Nauss with long hair about two years after he murdered Elizabeth Lande. (U.S. Marshals Service)

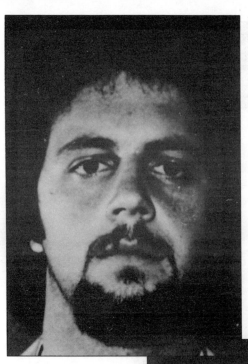

Bobby Nauss in May 1977, age 25, at the time of his arrest on rape and drug charges. (U.S. Marshals Service)

Nauss, clean shaven, in August 1977 at the time of his drug trial. (U.S. Marshals Service)

Nauss at the New Jersey shore during the summer of 1972 around the time he met Cookie Ciglinsky. (U.S. Marshals Service)

Close-up of parrot tattoo on Nauss's right bicep. (U.S. Marshals Service)

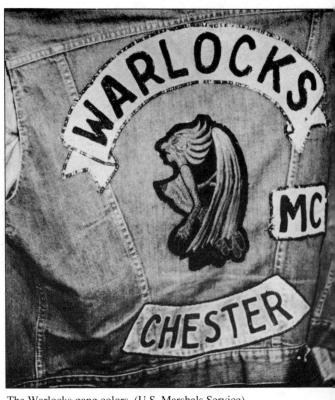

The Warlocks gang colors. (U.S. Marshals Service)

Elizabeth Lande's graduation photo, Overbrook High School, Class of 1967.

Elizabeth Lande lived with her parents in one of these rowhomes on the 7600 block of Overbrook Avenue in the Overbrook Park section of Philadelphia. (The author)

MISSING
REWARD $2,000

ELIZABETH (LIZ) ANN LANDE
(FOR INFORMATION LEADING TO WHEREABOUTS)

MISSING SINCE 12/12/71. LAST SEEN ENTERING
AN AUTOMOBILE AT 2:00 AM ON 12/12/71 IN
COMPANY OF MALE, AGE 21 YEARS.

$3,000 ADDITIONAL REWARD (TOTAL $5,000)
FOR INFORMATION LEADING TO THE ARREST
AND CONVICTION OF ANY PERSON OR PERSONS
HAVING COMMITTED BODILY HARM TO HER
PERSON.

ALL INFORMATION WILL BE TREATED CON-
FIDENTIALLY.

Reward poster printed by Frank Lande in 1972.

Apartment house where Bill Standen lived on Chester Pike in Folcroft. (The author)

Nauss murdered Elizabeth Lande in the loft of this garage. (The author)

Denise Seamen and Debbie Delozier before they were kidnapped and murdered. (U.S. Marshals Service files)

Frank Hazel in 1976 around the time of his election to district attorney of Delaware County. (Frank Hazel)

Jim DelBello sitting in Frank Hazel's office in 1977. (Jim DelBello/Photographed by William Johnson)

Anthony Truscello behind the bench. (Anthony Truscello)

The imposing walls of Graterford Prison in Pennsylvania, from which Bobby Nauss escaped on November 18, 1983. (The author)

U.S. Department of Justice
United States Marshals Service

WANTED
BY U.S. MARSHALS

NOTICE TO ARRESTING AGENCY: Before arrest, validate warrant through National Crime Information Center (NCIC).

United States Marshals Service NCIC entry number: (NIC: W392512647_____).

NAME: NAUSS, Robert Thomas, Jr.

ALIAS: "MATTRESS"

US MARSHAL SERVICE
E DIST PA PHILA
027853

DESCRIPTION:

Sex:	MALE
Race:	WHITE
Place of Birth:	PHILADELPHIA, PENNSYLVANIA
Date(s) of Birth:	MAY 10, 1952
Height:	5'9"
Weight:	190 LBS
Eyes:	BROWN
Hair:	BROWN
Skintone:	MEDIUM
Scars, Marks, Tattoos:	TATTOOS BOTH ARMS
Social Security Number:	161-44-2986
NCIC Fingerprint Classification:	19 CI CO PM 07 21 60 CI PI CI

SHOULD BE CONSIDERED ARMED AND DANGEROUS
NAUSS is reported to be a member of the Warlocks motorcycle gang. At the time of his last arrest, NAUSS was in possession of firearms.

WANTED FOR: ESCAPE

Warrant Issued: U.S. District Court, Philadelphia, Pennsylvania
Warrant Number: 8666-0219-0123-B

DATE WARRANT ISSUED: February 12, 1986

MISCELLANEOUS INFORMATION: NAUSS escaped from Graterford Prison in Pennsylvania on November 18, 1983, where he was serving a life sentence for first degree murder.

If arrested or whereabouts known, notify the local United States Marshals Office, (Telephone: _____).

If no answer, call United States Marshals Service Communications Center in McLean, Virginia.
Telephone (800)336-0102; (24 hour telephone contact) NLETS access code is VAUSMOOOO.

PRIOR EDITIONS ARE OBSOLETE AND NOT TO BE USED

Form USM-132
(Rev. 2/84)

Wanted poster after the U.S. Marshals Service created a task force to apprehend Nauss. (U.S. Marshals Service)

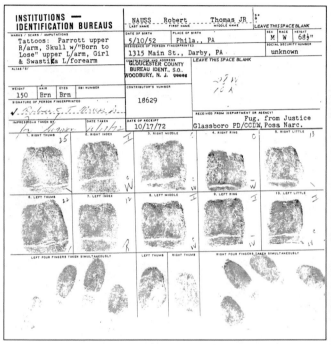

Nauss's fingerprints. (U.S. Marshals Service files)

Bob Leschoron with actor Don Johnson. Johnson will be portraying Leschoron in an upcoming HBO movie. (U.S. Marshals Service)

WANTED
ESCAPEE - MURDERER
CAUTION:
CONSIDER THIS SUBJECT ARMED & DANGEROUS

WANTED: ROBERT THOMAS NAUSS, JR.

1979

1979

1977

1974

1977

1977

1977

WHITE / MALE
DOB: 10 MAY 52   AGE: 34
HEIGHT: 5'9"
WEIGHT: 190 LBS. (IN 1983)
HAIR: BROWN
EYES: BROWN
SKIN TONE, MEDIUM, RUDDY COMPLEXION
WELL BUILT
FINGERPRINT CLASSIFICATION:
   N.C.I.C. – 19CICOPMO7216OCIPICI

TATTOOS: UPPER RIGHT ARM – PARROT
          RIGHT FOREARM – 3 SKULLS
          UPPER LEFT ARM – SKULL W/DAGGER &
                                BORN TO LOSE
          LEFT FOREARM – GIRL & SWASTIKA

SOC # 161442986
S.I.D. # 1 – 02 – 27 – 41
F.B.I. # 433 – 700 – J4

HENRY – 19 CI CO PM 07
          21 60 CI PI CI

PAGE 1 OF 2

Wanted poster showing the many faces of Bobby Nauss. Circulated
after his jailbreak from Graterford Prison.
(U.S. Marshals Service files)

The home in Luna Pier, Michigan, where Bobby Nauss lived as Rick Ferrer with his wife, Toni, and their three sons. The GMC wagon parked before the house is the vehicle he was driving at the time of his capture. (The author)

The Luna Pier marina where Nauss docked his 27-foot cabin cruiser. (The author)

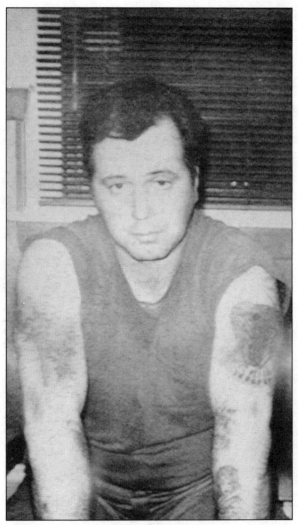

Nauss displaying his tattoos on the night of his capture in 1990. (U.S. Marshals Service)

"What did Mr. Nauss say?" Jim DelBello asked.

"He said, 'You know, the one we trained behind the airport. I strangled her. I pulled all her teeth out and I cut off her hands and feet. And I dumped two bags of lye on her when I buried her.'"

The courtroom fell shockingly quiet. Except for Frank Lande, who was staring at the floor and fighting back tears, everyone else was suddenly mesmerized by Raffa's unexpected testimony.

"And as he was telling me this," Mike Raffa continued, "he was going through the motions." He demonstrated what he meant by chopping his left hand on his right wrist.

Mike Raffa's testimony came as a shock to Ed Savastio. He and Bobby spent a good minute whispering back and forth, and Bobby kept shaking his head. Then Savastio rose.

"He told you he did this before he buried the body?"

"First," Mike Raffa replied, "he said he strangled her. Then he said he pulled her teeth out and cut off her hands and feet. When he buried her, he said he dumped two bags of lye on her—in case they ever found the body, they wouldn't know who she was."

Ed Savastio took a step back.

"Am I correct," he asked, and he sounded genuinely puzzled, "your testimony was that you are putting down your kickstand and out of the clear blue sky, Mr. Nauss walks up to you and says, 'I killed Liz?' And then he walks away? Nothing prior to when he walked up and said, 'I killed Liz.'"

"Nope."

Savastio walked to the defense table, shaking his head as he walked, and glanced at his notes. Then he returned to Mike Raffa.

"You mentioned you knew Liz, is that true?"

"Yeah."

"Am I correct that you stated she was the one you trained behind the airport?"

"Right."

"What does that mean?"

"It means when a bunch of guys get together and gang-bang a broad, rape her, whatever you want to call it."

"Am I correct that you were part of a train on Elizabeth Lande?"

"Yes."

"And that means," Ed Savastio said sarcastically, "a lot of gentlemen have intercourse with her one right after another. Is that correct?"

"There were about twenty or twenty-five guys when it happened," Raffa said matter-of-factly.

A murmur filled the courtroom and, once again, Frank Lande started staring at the floor.

"After all these years," Ed Savastio asked the witness, his voice vindictive, "why are you finally coming forward now?"

"I just wanted to get it all off my chest."

Under questioning from Savastio, Mike Raffa told the jury he was currently serving time in prison on rape charges. For agreeing to testify in this case, he admitted that the state had promised to commute the rest of his sentence from hard time to work release.

As soon as court adjourned for the day, the reporters raced out of the courtroom to file their stories.

The headlines in the *Daily Times* read, SLAIN WOMAN MU-TILATED; SEXUAL ORGY DESCRIBED. Although the jurors never saw the newspapers, it would be hard to imagine that Mike Raffa's testimony had not affected them the same way it had inflamed the press corps.

Meanwhile, Judge Toal was meeting in his chambers behind Courtroom 3 with Bobby Nauss, Ed Savastio, Roy De-Caro, and Jim DelBello. He was listening to motions for a directed verdict on the three charges facing Bobby: first-degree murder, voluntary manslaughter, and involuntary manslaughter.

"Your Honor," Savastio said, "taking the charges backward, I would like to demur to the charge of involuntary manslaughter."

"No problem," Jim DelBello replied, and Judge Toal dropped those charges.

"Jim," Ed Savastio asked, "What is your position as far as voluntary manslaughter?"

"The Commonwealth feels it's in the case," DelBello answered. He didn't come right out and say it, but he wanted to offer the jury an option besides first-degree murder. He knew his case was not airtight. If just one juror felt hesitant about sending such a young man to jail for the rest of his life, voluntary manslaughter was a compromise. Bobby could be convicted of the lesser charge, go to prison to be punished, and still have most of his adult life remaining after he paid his debt. Jim DelBello wanted to leave that option open to the jury.

To Ed Savastio and Roy DeCaro, it had been quite clear from the beginning that this was a classic case of "oath versus oath." One man's word against another's.

"I have advised my client," Ed Savastio informed Judge Toal, "that if the court sustained my application for demurer on voluntary manslaughter, it is an all-or-nothing proposition. It is either murder or zero. That is our posture."

"Mr. Nauss," Judge Toal asked Bobby, "do you understand what your counsel has said?"

"Yes, Your Honor, I do," Bobby replied.

"I will reserve my ruling until tomorrow."

A curious camaraderie had developed between Cookie Nauss and Frank Lande.

During many of the recesses in the trial, Cookie sought Frank out in the hallway outside the courtroom. They smoked cigarettes and made small talk.

Frank Lande didn't understand her motivation. Was it sympathy over the loss of his daughter? Was it compassion because his wife had stopped coming to court and Cookie wanted to keep him company? Perhaps she felt the trial was going poorly and by being close to Frank, some of his strength would rub off on her. Or was it guilt because she'd known all along that Bobby had murdered Liz?

For whatever reason, that evening when court adjourned, Cookie walked Frank to where his car was parked, talking along the way. Before Frank got into his car to drive home, Cookie took his arm and squeezed it gently.

As he pulled away, they were both crying.

CHAPTER
22

Before the trial resumed on day six, Judge Toal denied Ed Savastio's motion to drop the voluntary manslaughter charges.

Then Bobby's attorney called his first defense witness: Edward Emanuel, Liz Lande's former gynecologist.

"What was the nature of the patient's complaint at the time you were treating her?" Savastio asked him.

"Venereal disease," Dr. Emanuel said, explaining that Liz had tested positive for diplococci, which he spelled for the court reporter. "That's suggestive of gonorrhea, which I treated with the antibiotic Terramycin, four grams, intramuscularly."

"That means a shot, sir, I think," Ed Savastio said, "so she certainly knew she had gonorrhea, correct?"

"I would imagine so."

"No further questions," the attorney said. "You may cross-examine, Mr. DelBello."

"Now, Doctor," DelBello said, playing dumb in front of the gynecologist, "why didn't you hospitalize her?"

"There was no reason."

"It is not a hospital-treated condition?"

"It is not."

"Is it possible for a person to be cured of the condition and remain ambulatory?" DelBello asked, making his voice sound as if he didn't already know the answer.

"Yes."

"Was she in danger of death?"

"Not at all, in my estimation," the doctor replied.

Jim DelBello's first cross-examination had been short and powerful.

Raymond DiGiuseppe testified next. He was a Long Island–based psychologist, and Ed Savastio asked him about the nature of his work.

"I serve primarily as the crisis intervention person when we get a referral of someone we perceive to be some kind of threat to commit suicide."

"Doctor," Savastio asked, "have you compiled an empirical analysis of the predisposing factors of a suicide candidate?"

"I have," the expert witness replied. He then listed impulsive personality traits, compulsive personality characteristics, drug abuse, alcohol abuse, schizophrenia, any sort of depressive disorder, a past history of suicide attempts, a negative therapeutic history, and a chronically unstable family life.

Ed Savastio reviewed Liz Lande's emotional disorders in detail, then asked, "Doctor, are you able, with a reasonable psychological certainty, to give an opinion as to whether or not she was a suicide candidate?"

"My opinion is: most definitely suicidal."

To anyone keeping score, the tally stood at two to one in favor of the prosecution. Drs. McKenzie and Rosen, testifying for the prosecution, had deemed Liz Lande "not suicidal." Dr. DiGiuseppe, a defense witness, now suggested just the opposite.

When court reconvened after lunch, Dr. DiGiuseppe was back on the witness stand. Jim DelBello walked up and stood directly in front of him.

"In your private practice," he asked, his voice curt but polite, "have you ever had a suicide patient?"

Dr. DiGiuseppe said he had.

"Have you ever had a patient who actually committed suicide?"

"The only time I had a patient who committed suicide was when I was an intern."

"Was that a man or a woman?" Jim DelBello had done his homework. He was now facing the jury, his back to the psychologist, waiting for the answer he knew would come.

"A man."

"How did he commit suicide?"

"He jumped in front of a truck."

"Fully clothed?"

"Yes, sir."

Jim DelBello returned to his seat at the prosecutor's table and sat down. Once again, he'd scored points with the jury.

CHAPTER
23

The moment everyone had been waiting for came at 4:26 that afternoon.

"I now call Robert Nauss, Jr.," Ed Savastio said, and this clean-cut, well-dressed, good-looking young man, this accused murderer, stood. As the spectators in the packed courtroom fell silent, Bobby walked to the witness stand and raised his right hand.

All during his legal ordeals, Bobby had steadfastly refused to grant even one interview to anyone in the news media. As a result, he was now looking out at an audience which had been waiting a long time to hear his side of the story. What was he going to say about his relationship with Liz? About her death? About why, if she'd committed suicide as his lawyer was claiming, he'd kept it a secret all these years?

Bobby sat down in the witness box. He knew this was the most important event in his life. If he was going to win an acquittal, it would have to be won right now. His lawyers had prepared him and he'd rehearsed the script until he knew it by heart. But it would not be his words alone that influenced the jury. His guilt or innocence hung on his delivery. Would the jurors believe him?

Bobby glanced at his mother, then at Cookie. He'd been

told to look at the jurors, which he did. Then his lawyer approached.

"When did you first meet Elizabeth Lande?" Ed Savastio asked him.

Bobby described how he picked Liz up while she was sitting on a curb in front of the Bowlero Bowling Alley one night in February 1971. He said he took her to a bar, where they drank until closing time, then left together.

"Where did you go after you left the bar?"

"We went to my apartment," Bobby said, speaking in a voice that was little more than a drone, devoid of emotion. For now, he sat perfectly still. "Not the apartment Stanley had later in Folcroft, an apartment he had before that, when he used to live in Fernwood. He had a two-bedroom apartment and I rented one of the bedrooms."

"Did she spend the night with you?"

"Yes, she did," Bobby said, his eyes trained on his lawyer.

"Did you make love to her that night?"

"Yes, I did. Then I dropped her off at her house the next morning."

"Between February of 1971 and December of 1971, did you have occasion to see Elizabeth Lande again?"

"Every weekend."

"Through the entire period?"

"No, I stopped seeing her at the end of May."

Ed Savastio asked Bobby to describe how they spent their weekends between February and May.

"Every time I took her out," he said, "I spent the night with her. Sometimes we'd go out for one night, sometimes for the whole weekend."

"In May, what was the nature of your relationship?"

"I moved into an apartment in Yeadon. Parkview Court. In the middle of the month, she came over one night as the result of having a fight with her mother. I went out to her taxicab, got her clothes, and brought them into the house."

"For what period of time did she remain at your house?"

"Approximately two weeks."

"What happened after the two-week period?"

"As a result of constantly living with her, day in and day out, I got to know her better and she—under my—" Bobby shifted in his chair. "On my part, I stopped seeing her through that summer up until September."

"Do you know who she dated after that?"

"She dated William Standen in June."

Ed Savastio planned to develop a sexual relationship between Bill Standen and Liz Lande, and he paused to allow the seed some time to germinate.

"How often did you see William Standen and Elizabeth Lande together?"

"I saw them together one time—twice."

"And you began to see her again when?"

"I never began to see her again on a steady basis," Bobby said, his voice still a monotone, "but I occasionally saw her after September—just mainly for sexual purposes. She was, for that year, a new experience and probably the best sexual experience I ran into in my lifetime."

"Were you in love with her?"

Bobby looked straight ahead and his answer came out loud and clear. He said no, he wasn't.

Ed Savastio paused again to let it all sink in: Bobby was using Liz solely for physical gratification and there was no emotional attachment from his end. These were points he wanted to establish. Everything Bobby had said so far defined a loveless sexual relationship—and nothing more—his making love to her the first night they met, making love to her on the weekends that followed, her moving in, his kicking her out, going months without seeing her and not caring, then resuming their liaison, but only because she satisfied his lust better than anyone else he'd ever met. There was no love. No emotion. If there was no love, what was Bobby's motive for committing a crime of passion?

Cookie and Pauline Nauss were hanging on every word.

Frank Lande watched without batting an eye.

Ed Savastio wanted Bobby to deny some previous state-

ments by prosecution witnesses and that's where he steered
the next line of questioning.

"You have heard testimony, have you not, from Jackie
Weir, about an incident that allegedly occurred in Kostick's
Bar, where you slapped her in the face?"

"Yes, I have," Bobby said, nodding his head.

"Did that incident occur?"

"I'm not really sure. It's possible, but I'm not really sure."

"You have heard Mr. Foreacre describe an incident
wherein he said you threw a lock at Elizabeth. Can you describe that incident?"

"I hadn't seen her for a while and I was in my garage
working on a motorcycle one morning. I mentioned to her,
'What are you doing with that clown?' " For the first time,
there was some emotion in Bobby's voice. He explained that
he didn't like Foreacre. An argument took place and he told
Liz to get the hell out. One thing led to another and he got
mad and just threw the lock at her.

"It hit her in the mouth?" Savastio asked.

"No, it hit her in the teeth," Bobby said, pointing to his
own teeth, "left side, right here. It just grazed her."

Ed Savastio then asked Bobby about the shooting that had
supposedly taken place outside of Liz Lande's bedroom window.

"It has been testified," Savastio said, "that you called her
house and drove there with Mr. Weir. Is that correct?"

"No," Bobby said, "it is not." Then he leaned back.

"Bob, Mr. Weir also testified that late on the afternoon of
December 12, 1971, you called his house and asked him to
come over. Did you ever make such a call?"

"No, I did not."

"Did you have a car available to you that day?"

"I didn't have a car the whole weekend."

"Did you call Elizabeth that evening?"

Bobby said he didn't.

"Did you receive a phone call from Liz?"

Bobby said she called around midnight and told him she

was coming over. When she got there, they sat around for a while, then they went to bed and engaged in sex for most of the night and well into the next morning. They got up late the next day. Liz cooked them something to eat, then they sat around watching TV all afternoon. They were staying at Stanley's apartment because Stanley and his wife had gone away for the weekend and Stanley asked him to keep an eye on the place.

"Mr. Standen has testified that when he came home," Ed Savastio said, "you reported an incident to him wherein he alleges that you said you choked her. Did that occur?"

"No, it did not."

"What did happen?"

"She took several pills that day," Bobby replied, "consisting of ups and downs."

"Was that usual for her?"

"Constant," Bobby said with disgust, "and we always argued about the pills. That was the basic nature of all our fights. She would take them to the extent that she got irked out."

"What does that mean?"

"Just acts like a nut," Bobby replied, and there was contempt in his tone. "She got so wired out on ups that she would take downs. Several times it got to the point where I would be embarrassed to be seen with her. She would be so downed out, she'd start falling all around."

Bobby then explained that they had an argument around 6 P.M., mostly yelling back and forth at each other. Then Liz took a bath and came out of the bathroom a good hour later, all fixed up. For the next few hours, they sat on the back porch and listened to music.

Bobby leaned forward in his chair. He seemed relaxed. His voice sounded much more natural at this point, less contrived and more animated.

He said Stanley and his wife came in the back door around 10 P.M. Stanley's wife ran straight through the apartment into the bedroom. Stanley followed her, but she shut the door in his face and locked it. Stanley banged on the door several times, but she wouldn't let him in, so Stanley came back out to where Bobby and Liz were sitting.

Stanley asked him if they were still going out later that night to steal a car. Bobby said yes.

"We'll go in a couple of hours," Stanley told him. "I want to see if I can get things straightened out with her first." Then Stanley went into his bedroom.

Liz was just sitting there, dozing off from the pills she'd taken. Bobby told her she looked like a slob and said it was time she straightened up, which resulted in another argument.

"The pills make me feel good," Liz screamed at Bobby. "They aren't hurting me, and my doctor said they were okay."

Bobby yelled back at her, cursing and calling her names.

Liz ran into the bathroom and slammed the door and all the noise they were making must have bothered Stanley because he came back out of the bedroom.

"What's the problem?" Stanley asked him.

"She ran into the bathroom and locked the door," Bobby answered, "and she's in there taking pills again."

"I want her out of here," Stanley told him.

So Bobby went over and banged on the door and told her to come out.

"Just leave me alone," Liz yelled from inside and, according to Bobby, it sounded like she was crying. "I can't understand why nobody likes me. Nobody loves me. I just feel so worthless."

Stanley kicked down the bathroom door and stood in the doorway between Bobby and Liz. The medicine cabinet was open and pills had spilled in the sink.

"I don't know if she'd dropped them from—from her being startled from him kicking in the door," Bobby continued, "or because she was taking them. They were Thorazine pills.

"I could see Stanley was rather upset, plus the bathroom

was still a wreck from when she'd taken a bath. There were towels and makeup and stuff like that all over.

"I told Stanley, 'I'll take her home, lend me your car.' But she didn't want to go home, she wanted to stay with me. I told her I had to go out, but she said she didn't care, she'd wait for me until I got back. She was really high on drugs, staggering around, and Stanley didn't really help me. He more or less grabbed her and flung her toward me. I, like, put my arms around her waist and she put her other arm over my shoulder and we walked out through the kitchen and back room. I grabbed her coat and pocketbook and we went down the stairs and out to the garage, up into the loft."

At this point, Ed Savastio interrupted Bobby's testimony and asked him to describe the loft.

"There was a regular-sized bed up there. I would call it a twin, with a metal frame and box springs and a mattress, sheet, and covers. There was a night table beside it which was really a milk crate, an orange plastic milk crate."

"What else was there?"

"There were about ten of those crates," Bobby said. "We used them as chairs and we also used them to keep car parts in. There were quite a few tire pumpers, car doors, a few windshields—car parts, in general—carburetors, fuel pumps, stuff like that, and some boxes were just piled up with junk."

"Was there any illumination?"

"There was electricity up there, but I don't think I turned it on. I'm not sure. I turned on the radio, I turned on the electric heater, and I lit a candle. Then we talked, just getting her calmed down. She was really high. It seemed like every time we had one of those battles, we made up.

"So we made up and we went to bed and we had sex. We finished and we were just lying there when Stanley came upstairs and said—"

"Unannounced?" Savastio interrupted.

"Yeah," Bobby said, "Stanley just walked in without warning and I said, 'I'll be down in a minute.' He went back downstairs and I got out of bed right away, got dressed, and went downstairs. Then Stanley said to me, 'What's the chance of . . . ' " Bobby's voice trailed off, as if he were too embarrassed to say the rest out loud.

"Go ahead," his attorney coaxed, "say it."

"Like, what were the chances of him getting a piece?"

"What do you mean by getting a piece?"

"Having sex with Liz."

"What did you say?"

Bobby said he told Stanley he didn't think it was such a good idea because Liz was pretty upset at the time. But he said Stanley felt differently.

"I don't see where it matters," Stanley had supposedly said. "She's done it before, she'll do it again."

"If you want to go up," Bobby told him, "go ahead, but, you know, I don't want you to force her or anything like that."

While Stanley went upstairs into the loft, Bobby told the court, he started taking a VW apart in the garage. About twenty minutes, maybe half an hour later, Stanley came back down from the loft.

"Didn't it bother you," Ed Savastio asked Bobby, "that someone was upstairs making love to someone you'd just made love to?"

"No, it was pretty common with her."

"When Mr. Standen reappeared, did you have any conversation with him?"

"I said, 'How'd it go?' "

"Man," Stanley supposedly said, "she's so whacked out, I don't even think she realized a different person came in the room."

Bobby said he and Stanley then left the garage in Stanley's white Pontiac convertible. It was around 1 A.M.

Everyone in the courtroom was listening intently to every word Bobby said. But it was impossible to determine whether or not any of the jurors were buying into his story.

Wanting to keep the momentum rolling, Ed Savastio asked, "What was your destination?"

"We were going out to look for a 1970 red convertible, a Cadillac."

"A special one, or just any red Cadillac convertible?"

"It had to be fireman's red."

"What time did you get back to the apartment?"

"I think it was in the neighborhood of seven o'clock," Bobby replied. "It had just gotten light out. We parked in front of Stanley's house on Chester Pike and we got out of the car and walked up the driveway. Stanley went into his apartment and I went out to the garage, up into the loft."

"Did you see anything unusual?"

"Yes, I did."

"What did you see?" Savastio asked. Glancing at the jurors, he saw they were paying close attention.

"I got to the top step of the loft," Bobby said, and he hesitated. Then he let out a sigh. "And Liz was hanging by a rope with a milk carton right under her feet."

"What did you do?" Ed Savastio asked, his voice low and dramatic.

"I froze for a minute," Bobby said, looking around the courtroom as if he wanted to share the horror of his discovery with everyone, "and I just shook."

Ed Savastio made Bobby pause for a moment. Then he asked Bobby what happened next.

Bobby said he ran out of the garage, down to Stanley's apartment. There, he found Stanley in the kitchen, getting something to eat.

"Stanley," Bobby had supposedly said, "Liz is dead. She hung herself."

"Get out of here," Stanley responded.

"I'm not kidding. Come on out and I'll show you."

They walked out to the garage and climbed the stairs to the loft. Stanley went first. When he reached the top, he stopped.

"Holy fuck!" Stanley shouted. "Of all places for this to happen."

They walked over to where Liz was hanging.

"Stanley," Bobby asked him, "do you think she's dead?"

Stanley shook her.

"Yeah," Stanley said, "she's had it."

"What are we going to do now?" Bobby asked him.

"One thing's for damn sure, let's get her the hell down from there."

Bobby took the sheet off the bed and went over and kicked the crate out from under her and laid the sheet down. Liz was facing the front of the garage and he went around in back of her, grabbed hold of her, and lifted her up. At the same time, Stanley was untying the rope from around her neck. Suddenly Liz started falling and she was too heavy for him to support. She fell down and landed on the floor on top of the sheet. Bobby covered her, and he and Stanley carted her downstairs.

"What should we do?" Bobby asked Stanley.

"I know a place where we could put her," Stanley replied, "that I don't think anybody will ever find her."

Bobby's attorney stopped him and asked, "Why didn't you call the cops, Bob?"

"There were several cars down in the garage that were half apart," he replied. "Cars without serial numbers."

"Were they stolen cars?"

"Yes, they were," Bobby replied, but suddenly his voice turned wooden again, too rehearsed, "and we could have never cleaned out the garage in time. A second reason was it would have uncovered Stanley, who was wanted for arrest in New Jersey."

Bobby kept going. He said it was light by then, somewhere between 7 and 8 A.M. Stanley suggested calling Jackie Weir.

"For what?" Bobby asked him.

"Well, for one," Stanley began, "we can get rid of her clothes at his uncle's garage in the fire barrel. For two, Jackie knows New Jersey a lot better than I do."

Bobby grabbed Liz's clothes and Stanley handed him her coat and the rope and Bobby put everything in a shopping bag. Then they put Liz's body in the trunk of a broken-down black Cadillac that belonged to Bobby, which was parked in the garage, and he sat and waited in the Pontiac while Stanley went into his apartment to call Jackie Weir.

When they arrived at Jackie's uncle's garage in Yeadon, Jackie was standing outside next to the fifty-five-gallon drum and a fire was already burning. Bobby handed Jackie the brown paper shopping bag and he threw it—clothes and all—right into the flames.

Bobby and Stanley then drove back to Folcroft to pick up Liz's body, but they soon changed their plan. They agreed it wasn't such a good idea to drive around with a corpse in the trunk. So first they drove to the Jersey pine barrens and found a secluded location. They dug a deep hole in the sandy soil and covered it with pine boughs. Then they returned to Folcroft and transferred Liz's body from the broken-down Cadillac to Stanley's Pontiac.

"I believe Mr. Standen mentioned that there was some trouble closing the trunk," Ed Savastio said to Bobby. "Is that accurate?"

"No, it's not," Bobby replied. "The trunk on that car is probably the biggest trunk on any car ever, and there was nothing in it other than the shovels and maybe a spare tire."

One of the jurors must have once owned a Pontiac Bonneville because a glimmer of recognition came into his eyes, and he nodded his head ever so slightly.

But, Bobby explained, when they returned to where they'd dug the hole, a red Jeep was parked on the dirt road and a two-man surveying crew was working. So he and Stanley drove away to look for another spot for Liz's grave. This time they dug a shallow hole, threw the body in, covered it with dirt, and sprinkled pine needles on top.

At this point, Ed Savastio turned his back on Bobby and walked slowly toward the defense table. He wanted a long silence. All he needed was one juror to start doubting the prosecution's case and he wanted the jurors to absorb everything Bobby'd just said. He shuffled through his notes for a few moments. He was almost finished with Bobby—just a couple of points left to refute—then he asked his next question.

"Bob, you heard Mike Raffa testify, didn't you?"

"Yes, I did."

"Did you ever have that conversation with him?"

"No, I did not," Bobby said, and his tone was his most forceful thus far.

Ed Savastio changed the subject. He knew Jim DelBello would bring up the fact that Bobby sometimes failed to tell the truth. He thus felt Bobby's interests would be best served if the jurors heard it from Bobby's lips first.

"Bob, when you told police officers, at various times, that you didn't know where Liz was," the defense lawyer said, "were you lying to them?"

"Yes, I was."

And now it was time to deny, deny, deny.

"Bob, did you have anything at all to do with the death of Elizabeth Lande?"

"No, I did not."

"Did you hang her?"

"No, I did not."

"Murder her in any fashion?"

"No, I did not."

"As far as you know, who was the last person to have seen Elizabeth Lande alive?"

"Stanley," he said.

When Bobby finished his testimony at 6:30, Judge Toal adjourned for the day.

CHAPTER
24

At 10 the following morning, a Wednesday, December 7, Jim DelBello stood for Bobby's cross-examination. He checked his notes one last time, then strode to the witness stand. Bobby, dressed like a businessman in a pin-striped white shirt, a solid blue tie, and a dark blue suit, sat with his hands on his thighs. As it had been throughout the trial, his face was devoid of color. Reporters were describing him as pallid.

"Do you remember hearing Detective Raleigh Witcher testify to statements you made to him?" DelBello asked.

"Yes, I do," Bobby replied, looking DelBello in the eye, his voice cool and steady.

"Do you recall Detective Witcher stating that you told him you took Liz Lande to the clubhouse during the summer?"

"No," Bobby replied, shaking his head. "I might have said that, but anything I told him was a lie."

"Anything?" Jim DelBello asked politely.

"Anything," Bobby replied emphatically.

"Well, then," the prosecutor baited Bobby, "was it a lie when you told him you received a Christmas card from Elizabeth Lande?"

"That was not told to Detective Witcher by myself,"

Bobby replied in a jerky voice. "It was told to him by my mother."

"Why did you lie to him?" Jim DelBello asked, walking away from the witness stand to a point directly in front of the jury.

"I figured," Bobby said confidently, "better than not telling him anything at all, I would tell him a little bit of everything—whether it was true or false—just so he might believe a little bit of what I was saying."

"Are you saying you mixed up a little of the truth with a few lies when you talked to him?" DelBello qualified.

"Yes."

"Is that what you're doing now?" Jim DelBello said under his breath, but loud enough for the jury to hear.

When Ed Savastio objected, DelBello withdrew his remark an instant before the judge sustained the objection. But DelBello had made his point.

"In the summer of 1971," Jim DelBello continued, moving on to the next item on his agenda while he walked back toward Bobby, "did Jackie Weir ever drive you to the Lande residence?" He had emphasized the word *ever*.

"No," Bobby answered curtly.

"You are stating that Jackie Weir never drove you to the Lande residence, is that correct?" This time, he put the emphasis on *never*.

"That's correct," Bobby said, and he leaned forward.

"Jackie Weir's testimony describes your striking Elizabeth Lande in Kostick's Bar and you testified that it might have been true. Why do you say that?"

"I remember striking her," Bobby said, almost apologetically. "I just don't remember if I struck her in a bar or not."

"Did you ever strangle her?" Jim DelBello asked.

"No," Bobby said, and he shook his head.

"Ever hit her with an implement?"

"What do you mean by that?" Bobby asked.

"A stick," DelBello suggested, "or a baseball bat."

"No," Bobby said, and he seemed offended.

"Anything?"

Bobby was still shaking his head, then he blurted out, "A padlock." It was not a startling confession, since he'd testified to that fact a day earlier.

"You stated that Mr. Standen dated Liz in the summer of 1971, between June and September, is that right?" Jim DelBello asked, and his tone was nonthreatening once again.

"That's right."

"When and where did you see them?"

"The first time was in the car," Bobby said. "I'm not sure where."

"When?" DelBello immediately shot back.

"Sometime shortly after I stopped seeing her."

"Where was it?" Again, he'd posed his question quickly.

"I'm not sure where it was."

"Let me see if I've got this right," DelBello said, sounding incredulous, grinning at the jury and shaking his head. "You just happened to drive past somewhere and you saw them together? Is that what you're telling the jury?"

When Bobby said yes, DelBello rolled his eyes.

"Okay," the prosecutor said, and it sounded as if he were about to change the subject. He walked to the prosecution table as if he were checking his notes, but he knew quite well what his next question was going to be: "When was the second time?"

"The second time," Bobby said, and he hesitated slightly, "was when he was with her on the night of her death."

"Wait a minute," Jim DelBello said, letting the slightest grin curl his lips, "I thought you said you saw them twice between June and September. Now you're saying it was in December." The prosecutor shrugged his shoulders and extended his arms toward Bobby, palms upward. "Which is right?"

"I really didn't consider the time frame," Bobby said, and his mouth remained open until he added, "but I saw them twice."

"Exactly when did you *see* Mr. Standen with Elizabeth

Lande on the night of her death?" Jim DelBello asked Bobby point-blank.

"I can't say I ever *saw* them, but he was with her."

"I'm asking you what you *saw*," DelBello demanded.

"I know he was with her."

"I'm asking what you *saw*."

"I didn't see anything," Bobby conceded.

Jim DelBello then changed the nature of his questions. And once again, he was speaking calmly.

"You used a couple of terms some of us might not understand. Did you say she was wired out?"

"At times, she acted wired out," Bobby clarified.

"Tell the jury what wired out means."

"Just when someone acts like a nut," he said, forcing a nervous laugh.

"You also said she was downed out. Tell the jury what that means."

"Downed out would be the same situation as a person who was very drunk, nodding out. Stuff like that."

"How do you know these terms?" DelBello asked.

"During the past four or five years, I've been involved with drugs," Bobby said, his eyes now looking at the floor. "I've done drugs myself."

"I see," Jim DelBello said, acting surprised. "Now, did you ever tell William Standen you could kill Elizabeth Lande?" This was DelBello's first reference to Bobby's talking about killing Liz. It would not be his last.

"No, I did not," Bobby refuted hotly.

Jim DelBello walked to the witness box and placed both hands on the wooden railing, right in front of Bobby. As he asked the next question, he went eyeball to eyeball with Bobby. "Are you certain?"

"I'm positive," Bobby said.

"Did you ever tell anybody you could kill her?" Jim Del-Bello stressed *anybody*.

"No, I did not," Bobby said once again.

DelBello moved to the middle of the courtroom.

"How many times were you at the Lande house?" he asked.

"In the neighborhood of six times."

"Did you ever go to the house to pick her up with anybody else?"

"No."

"Are you telling the jury you were always by yourself when you went to pick Elizabeth up?"

"Yes."

"Never with Weir?"

"No."

"Did you ever tell anybody else you killed Elizabeth Lande?" Jim DelBello asked again. It was now obvious he was trying to paint Bobby into a corner.

Bobby glanced at his lawyers, then said he'd never told anyone he killed her.

"Are you absolutely certain of that?" There was a tone of finality as Jim DelBello drove home the word *absolutely*.

"Positive."

"That's all I have."

Ed Savastio's strategy for redirect examination called for only one question.

"What is the reason you never told anyone you killed Elizabeth Lande?" he asked Bobby.

"Because I didn't kill Elizabeth Lande," Bobby said.

Three names were listed on Jim DelBello's yellow legal pad under the category of rebuttal witnesses. He called Jackie Weir first.

"Mr. Weir," DelBello began slowly, "earlier in this trial you testified to an occurrence during the summer of 1971 when you went to the Lande residence. I want you to put that out of your mind. Approximately how many other times did you go there?"

"Four or five times," the witness replied.

"When you went there those other four or five times, who was with you?"

"Robert Nauss."

Bill Standen was second.

"Between the time you got home with your wife on Sunday evening," Jim DelBello said, referring specifically to the night of the murder, "and the time you loaded the body into the trunk of your car, did you drive around with the defendant looking for a fire-engine red Cadillac to steal?"

"No, I did not," Bill Standen said firmly.

"Did you ever have sex with Elizabeth Lande?"

"No, I did not," he replied convincingly.

A blond woman around Bobby's age was third. She identified herself as Kathy Gardner, and she was a former girlfriend of Steve DeMarco.

"Do you know Robert Nauss?" Jim DelBello asked.

"Yeah," she said. Her tone and manner were informal.

"Look around the courtroom," he instructed her in a reassuring tone, "and tell me if you see him."

"Yeah," she said again, and she nodded.

"Could you point him out, please?"

"Right there," she replied, and she pointed toward the defense table where Bobby was sitting between Ed Savastio and Roy DeCaro.

Jim DelBello asked her if, right before Christmas in 1971, she had been in the company of Robert Nauss. She said she'd been sitting in a car outside of her home in Glenolden when Bobby walked up.

"Who else was with you?" DelBello asked.

"Steve DeMarco."

"At that time," Jim DelBello said, "did Mr. Nauss say anything to you?"

The courtroom had fallen silent. As of yet, none of the spectators knew who this woman was or what she had to do with the case. But being called at this late stage, everyone assumed she had something important to say.

"I asked him where his girlfriend was," Kathy Gardner said, "and he told me he killed her."

The courtroom started buzzing. So this was what DelBello had been setting up when he cross-examined Bobby. Judge Toal rapped his gavel to restore order. When the noise subsided, Jim DelBello continued.

"Subsequent to that," he said, "did you have occasion to be in an apartment accompanied by Steve DeMarco?"

"Yes, a couple of months later. At a party."

"Did you hear the voice of Robert Nauss at that time?"

"Yes."

"Did you see him?"

"Well, I wasn't in the same room," she replied, her voice clear and even, "but I had seen him before I went into the other room."

"Prior to the time you heard that voice, did you know Mr. Nauss's voice?" Jim DelBello asked her.

She said she knew it well.

"The voice you heard in the other room in that apartment, did it belong to Mr. Nauss?" DelBello asked.

"Yes."

"What did he say?"

Again, the courtroom stilled.

"There were other people in the room," she said easily, "and he said, 'She was making me mad and I couldn't stand her anymore. I put my hands around her throat and started strangling her, and I just went too far.'"

Ed Savastio recalled Bobby for rebuttal purposes.

Savastio asked Bobby if he'd heard Kathy Gardner's testimony. Bobby said he had.

"Did you ever make those statements to her?"

"Absolutely not," he said, shaking his head vigorously.

"At any time, any place, anywhere?"

"Never," Bobby said forcefully.

Except for closing arguments and the verdict, the trial was over.

CHAPTER
25

On the morning of Thursday, December 8, Frances Lande returned to court. She had been absent for a week.

She could not bring herself to listen to the witnesses denigrating her daughter. Now that the testimonies had all been concluded, Frances felt it was safe to come back. Above all, she wanted to be present in the courtroom if Bobby Nauss was pronounced guilty.

While she and Frank were settling into their seats in the first row behind the prosecution table, Ed Savastio, Roy De-Caro, Jim DelBello, and Bobby were all sitting in Judge Toal's chambers, across a big mahogany desk from the judge.

"Mr. Nauss," Judge Toal said, "I have directed a verdict of not guilty on the charges of voluntary manslaughter." In plain English, it had boiled down to the double-or-nothing proposition that Ed Savastio had requested at the trial's onset: Bobby was either going to be found guilty of murder or he was going to be found innocent. There would be no lesser charges for ambivalent jurors to fall back on.

Then everyone except Judge Toal left his chambers. The attorneys walked briskly, passing through a wooden swinging gate on their way to assuming their positions at their re-

spective tables. Moving somewhat slower, deputies escorted
Bobby to his seat at the defense table. Before sitting down,
Bobby glanced at his family members, but he didn't even
glance at Frank and Frances Lande. There was no expression
on his face.

When Judge Toal appeared a few moments later, the clerk
called this session to order.

Ed Savastio followed ceremony.

He stood before the jurors and thanked them for their attention and patience during what he called a long, complex
trial. He praised them for enduring the hardships of being removed from the comforts of their homes and being separated
from the companionship of their loved ones. Then he got
down to business.

"Ladies and gentlemen of the jury," he said in a loud,
somber tone, "the burden in this trial is now shifting to you."
He started walking slowly, away from the jury, crossing the
courtroom until he was standing behind the defense table, directly in back of Bobby. The defense attorney placed both
hands on Bobby's shoulders. "This is the last chance for anyone to talk to you on behalf of Robert Nauss and sometimes
jurors have a misconception. They figure if they make a mistake, someone else will straighten it out. But this is it. If you
make a mistake, no one will straighten it out for you." He removed his hands from Bobby's shoulders and extended them
toward the jurors, symbolically putting his fate in their
hands. "The burden is now on your shoulders."

Ed Savastio approached the jury with measured steps.
When he began speaking again, he spoke with deep emotion
and his eyes moved from one juror to the next. Piece by
piece, he reviewed the evidence. One by one, he reviewed
the witnesses. Incident by incident, he reviewed Liz Lande's
history of emotional problems and her threats to take her
own life. He called her a walking, suicidal time bomb. Then
he reminded the jury that Bobby was innocent until the prosecution proved his guilt beyond a shadow of doubt.

"A story is either true or false," he told the jurors. "Something happened to Elizabeth Lande. There is no doubt about that. But the issue is: Did Bob Nauss willfully, deliberately, and with malice aforethought hang her?

"That is what you are here about.

"Let's talk about the witnesses—Foreacre, Standen, Weir, and Raffa—they are the guts of the Commonwealth's case. But if you don't believe those four characters, then there is no case at all.

"Mr. DelBello has made something of the fact that Mr. Nauss lied to the police. But how about his classic foursome—Foreacre, Standen, Weir, and Raffa? Were they ever lying to the police? How many times did they lie in their stories?"

He paused to heighten the drama.

"Maybe it was an accident," he threw out rhetorically. "Maybe it was a suicide. But ask yourselves this: Was it a homicide?

"I suggest to you that in considering all of the evidence, disregard that which is inconsistent. If you do just that, then you will have no alternative but to find Bob Nauss not guilty."

During Ed Savastio's entire emotion-filled summation, Bobby kept his head tilted down, his eyes trained on the top of the defense table. And most of his family members were either crying or on the verge of crying.

Jim DelBello had been rehearsing his closing argument since July, ever since he realized he was stuck prosecuting a homicide without a corpus delicti, forced to rely on a cast of shady characters as witnesses. He planned to speak softly, but with dramatic flair. He would blend fact with common sense and interject emotion whenever the opportunity presented itself.

"With regard to the inconsistencies in testimony that Mr. Savastio has so ably pointed out," DelBello began, using his hands to help deliver his message, "was Mr. Standen in the bedroom when Mr. Nauss came over and woke him up? Or was he already awake in the kitchen getting something to eat? When they were burying the body, was it a green Jeep that drove up on them unexpectedly? Or was it a red Jeep that was already there when they arrived?"

Jim DelBello was standing in front of the jurors. One minute, he was at one end of the jury box. The next, he was right in the middle, or at the far end. His words flowed smoothly and he talked the jurors all the way through the trial, using his eyes, his hands, and the inflections in his voice to convey his message.

He mentioned the passage of six years and how time has a way of eroding even the best of memories. He hinted at the possibility that Bobby had purposely distorted the details to artificially create doubt in their minds. Then he offered some homespun philosophy to illustrate his point.

Once, he told the jury, he'd gone to a football game with a bunch of friends. He was off buying hot dogs at the concession when somebody scored a touchdown. When he returned to his seat, he asked his friends who'd scored. Instead of naming the player who'd just scored, his friends started arguing about who'd thrown the key block. All he cared about was who scored the touchdown, but nobody knew. So he told them, next time, don't take your eyes off the ball.

"Ladies and gentlemen of the jury," DelBello said, clutching his chest, both hands tightly clenched into fists, "it doesn't matter whether it was a forest ranger or a survey crew that spooked Mr. Nauss and Mr. Standen away from the first burial site. All that matters is that they were there to bury Liz Lande because Bobby Nauss hanged her."

Jim DelBello's hands were now outstretched in a pontificating posture. "This is just like that football game," he told the jury. "Don't take your eyes off the ball."

Nearing the end of his closing argument, he said, "A witness was called by the defense to indicate that Miss Lande had a venereal disease." His voice was low and rumbling. "Different facts and different factors were brought out—over and over again—to make you believe that Elizabeth Lande was some kind of dirt.

"And what is dirt?

"A color of earth.

"Several hundred years ago, the poet John Donne wrote, 'If a clod be washed away by the sea, Europe is the less. Any man's death diminishes me because I am involved in mankind. Therefore, never send to know for whom the bell tolls; it tolls for thee.'

"Notwithstanding anything that may have been brought out about Elizabeth Lande, this young woman was a human being. If you accept the evidence as presented by the Commonwealth, you will have to arrive at the conclusion . . . this woman . . . this human being . . . regardless of what her background was or what she may have done . . . she was alive . . . she was a human being. The law protects her and considers her the same as any other person.

"Ladies and gentlemen of the jury, don't take your mind off the important facts in this case." Jim DelBello was using his voice like a musical instrument and a resonant crescendo was starting to build. "Ladies and gentlemen of the jury, there is a bell tolling in this courtroom at this very second. It is being tolled by the evidence in this case. And based on that evidence, I ask you to find the defendant guilty of murder in the first degree!

"Don't take your eyes off the ball!"

As the jury left the courtroom to deliberate whether or not Bobby Nauss would spend the rest of his life in prison, hardly anyone left the courthouse.

They loitered in the corridors, making small talk and smoking cigarettes. But two hours passed without a verdict. Finally, at 10:30 P.M., Judge Toal adjourned and sent the jurors back to their motel rooms for one last night.

December 9 began with a chill. Winter was definitely on its way.

Long before sunrise, the lights came on inside the Nauss home in Darby. Cookie, Pauline, Tommy, Bob, Sr., and the rest of the clan were at various stages of getting out of bed, showering, dressing, and eating breakfast. Three miles away in Overbrook Park, Frank and Frances Lande were doing the same thing. Frank picked out a tan sport coat and brown slacks. Frances selected a black dress, the same one she'd worn when she testified, the same one she would have worn to Liz's funeral—had there been one.

In his tiny cell, Bobby Nauss was also getting dressed. For him, it had pretty much been a sleepless night. In a few hours, his fate would be decided by a dozen of his peers. Granted, he'd already been convicted of drug trafficking and rape, but those sentences had finite terms. With time off for good behavior, Bobby could see himself out of jail at some point in the future. However, in this case, spending the rest of his life behind bars was a distinct possibility and that thought made him feel squeamish.

The jury deliberated all morning.

Right around noon, the foreman sent a note to Judge Toal. It read:

Judge Toal—

We have reached a verdict.

Shortly after noon, Courtroom 3 was overflowing with people and noise.

In addition to the nine or ten reporters who'd been following this story since its inception, almost all of the region's half dozen television stations had sent crews to cover the verdict.

Metal detectors had been installed at all the entrances and sheriff's deputies scanned everyone who entered. At Frank Hazel's request, all of the task force officers were present, along with an extra contingent of armed law enforcement personnel.

Bobby was led in. He did not look up until he was seated at the defense table for the last time. Three times, he rapped his left fist on the tabletop. Then he turned around to face his family. With both hands, he made thumbs-down gestures.

The wait for Judge Toal seemed to take forever. When his door finally opened and he made his entrance, the courtroom hushed.

At 12:30, the foreman of the jury stood.

Bobby sat motionless. His family members held their collective breaths. Frank and Frances Lande joined hands. Frank lowered his head and shut his eyes tightly. His wife stared at the ceiling.

In the silence of the courtroom, the foreman read the verdict and the word that some hoped for and others dreaded resounded: "Guilty."

"No! Oh, no!" Bobby's family members called out loud as soon as they heard the verdict. They wept bitterly in shock and disappointment.

Bobby never moved. He showed no emotion whatsoever.

Frances Lande threw her arms around her husband's neck and the two of them sobbed openly.

"I want to thank God," Frank Lande told reporters on his way out of the courtroom. Tears were rolling down his cheeks. "It's been a long ordeal, almost six years to the day of our daughter's death, but I just can't talk about it right now."

"He's such a pussycat," Frances Lande said to the reporters who were following them out of the courtroom. "We feel relieved, but we're not happy. My husband's tears are for everyone—our daughter, Bobby Nauss's wife, his son, and his parents. The burden has been lifted off of our shoulders and is on them now, his family, and we know how they'll feel for the rest of their lives."

PART THREE

The Next Chapter

December 1977–December 1990

CHAPTER
26

It took nearly two years to sentence Bobby Nauss for his crimes. During that time, he was transferred from Delaware County Prison to Huntingdon Correctional Institute, a state prison, where he was an unassigned inmate.

The drug trafficking came first. A federal offense, it carried a three-year jail term followed by three years of probation. The time was to be served upon completion of whatever sentence Bobby eventually received for murdering Liz Lande. As with every one of his convictions, an appeal had been filed and was slowly making its way through the legal system. This appeal had gone to the U.S. Third Circuit Court of Appeals.

Two months after the murder trial ended, a Chester County judge fined Bobby $1,000 and sentenced him to serve six to twenty-three months, plus a five-year probation, for violating the terms of the parole in Bobby's 1974 armed robbery conviction.

More than a year and a half later, Bobby returned to the Media Courthouse for sentencing on both outstanding cases: the rape and the murder. The date was August 3, 1979.

At 8:30 A.M., Malcolm Berkowitz asked for a continuance in the rape case. He wanted Bobby to undergo psychological testing prior to being sentenced. The judge delayed the sentencing for sixty days and ordered the tests.

Later that same day, at 2:32 in the afternoon, Bob and Pauline Nauss, Cookie and Tommy, sisters Nancy and Sharon, a sister-in-law, a handful of friends, and Father Vincent Gallagher, who'd baptized Bobby and served as the family's parish priest for twenty-five years, entered Courtroom 3 to show their support.

Bobby's hair was longer. It covered his ears and reached his collar. He'd grown a mustache and some color had returned to his cheeks.

"Your Honor," Roy DeCaro said to Judge Toal, "Mr. Nauss's father has had five heart attacks over the years, one of which occurred when the verdict of guilty came down in the murder trial. In addition, Robert's mother is in ill health; his wife has suffered two nervous breakdowns since the verdict came down; and his six-year-old son has been harassed in school because of it.

"For the sake of the family, I hope you will recommend he stays within this area, particularly Graterford Prison."

The prosecutor representing the District Attorney's Office seemed confused.

"Your Honor," he said, "this morning in another case, Mr. Nauss's mother and wife made rather an emotional and heartfelt plea that he have a neuropsychological evaluation before he was sentenced. But I hear no such request only two and a half hours later."

Roy DeCaro stood.

"We make no request to have a psychiatric report on this matter," he said.

"And you wish to be sentenced?" Judge Toal asked.

"We do," DeCaro said.

"Is that correct, Mr. Nauss?"

Bobby said it was.

"You understand, Mr. Nauss," the prosecutor pointed out, "that there conceivably could be something that comes out of this examination that might benefit you?"

"I understand," Bobby replied, "but I will put my faith in the higher court and Mr. DeCaro." Bobby was referring to the appeals DeCaro had already filed.

Judge Toal sentenced Bobby to life imprisonment.

The cold gray stone walls rise nearly twenty-five feet in the air. A maximum security facility some fifteen miles northwest of Philadelphia, Graterford Prison sits on seventeen hundred acres of rural Montgomery County real estate.

In prison parlance, Bobby's "reception" at Graterford took place on August 22, 1979. Officially, he became prisoner #AM2456.

The very next day, a prison counselor started working with Bobby. Bobby took the correction department's standard aptitude test and scored in the "bright normal" range. He rated highest in reading, lowest in math. His academic potential was listed: junior college level. The counselor recommended Bobby for remedial math courses. If Bobby succeeded, he felt Bobby should take college courses.

The counselor also tested Bobby's vocational aptitude. Bobby's vocational potential fell into the skilled technical range.

At their first meeting, the counselor asked Bobby to tell him about himself and his family background. Bobby started out by talking about his parents. He described them as literate, said his mother had told him she'd experienced a normal prenatal period and childbirth with him. He said he'd received adequate love, discipline, guidance, and supervision from both of his parents during his formative years. In fact, he'd worked in his father's auto repair shop for thirteen years and he considered himself a pretty damn good mechanic.

As their meetings continued, Bobby seemed cooperative and indicated an interest in being rehabilitated. He said he really enjoyed working with cars and had a mild interest in sports. As far as religion was concerned, he'd been raised Catholic but had stopped practicing.

He mentioned the birth of his son, Tommy, and how much

he loved him. He spoke of his marriage to Cookie, but said their relationship had been going downhill ever since his arrest.

Bobby told the counselor he didn't anticipate any problems with his former associates in the Warlocks who were also being housed at Graterford, but he didn't want to be in the same prison with Mike Raffa.

When Bobby was asked to write down the reason for his present incarceration, he wrote:

> I was accused of the murder of Elizabeth Lande on the 12th or 13th of December 1971. I was arrested on July 15, 1977. William Standen testified that I told him that I killed the girl. However, she committed suicide and I admitted burying her to avoid questions from the police. I feel sorry about the case. The girl was never found. I had no co-defendants.

In making his official assessment of Bobby, the counselor wrote:

> Robert Nauss is a depressed, anxious inmate with a history of drug and alcohol addiction. Also working against him is his prior membership with the Warlocks Motorcycle Gang. As a member of the gang, he had been subject to continual violence and lived in an antisocial environment. Additionally, he shows no remorse for his previous behavior. Instead, he tries to give the impression he is a victim of circumstance. Although the prisoner presents himself as a passive individual, he harbors a lot of underlying hostility. Due to the possibility of his acting out under stress, he appears to be a potential behavioral risk.
> I recommend that he take part in therapy for drug abuse and alcohol abuse, and that he be placed in a program for sex offenders.

The prison psychologist took over where the counselor left off. He began the psychoanalysis by asking Bobby if any significant event stood out as a turning point in his life.

When he was eighteen, Bobby said flat out, his high school sweetheart dumped him and he became seriously depressed for months afterward. He'd started drinking and he started using "crank." Then he joined the Warlocks. To comply with the gang's philosophy, he started stealing cars. One thing led to another.

To the psychologist, it was an oversimplification of a complex psychological manifestation. But he didn't challenge Bobby. Already he'd learned that Bobby was trying to dazzle him with footwork, trying to present himself as articulate and intelligent when, in reality, he was neither.

To the psychologist, Bobby appeared to be quite anxious and extremely tense.

Bobby eventually got around to talking about dealing drugs and he mentioned his rape conviction. In detail, he explained how Liz Lande had committed suicide. Here, the psychologist got a good glimpse into Bobby's psyche and concluded he was dealing with an extremely self-serving individual. Each one of Bobby's "confessions" about his crimes had been highly detailed concoctions of his imagination. In each scenario, Bobby blamed someone else for his misfortune. He was never at fault.

Next, Bobby described his high school years. In telling about them, he let a few things slip. His size bothered him. He didn't like being small. He felt he never got enough attention and he lacked a strong male role model. In the traditional sense, he accomplished nothing in life and he was unsure of his manhood. To the experienced psychologist, Bobby's emotional scars ran deep.

The psychologist theorized that Bobby believed he was a failure in his father's eyes. In his own, he was not a man. That was where the motorcycle gang fit into the puzzle. It became a surrogate family. There, he felt wanted and needed. For once, he actually felt like he belonged to something.

And a life of crime filled other voids. It gave Bobby a feeling of satisfaction and sense of accomplishment. Gratification was instantaneous. He was able to exercise more control and attain more stature in the biker environment than he could in the "straight" world. In his own way, he was also showing his father he could be successful at something while he was proving to himself that he was strong and courageous.

Perversely, getting caught brought him the attention he craved. From a deeper psychological viewpoint, committing crimes eased the subconscious feelings of guilt that Bobby, like everyone else, possessed. He knew he was doing wrong, so that gave him a concrete reason to feel guilty. Carrying a gun reinforced and enhanced the image of machismo that Bobby wanted so very much to convey to others.

The psychologist also put Bobby through a series of psychometric and projective tests. The results were consistent with what the psychologist had already observed firsthand. They revealed Bobby's feelings of inferiority and worthlessness. They showed that, to overcompensate for those feelings, Bobby strove for perfection which, in and of itself, was self-defeating. When the attempts fell short of perfection, which they inevitably did, his ego suffered all the more. He became hostile, resentful. His impulse control was weak. His thoughts became obsessions, his actions compulsions. Paranoia played tricks on his sense of reality. Alcohol and drugs rendered him completely out of control. As a result of all factors, Bobby was apt to say or do almost anything to relieve his frustrations. And when it was all over, he blamed someone else for whatever he'd done.

In summation, the psychologist prescribed psychotherapy to attack the neuroses that had originally triggered Bobby's alcohol and drug abuses.

On October 5, 1979, the psychiatric testing behind him, Bobby reappeared for sentencing on his rape conviction.

The judge informed Bobby that she could neither overlook

nor excuse the baseness of Bobby's actions. Therefore, she was sentencing Bobby to ten to twenty years for raping Catherine Ingram and an additional ten to twenty years for forcing her to commit involuntary deviate sexual intercourse. The terms would run consecutively to each other, but would not begin until Bobby's life sentence for murdering Liz Lande had been satisfied.

Malcolm Berkowitz appealed the sentences as too harsh. In essence, his client would be spending the rest of his life in jail—plus an additional forty years. Bobby's only chance at freedom rested on successful appeals, or so it seemed.

Cell 317 became Bobby's new home. Its dimensions were six feet by eight feet. Located in Cellblock B, it had a bunk, a toilet, and a sink. If Bobby wanted to shower, he had to use a communal facility. He had his own radio and TV. The cell door was locked nightly at eleven, at which time the lights were turned off. It was unlocked the following morning at seven. He was allowed to make phone calls, send and receive mail, and host visitors.

On one of her first visits, Cookie Nauss was surprised to see how well Bobby was adjusting to prison life. Prior to his transfer to Graterford, Bobby had spent a year and a half as an unsentenced prisoner at the Huntingdon Correctional Institute, which was situated halfway across the state in the boondocks of central Pennsylvania. He'd hated it there. He hadn't eaten well, he'd made no friends, and it was just far enough away from home to make visitations sporadic.

It was different at Graterford, he told Cookie. He was lifting weights and he'd been assigned to the woodshop, where he was learning carpentry. In addition, he told Cookie he'd read the trial transcripts, done some research in the prison library, and written letters to several agencies trying to speed up his appeals. And dig this, he told Cookie, he'd bought an acoustic guitar and was learning how to play.

"Ace is here," he said, "plus Russian and a whole bunch of guys from the club."

Bobby also mentioned a new friend he'd made.

Hans Vorhauer was a Graterford Prison inmate because, one night back in 1970, he'd dressed himself as a security guard—uniform, gun, mace, and handcuffs—taped sponge rubber to the bottoms of his shoes, and broken into the Woolco Department Store at the MacDade Mall. By the time police officers responded to the silent alarm, Hans Vorhauer had already drilled and blown the safe and stolen $39,000 worth of jewels. The only problem was, the cops arrived before he made his getaway.

He was less than halfway through a twenty-three to forty-seven-year jail term and he sorely missed his wife and children.

Born in Germany to a father who was an artist and a mother who was a nurse, his IQ was 119. In Germany, he attended a school that specialized in chemistry. After his parents divorced, his mother brought him to America.

In the United States, his mother moved frequently—New York, New Jersey, New Hampshire, Florida, Pennsylvania, and Delaware. Despite shuffling in and out of one school after another and having to adapt to a foreign culture, he graduated from Mt. Pleasant High School in Wilmington with a B average. He was neither a truant nor a disciplinary problem.

However, at the age of twenty-two, he was arrested for burglary in New Jersey and served three years at Trenton State Prison. After his release in 1967, he "went straight." He got a job managing a bar and he fell in love with a woman named Phyllis. She was married at the time and the mother of two small daughters, but she'd been abandoned by her husband.

Hans and Phyllis started living together. Eventually, they married and had two sons of their own. In 1970, they found their dream home and applied for a mortgage, but they were rejected because of his criminal record. That was when he decided to rob the Woolco Department Store.

At Graterford Prison, he lived in Cellblock B, Cell 327, just a couple of doors down from Bobby. He, too, worked in the prison woodshop. And he was always talking to Bobby about escaping. But Bobby was convinced his appeals were going to be upheld.

For the time being, Bobby told him, he just wanted to sit tight.

Bobby took the guitar seriously. Quickly, he learned how to strum a few chords. When he got good enough, he bought an electric guitar and amplifier. At some point almost every day, he sat in his cell, plunking out tunes and singing along. He performed his own versions of Crosby, Stills, Nash, and Young; Lynyrd Skynyrd; and even the Rolling Stones.

Three years passed. By then, Bobby was once again involved in something he did quite well: trafficking methamphetamine. Warlock friends cooked it in labs in the Pocono Mountains of northeastern Pennsylvania. "Mules"—often old girlfriends—concealed meth-laden balloons in various body cavities and smuggled it in to him. At times, larger quantities were hidden among supplies coming into the woodshop. Once the meth was in his hands, Bobby distributed it to a network of pushers, who sold it to the convicts.

On August 9, 1982, nearly five years after the verdict in the Liz Lande murder trial, the Pennsylvania Supreme Court rejected Bobby's appeal. Forlorn and unwilling to spend the rest of his life behind bars, Bobby was ready to listen to Hans Vorhauer's escape plans.

CHAPTER
27

Late on a Thursday afternoon, November 17, 1983, an inmate motioned a guard to come closer.

"I overheard two white dudes saying somebody was gone," the inmate whispered.

The guard phoned the control tower at once.

"Got all your men?" he asked the sergeant of the guard, who then relayed the information to the squad commander, who ordered an immediate head count.

The prison superintendent was on his way to a conference at Huntingdon Prison, so the problem fell into the lap of the deputy superintendent. Too well, he still remembers the squad commander telling him the count came up short by one.

"Got a name?" he asked.

"Hans Vorhauer," the squad commander replied.

"Proceed with a bunk check and confirm," the deputy super instructed the squad commander. To an aide, he said, "Get Mr. Hart on the phone."

Robert Hart was the supervisor of the hobby shop. He answered his home phone at 5:10 P.M.

"Did Vorhauer work today?" the deputy super asked him.

"Hans had a visit," Hart answered, which was prison jargon meaning he'd been expecting a visitor.

"When was the last time you saw him?"

"He left his job between eight-thirty and nine this morning," Hart said. "He left with Robert Nauss."

"Do you remember anything unusual? Was he acting strange? Did he say anything out of the ordinary?"

"Nothing I can think of," Hart replied. "Just that they both left together and I gave them both passes because I was of the impression they were both going on a visit."

Although it didn't register at the time, the deputy super later thought that Hart hadn't sounded very surprised when he first mentioned the escape to him.

Two guards made a visual inspection of Cellblock B. Not only was Hans Vorhauer missing, so was Bobby Nauss.

Teams of guards were dispatched to search the woodshop, the front gate, the tunnels, the roofs, the industrial shops, the greenhouse, inside and outside the walls—everywhere.

Meanwhile, the deputy super had a list of phone calls to make: the state police, the duty officer at the Bureau of Corrections at the state capitol in Harrisburg, and the news media. He instructed administrative personnel to pull the missing prisoners' files and to start printing escape fliers—it was all prescribed escape procedure—and all the while, he kept trying to contact the superintendent.

Guards searched both sides of the walls for signs of escape apparatus. They found none, which meant the possibility existed that Vorhauer and Nauss were hiding somewhere inside the walls. Search parties were ordered to begin searching all over again and the word was passed to the guards in the towers to maintain a constant vigil for the two men.

The prison siren began wailing at 6 P.M. The manhunt for Hans Vorhauer and Bobby Nauss was officially under way.

Hart was called once more for descriptions. He said both men were clean-shaven and dressed in prison garb—although he remembered Nauss wearing a light blue warm-up jacket over his uniform.

State troopers arrived at Graterford at 6:35 and immediately took charge.

Wanted alerts were teletyped to all regional law enforcement agencies. They described Hans Vorhauer as a thirty-seven-year-old white male, five-nine and 150 pounds with a medium build, brown eyes, thinning red hair, and a missing front tooth. Bobby was described as thirty-one years old, a white male, five-nine and 195 pounds, medium build, brown hair and eyes, and a ruddy complexion. Both fugitives were considered dangerous.

By 7 P.M., the phones were ringing off the hook. Police departments, newspapers, and television stations all wanted more information about the jailbreak. But there was none to give: The prisoners were last seen around 9 A.M. by Hart, the woodshop supervisor. And that was it.

Shortly before midnight, criminal complaints were issued charging Hans Vorhauer and Bobby Nauss with escape and criminal conspiracy. Their names were then entered into the NCIC and WIN computer networks.

CHAPTER
28

The next day's headlines in the *Daily Times* would read, BRUTAL KILLER WARLOCK ESCAPES GRATERFORD. The type was still being set when task force officers Bill Davis and Paul Schneider knocked on the front door of the Nauss residence in Darby.

Bobby's mother answered the door. His wife was sitting at the kitchen table. The two women had been drinking coffee when the officers arrived and Pauline Nauss asked the men if they'd like a cup, but they declined. Instead, they got right down to business. Did they know where Bobby was?

"I have no idea," Pauline told them. She was understandably upset, but her manner seemed appropriate under the circumstances. "The last time I saw him was about a week ago, and he gave me no idea he was planning to escape."

"Has he phoned you?" Bill Davis asked, watching her eyes. So far, Pauline's voice sounded just right. There was a bit of nervousness but not a hint of deception.

"No," she replied in the same tone.

"If he does," Davis said, noticing that Cookie Nauss kept twirling strands of blond hair around her fingers, "I hope you'll urge him to surrender."

Pauline promised to do exactly that.

Bill Davis looked straight into Cookie's eyes and played a hunch. "I know Bobby called you."

A nervous silence followed.

Finally, the pressure got to Cookie.

"Okay," she said, "yesterday I was at my friend's house and Bobby called around noon. But I thought he was calling me from Graterford—I swear. Bobby asked me how Tommy was. Then he asked me if I knew where Stanley and Jackie Weir were. But honestly, I had no idea he'd already escaped."

Neither officer believed her, but they didn't press the issue.

Bobby's trail was ice-cold by the time State Trooper Bobby Kline arrived at Graterford Prison shortly before noon. While teams of troopers continued searching the prison grounds for clues as to how Vorhauer and Nauss had escaped, Bobby Kline went directly into the security office. There, Hart and a group of prisoners were waiting to be interviewed.

Kline introduced himself and said he was the criminal investigator in charge of the escape and needed to ask them all a few questions. With fifteen years as a trooper, he knew what he was doing and it showed. He announced that Hart would go first, then he led the woodshop supervisor into a private conference room.

"Shortly after seven A.M.," Hart said in an uneven voice that made an immediate negative impression on the trooper, "Robert Nauss came to my desk with Hans Vorhauer. He said he was going back to the block to get ready for a visit and Robert Nauss also said he was going back to the block. So I issued passes to both men."

Vorhauer's routine, Hart explained, was to report to the woodshop every morning at seven. He said Vorhauer was a steady worker who only missed time when visitors came calling. On the days he got visitors, he always left by nine.

Hart's demeanor didn't sit well with Bobby Kline. The trooper thought Hart knew more than he was telling.

After Hart, Kline took the prisoners one at a time. The first two worked in the woodshop. Both said they remembered seeing Nauss and Vorhauer first thing Thursday morning in the woodshop, but not after that. The next four convicts worked in the storeroom, which was adjacent to the woodshop. They proved equally worthless. To a man, all six prisoners swore they'd seen nothing unusual all day. Nobody knew anything about the escape—which was exactly what Bobby Kline expected.

That's how it went all day.

The search of the prison grounds continued all weekend without turning up a trace of Bobby Nauss or Hans Vorhauer, or finding a clue to determine how they'd made their break.

Trooper Kline returned to Graterford the following Monday morning to begin interviewing prison employees.

"This is embarrassing," the prison's business manager told the trooper, "but it turns out a piece of furniture left the prison on the day of the escape." He explained to Bobby Kline that the woodshop took outside orders for furniture. The profits from those sales went into a welfare fund for the inmates.

Kline asked him to explain SOP.

"That's just it," the business manager replied, and his face flushed. "There is no official policy. No paperwork."

"You're shitting me!"

The business manager assured Kline he wasn't.

"All orders go through Mr. Hart," the business manager continued. "He orders the materials and supervises the construction. When an order's finished, he arranges the delivery and collects the fee. If Mr. Hart collects the fee during the normal business hours, he usually brings the money into the business office and picks up a receipt. If he collects after hours, he puts the money into an envelope, writes the customer's name on the outside, and drops it into a vault outside the business office. On the morning after the escape, our clerk found this envelope inside the vault."

The business manager handed an envelope to Bobby Kline. MR. THOMPSON, $240, BREAKFRONT was written on the outside. Twelve twenty-dollar bills were inside.

"Mr. Hart said it simply slipped his mind on Thursday," the business manager said, anticipating Kline's next question, "so he dropped it in the vault as soon as he got to work Friday morning. Around six-thirty."

The trooper wrote out a property receipt for the money and told a security officer to get Hart in here pronto.

Hart arrived a few minutes later and sat down.

"I've just gotten some information I'd like to go over with you," Bobby Kline said to Hart. His tone was matter-of-fact and concealed the pique he'd felt only moments earlier. "It's about the breakfront that was shipped out of the shop last Thursday."

"A Mr. Thompson contacted me during the last week of July or first week of August," Mr. Hart began. He appeared to have been anticipating the question. "Said he'd seen one of our furniture displays at the Plymouth Mall and wanted a breakfront made to order. A few days later, he dropped off a set of plans. I worked up an estimate and called him back about a week later with the price. He agreed and asked, could I have it ready in time for Christmas?

"I assigned it to Hans Vorhauer and he completed it on November ninth, at which time I called Mr. Thompson and told him it was ready. He said he'd make pickup arrangements and get back to me."

"Then what happened?" Kline asked.

"Nothing," Hart said. "He never called back. But then last Thursday, the reception desk called and said that a Mr. and Mrs. Thompson had arrived to pick up a piece of furniture. So I sent two inmates to wheel it up to the vehicle lock."

Bobby Kline got the names of the two inmates and jotted them down.

"Then what happened?"

"Well, I went up there with them," Hart replied, and his voice was a lot steadier than it had been earlier, "and we just stood around and waited for about fifteen minutes."

"Why's that?"

"Some sort of commotion was taking place inside the vehicle lock. Anyway, while we're waiting, some guards yelled out the window and asked what was on the handcart."

"Which guards?"

"The only one I recognized was the tall blond," Hart replied, "but I don't remember her name. Anyway, I opened the door of the breakfront and showed them the interior."

"I'd like to have Mr. Thompson's phone number," Kline said.

"I don't have it."

"What do you mean you don't have it?"

"The only place I had it written down," Hart explained, "was on the diagram, and I packed it inside the breakfront when I delivered it."

"Of course," Kline said, his voice irritated.

"But," Hart said, "I remember his exchange: four-six-four."

"So you're waiting for the commotion to die down," Kline prompted, "and then what?"

"Well, I went into the lobby and met Mr. and Mrs. Thompson."

"What did they look like?"

"Mr. Thompson was a white male," Mr. Hart replied, "about thirty-five. He was five-nine or five-ten and weighed about a hundred and forty-five."

"Hair?" Kline asked without looking up from his note-taking.

"Well, his hair was short and dark and he was clean-shaven."

"And Mrs. Thompson?"

"To tell the truth," Hart said, and he laughed nervously, "I didn't pay much attention to Mrs. Thompson."

Kline then asked him to describe the breakfront.

"The base," Hart said, "was made out of inch-and-a-quarter oak, and sides and shelves were three-quarter white pine, and the back was quarter-inch plywood. The finished product was stained dark brown and weighed around two hundred pounds. We helped Mr. Thompson load it into a U-Haul and came back inside."

Bobby Kline looked into Hart's eyes. He had a knack for reading people and he suspected that Hart was implicated in the escape. It was preposterous to think that two prisoners could be wheeled out of a maximum-security prison in broad daylight while hidden inside a piece of furniture they'd made with their own hands inside the prison woodshop. So preposterous, Kline assured himself, it had to be true.

Trooper Bobby Kline was now interviewing the three guards who'd been on duty in the vehicle lock on the day of the escape.

The first guard said some deputies from the Bucks County Sheriff's Office had been delivering a prisoner shortly after 10 A.M. When they had trouble removing the handcuffs, the prisoner started kicking and screaming. So, the guard said, he'd entered the vehicle lock himself to help out, but he couldn't get the cuffs off, either. So a second guard came to help him out. The disturbance ended at 10:20. At that time, he noticed Hart standing there, waiting to enter the vehicle lock with some furniture. But the guard had paperwork to fill out. By the time he finished it and returned, Hart and the furniture were gone.

The second guard told Bobby Kline he saw Hart with a cabinet or something, but he, himself, left to escort the new prisoner to the Assessment Unit.

The third guard said he was instructed to deliver the new prisoner's commitment papers to the Assessment Unit. He didn't remember seeing Hart or any furniture, but he did see a prisoner hanging out in the yard between the vehicle lock and the stairs leading to the main corridor.

The prisoner's name?

Marty Riley.

At that point, Bobby Kline was out of people to interview for the day. Then another guard handed him a sealed envelope with a note inside. It said that if secrecy could be guaranteed, an inmate wished to speak to him.

Using extreme caution, the trooper met the inmate in another room.

"I was outside the vehicle lock," the inmate said, his eyes gazing straight ahead into Bobby Kline's, "looking through a peephole." He said he was paying close attention because he wanted to see if the guards were going to work the prisoner over.

Bobby Kline said he understood.

"When the guards took him out," the inmate continued, "Mr. Hart entered the vehicle lock with two handcarts. A piece of furniture was on each. Then the front door opened. Mr. Hart asked me to pull one of the carts and he pulled the other one. That's when I became suspicious."

"Why's that?"

"Because it was heavy as hell," the inmate said, "and none of the guards bothered to look inside or tried to lift it up to see how heavy it was. But I was afraid to say anything."

Kline nodded. He was familiar with prison protocol.

"You said there were two pieces," Kline said.

"Right. Two."

"How big were they?"

"One piece was around four-by-six-by-four."

"Feet?" Kline said.

"Right. Feet. The other was smaller, but . . . "

"But what?"

"The big piece," the inmate continued slowly, "was big enough to hide two men inside."

"So you and Mr. Hart are pulling these two pieces of furniture," Kline cued the inmate back to where he'd left off, "and then what happened?"

"We parked the carts by the stairs leading to the main

lobby and Mr. Hart went inside. A few minutes later, he came out with a man and a woman."

"What did she look like?" the trooper asked, his pen poised to write down her description.

"She was five-five," the inmate replied, "about a hundred and fifteen pounds. Blond. And she was wearing a blue print dress."

"What about him?"

"He looked like a biker," the inmate said. He and Bobby Kline then exchanged knowing glances. "He was wearing jeans, a black leather jacket, boots, and he had a long silver chain attached to his belt."

Bill Davis received a phone call from a confidential informant later on the same day. The informant told him he'd received a call from William "Worm" Walhower on November 11—six days before the jailbreak. The informant said Walhower asked him for a favor.

"What kind of favor?" Davis asked.

"He asked me if I'd drive up to Graterford, pick up two tables for Bobby Nauss, and deliver them," the informant replied. "He offered me twelve hundred dollars to do it."

Bill Davis whistled. "What happened?"

"I told him I'd do it the first day it rained," he said to Davis, "and told him to get back to me."

"And?"

"He never called me back until the day of the escape, and then only to ask me if I'd heard Bobby had escaped earlier that day."

As soon as the call ended, Bill Davis phoned Bobby Kline to pass along what he'd just heard. When the two lawmen compared notes, they added up. To Davis, Worm Walhower fit Mr. Thompson's description. He told Kline he'd send some photos to him ASAP.

It was the following morning and Bobby Kline was back at Graterford Prison conducting more interviews.

The tall blond female guard came first. She said she'd observed two inmates wheeling two large pieces of furniture on two handcarts.

"I yelled out the window and asked them what it was," she told Kline. "One of them said it was a bedroom set and opened the doors so I could look inside."

"And?"

"And nothing. It was empty."

Two prisoners came second and third. They told Kline similar stories: Hart told them to get the furniture. It had already been loaded onto carts. They rolled both pieces to the vehicle lock, then returned to the woodshop.

Right after lunch, Bobby Kline checked the records of the phone calls Hart had placed through the prison switchboard. He went all the way back to July, but there was not one listing of an outgoing call to a number with a 464 prefix. When Kline returned to the security office, a prisoner was waiting for him. Marty Riley.

"I got to the shop right after seven," Riley told the trooper, avoiding Bobby Kline's eyes. "Vorhauer was already there, Nauss got there at eight, and they both left a little while after that."

"What do you know about the furniture that was shipped out that morning?"

"Later," the prisoner replied, "a call came in and Mr. Hart told me to get it ready for delivery."

"Which meant what?"

"I had to load it onto carts."

"Who helped you?"

"Nobody," Marty Riley said, his eyes downcast.

"It wasn't heavy?"

"I didn't think so."

"And what do you know about the escape?"

"Around six o'clock that evening," Riley replied, looking up, "another inmate told me about it. That was the first I heard."

Before Bobby Kline went home for the night, he called

Hart and asked him if he'd mind coming in to the barracks to make an official statement.

Hart consented.

It was nearly four o'clock the next afternoon when Robert Hart arrived at the state police barracks in Limerick. It was Wednesday, November 23. Just before the interview started, Bobby Kline flipped on the tape recorder and said, "I have a question."

Hart looked at him.

"Exactly how many pieces of furniture are we talking about?"

"The breakfront was really two pieces," Hart said.

"I thought you told me it was one piece."

"I originally called it one piece," Hart explained, "because when it's put together, it is one piece. It was an honest mistake on my part."

The rest of Hart's statement was a rehash of what he'd told Kline on earlier interviews at the prison.

Bobby Kline knew full well that lie-detector results were not admissible in court. But he also knew mentioning the word *polygraph* often resulted in unnerving people who were trying to hide something.

"There's no legal obligation on your part," is the way Kline put it to Hart, "but I'd like to see you take a polygraph examination."

"Well," Hart replied, "I've heard good things about the polygraph and I've heard bad. If you don't mind, I'd like to consult my attorney before I make such a decision."

"Do you have an attorney?" Bobby Kline asked.

"No," Hart replied, "but I plan on getting one."

Bobby Nauss was beginning his third week of freedom by the time Trooper Kline returned to Graterford Prison to confront Hart again. It was Friday, December 2.

Kline placed a photo of Worm Walhower on the table.

"Ever seen this man before?" he asked.

Hart picked up the photo and took a good look at it. Then he shook his head.

"Can't say I have."

"That's not Mr. Thompson?"

"Not even close."

"As of yet," Kline said, changing the subject, "have you retained an attorney?"

"Yes, I have."

"What has he advised you regarding submitting to a polygraph?"

"To tell you the truth," Hart replied, his face turning red, "I forgot to mention it specifically. But he told me not to make any more statements. Based on that advice, I feel it's best to decline taking one right now."

By Christmas, the state police investigation had run out of gas.

After more than a month, there were no tangible clues. Worm Walhower had proven to be a dead end. The Thompsons had not been identified. The U-Haul had not been traced. The FBI lab was unable to detect a single fingerprint on the twenty-dollar bills used to pay for the breakfront. Other than suspicion, there was nothing to implicate Hart. Ditto Marty Riley. And the fugitives had left no trail.

CHAPTER
29

"This was a fucked-up case," said the man who would become Bobby Nauss's nemesis.

His name was Tom Rapone and he grew up in Drexel Hill, a mile or so down the road from where Bobby had lived in Darby. Because every strand of his coarse dark hair was always in place, his classmates at St. Bernadette's Grade School called him "Rughead."

Like Bobby Nauss and District Attorney Frank Hazel, he also graduated from Monsignor Bonner—two years ahead of Bobby—although he says he never knew Bobby in high school. The school was too big. However, during those early years, one person he did become friendly with was Rick Martinson—who would eventually become the suspected leader of the Warlocks.

After high school Tom Rapone's life headed in an opposite direction from those of Bobby Nauss and Rick Martinson. While they were rising through the ranks with the Warlocks, Rapone was earning his bachelor's degree from the Philadelphia School of Textile and Sciences. For postgraduate studies, he began taking courses in criminology at West Chester State University. He married, started a family, then landed a counselor's job at the Delaware County Prison.

His duties consisted of spending time getting to know the inmates, working with them, and trying to rehabilitate them. In that capacity, he met Bobby Nauss and got to know him quite well.

By the time Bobby was arrested for murdering Liz Lande during the summer of 1977, Tom Rapone had been promoted to prison warden. He was thus responsible for Bobby's care and feeding during the six months of Bobby's pretrial and trial proceedings. Then, shortly after the trial ended, it was Rapone who recommended Bobby's transfer to Huntingdon Prison for security reasons. And that was his last brush with Bobby Nauss—or so Rapone thought.

Six years later, their lives began to turn onto a collision course. Just seven weeks prior to Bobby's escape from Graterford Prison, President Ronald Reagan appointed Rapone as the U.S. marshal for Pennsylvania's Eastern District.

Empowered by George Washington near the turn of the eighteenth century, the Marshals Service is the oldest, most versatile law enforcement agency in the world. Among its functions are providing judicial security, protecting witnesses, seizing assets, and apprehending fugitives. However, those fugitives must fall into one of three categories: fugitives who've escaped from federal confinement, fugitives who've escaped from state confinement if they owe federal prison time, or fugitives who've escaped from the custody of federal officers.

Of all of Bobby's convictions, the one for drug trafficking was his only federal crime—for which he received a three-year sentence. Since he served six years in prison prior to his escape, law enforcement assumed he'd satisfied his federal debt. As far as anyone knew, he was a *state* prisoner who'd escaped from *state* confinement and he owed no *federal* prison time. Therefore, when Bobby escaped, the state police force assumed the role of primary investigative agency and retained that position during the months that followed—even

though its chances of ever apprehending him were virtually
nonexistent.

"You need time and resources if you're ever going to capture Bobby Nauss," Tom Rapone lamented. "You need the
manpower and apparatus of a national law enforcement
power. You've got to be able to go from jurisdiction to jurisdiction, to pick up a phone and call anywhere in the country,
and say, 'Meet me at the airport in the morning.'

"It's very bulky without a federal umbrella."

For nearly a year and a half, Tom Rapone and the federal
marshals sat on the outside looking in.

In March 1985, Tom Rapone received an anonymous tip
that Bobby Nauss was hiding on the outskirts of Raith, a
small town in Ontario, Canada. Rapone's source said he was
living with a woman named Claudia, a white female with
long dark hair, in a home on Route 102 a few miles northwest of Thunder Bay.

Rapone called headquarters and passed the information
along to the Enforcement Division. He suggested that the
Royal Canadian Mounted Police be contacted and that a surveillance be established which included deputy marshals,
mounties, and Pennsylvania state troopers. At the same time,
he began promoting the case. With fifty-eight thousand cases
in its files, the Marshals Service prioritizes its workload. In
regard to Bobby Nauss, his name was not even on file. But
Tom Rapone planned to change that situation. He sent the
following memo to Bob Leschoron, the marshals' chief of
domestic operations:

Be advised that the Nauss escape and his association with the Warlocks Motorcycle Gang, who were
believed to be involved in a number of unsolved
homicides, have generated an extensive amount of
publicity.

Certainly the potential press generated by the
United States Marshals Service assisting in an arrest

of this type would generate national publicity for
the USMS and the RCMP.

The mounties moved on the suspect's residence. A long-
haired brunette answered the door and said her name was
Claudia and the suspect bore a striking resemblance to
Bobby Nauss. But he was not Bobby.

Although it failed, the incident made Tom Rapone's
adrenaline flow. But no federal warrant existed. Once again,
he was forced to watch from a distance, an interested but un-
involved spectator.

Another eight months passed with no progress in the investigation.

An anonymous caller phoned the superintendent's office
at Graterford Prison on Thursday, January 23, 1986.

A secretary answered the phone.

"I have information about an escape that occurred two
years ago," the man's voice said.

"Please hold," the secretary said, then tried to find someone to take the call. The superintendent was in a meeting and
the deputy superintendent was out of his office. Finally she
found one of the superintendent's assistants.

"I'm talking about Robert Nauss and Hans Vorhauer," the
caller said when the assistant came on the line.

"How do I know you're not some crackpot?"

"Just listen," the caller replied, and he spoke in choppy
sentences. "Other inmates sealed them inside a large piece of
furniture. Wheeled them outside to a U-Haul van. They
bribed a guard named Hunt. It was a one-time payment made
on the morning of the escape. The van was owned by Adrian
Mailers. That's a business at 1233 Cherry Street in Philadelphia. The driver's name is Cindy Lougee. She rented the van
from her mother's company. Adrian Mailers. Her boyfriend
went with her. He helped with the loading and unloading."

The assistant asked where this Cindy could be found.

"She hangs out at Charlie's Bar. In Manayunk. Sometimes on the weekends, Nauss meets her there."

Then he hung up.

Tom Rapone got wind of the phone call a few days later. He then contacted the U.S. Attorney's Office and asked for an opinion on the case.

In February, he got an answer: The judge had scheduled Bobby's drug sentence to run consecutively to his murder sentence. Bobby Nauss still owed the federal government three years.

A federal warrant for the arrest of Robert Thomas Nauss, Jr., was issued on February 12, 1986. From that moment on, twenty-five hundred deputy marshals were officially on Bobby's tail.

In addition, a federal detainer would subsequently be located on Hans Vorhauer.

On February 12, Hurley Trout started his workday by key-punching the new data into the WIN and NCIC computer terminals. Trout was the deputy marshal Tom Rapone put in charge of what would become the biggest case to hit the Philadelphia office in years.

Hurley Trout was a slender investigator of medium height with salt-and-pepper hair and he possessed the temperament and self-control of a man who never seemed to get mad at anything. At the moment, he was working from a long list in front of him: new files to initiate, related files to locate, time lines and linkage charts to draw, documents to inspect. It was all SOP and with better than twenty years on the job, he'd done it at least a thousand times before.

Compared to the younger deputies who often wore jeans and running shoes, Trout was a throwback to the old days— not that he looked like he just stepped out of the pages of *GQ*, but he always wore a suit and tie.

"He never gave up," recalled Janet Doyle, a deputy who

worked several cases with Trout. "We called him 'Hound Dog' because once Hurley got on your trail, he didn't stop until he got you."

Hurley Trout was lighting a cigarette when Tom Rapone and Paul Schneider entered the Marshals Office. He crushed out a butt that was still smoldering in the ashtray and took a deep drag on the one he'd just lit.

Rapone smiled a cheshire grin and handed Trout a huge stack of documents he and the Delaware County task force officer had just obtained at Graterford Prison: visitors lists, phone records, and mail logs.

"Good luck," Rapone said, then asked Paul Schneider to fill Trout in.

"Cindy Jill Lougee," Schneider said, handing Trout a manila folder.

Trout opened the file and looked at her picture. Mousy-haired. Plain-looking.

"Thirty-two," Schneider continued, "a known junkie, and it's a commonly held notion that she shared a sexual relationship with Nauss for years."

"She's a regular on the visitors list," Tom Rapone interjected.

"John Lougee's widow," Schneider continued, "a chapter president until his body was found in an apartment two years ago. THC overdose."

"Look," Rapone said to Trout, "here's where I want you to start: One, establish a surveillance at the Lougee girl's house; two, get a picture of the boyfriend; three, establish a surveillance at Charlie's Bar in Manayunk; and four, see what you can dig up on Adrian Mailers."

Hurley Trout went to Manayunk on Valentine's Day to look for Charlie's Bar. It didn't take long to find someone on the street who told him, first of all, it used to be Uncle Charlie's Bar. But it'd changed hands recently and was now called German Mike's. The man said it was on the corner of Dawson and Cresson streets.

Trout staked out the parking lot for two days. He copied license numbers and snapped pictures of the patrons entering and exiting the establishment. Many of them were known Warlocks, but neither Bobby Nauss nor Cindy Lougee made an appearance.

The following weekend, February 21 and 22, Hurley Trout moved his surveillance to 4713 Fowler Street, just a hop and a skip from German Mike's, to Cindy Lougee's two-story row house.

The first night on Fowler Street, he started out by copying tags and snapping pictures. A steady stream of biker types going in and coming out kept him busy for several hours. To seasoned eyes, it was obvious she was running a drug house—but again, there were no signs of Bobby Nauss.

In between those surveillances, Hurley Trout investigated Adrian Mailers in the city. What he found was a busy mail drop and what he learned was that the business was owned and operated by Louise Parness, who was Cindy Lougee's mother.

The Delaware County Major Crimes Task Force, the Pennsylvania State Police, and the U.S. Marshals Service were now unofficially working together to apprehend Bobby Nauss and Hans Vorhauer. One of the biggest stumbling blocks facing the investigators was the identification of the two fugitives. Vorhauer's file photos from Graterford Prison were thirteen years old at the time of the escape and none of the investigators working the case had ever seen him face-to-face. While Bobby's prison photos were more current, he'd gained weight and his looks had changed somewhat. Other than Tom Rapone and the task force officers, the other investigators had never seen him.

"At that time," Rapone explained later, "Frank Bender comes on the scene." Bender was a forensic artist and sculptor. "I was at the city morgue one day identifying a fugitive's body," Rapone continued, "and I ran into Frank Bender. He was doing some work on another case, but he got wind of what we were doing. As a result, he started hanging around the Marshals Office, talking about this case and that case. Then he offered to put on a presentation."

Rapone took him up on the offer. He called all of the agencies involved and invited key personnel into the Marshals Office, at which time Frank Bender put on a presentation—a reconstruction of decomposed bodies and a demonstration of how the aging process works.

Afterward, Bender volunteered to help him out.

"Okay," Tom Rapone said to him, "you're working on the Nauss-Vorhauer case. We've got pictures more than ten years old and that's it."

In the days that followed, Frank Bender sought out the investigators who'd been involved in the original arrests of Vorhauer and Nauss. He picked each investigator's brain, sketching as they talked, adding something here, taking away something there, fine-tuning his renderings until they looked lifelike, more and more contemporary.

Luck plays a larger role in cracking cases than most investigators like to admit.

"During rush hour one morning," an Upper Darby police officer said, describing the first major break in the case, "this asshole jumps out into the middle of Marshall Road and holds up traffic so his buddy can back his car out of the driveway—and Marshall Road can get pretty busy during rush hour.

"What the guy doesn't know is that one of the people he's holding up is a law enforcement officer on his way to work. The officer recognizes the guy, checks him out, and learns there's an outstanding warrant on him. And it works out that he's an associate of the Warlocks.

"Prior to that contact, we had no idea the Warlocks were in that house."

On April 14, a surveillance was established at 6710 Marshall Road. An activity log was started and still and video photos were taken. Later, back at the Marshals Office, Frank

Bender kept scrutinizing one of the surveillance photos. It was quite hazy.

"That's Vorhauer," he said finally, and he tossed the photo onto the table for the others to see.

"Everyone remotely involved," recalled an Upper Darby police officer, "was deputized on a detainer from the federal government. Day and night, we followed Phyllis Vorhauer from her residence to work, shopping, wherever she had to go, using five or six unmarked cars so she wouldn't spot the same car."

Frank Bender, along with ATF and DEA agents, joined the surveillance unit at the home on Marshall Road the next day. Around noon, the original suspect exited the house accompanied by an unidentified white male who was openly carrying a weapon. While Bender snapped close-ups of the two men through a telescopic lens, the ATF agent trained his binoculars on the weapon.

"KG-99SS," the ATF agent said, "nine-millimeter semiautomatic pistol. Easily convertible to a fully automatic machine gun."

The stakeouts lasted all spring and summer.

"We operated cool, calculated, and efficient," Paul Schneider explained later, "and we were certain we'd made visual contacts with Vorhauer. But the circumstances hadn't been right to make a move. Our number-one priority was that no one would get hurt—including Hans Vorhauer himself.

"We spotted him a total of three times. One of those times, there were five or six kids playing ball in the street all around him. So we waited."

CHAPTER
30

Phyllis Vorhauer drove to the Quality Inn at 26th Street and Penrose Avenue in South Philadelphia on the first Sunday night in September. It was Labor Day weekend and her husband had already registered under an assumed name.

She knocked twice and the door opened.

Two Upper Darby police officers had followed her from home and were sitting in an unmarked car in the parking lot watching the whole thing. They called for backup and deputy marshals, state troopers, county task force officers, and policemen from Upper Darby, Haverford, and Springfield began converging on the scene.

In the privacy of their motel room, Hans and Phyllis Vorhauer made love, then fell asleep watching television. In contrast, the officers remained outside in the heat and humidity, drinking coffee to stay awake and smoking cigarettes. Reminding themselves they were stalking a dangerous fugitive.

They waited all night.

Hans Vorhauer opened the motel room door at 11:15 the next morning and he and Phyllis stepped right into the trap. Taken totally by surprise, he offered no resistance. His wife was also arrested and charged with hindering the apprehension of a fugitive.

It had taken nearly three years, but law enforcement now had Hans Vorhauer back in captivity.

Vorhauer refused to talk to his captors.

Hurley Trout searched him. He found a Michigan driver's license, Michigan registrations for several vehicles, a Visa and Mastercard, and the return portion of a round-trip USAir ticket between Detroit and Philadelphia. The name on all of the seized documents read Elmer Colombo, the address: 8939 Fargo Road, Yale, Michigan.

At the same time, Paul Schneider and a team of Upper Darby police officers were searching Phyllis Vorhauer's car and her residence at 22 Wellington Road. Altogether, they found and seized several years' worth of diaries which detailed secret meetings between Hans and Phyllis. Schneider carted everything back to the Marshals Office to be inventoried and examined.

Yale is about fifty-five minutes northeast of Detroit by car. By the time a deputy marshal from the Detroit office picked up Hurley Trout at the airport and drove him to 8939 Fargo Road, officers from the St. Clair County Sheriff's Drug Task Force and Michigan state troopers were already there.

Trout got out of the car and stared at a slice of Americana that was straight out of a Norman Rockwell painting. It was a big stone farmhouse surrounded by acre after acre of tall green cornfields. Out back was a weathered barn. Next to the farmhouse sat a silo with its roof missing. But inside was where Hans Vorhauer's masterpiece was located: the most sophisticated meth lab any of the investigators on the scene had ever witnessed.

The DEA flew in a chemist from Chicago. He called it the

"California System," photographed it, then began dismantling it.

The investigators searched the premises for two days. They found $37,000 in cash and enough chemicals to manufacture ninety-two pounds of methamphetamine, which carried a wholesale value at that time of nearly $400,000. They also found a set of books for a company calling itself Dathko Sales. The books listed an address in Southfield, Michigan, and identified its purchasing director as a Joseph N. Dome. A check of the Michigan motor vehicle computer found no listing for Joseph Dome and a trace of the company's address and phone number led the investigators to a mail-drop and answering service.

The last entry in the ledger was for one hundred kilograms of ephedrine hydrochloride, purchased from the Graymor Chemical Company in Pine Brook, New Jersey, the previous June. It had been shipped to the R.C. Trucking Company in Philadelphia. Hurley Trout called his office and Tom Rapone dispatched deputies to the address listed for R.C. Trucking Company. But they arrived three months too late. All they found was an empty warehouse.

Back at the farmhouse in Yale, the investigators also found a file of nearly thirty false identities that Hans Vorhauer had been in the process of procuring via Michigan birth and death announcements. They found no signs of Bobby Nauss, but Vorhauer's neighbors identified Bobby's photos as those of a man seen riding a motorcycle in the vicinity of the farmhouse on several occasions.

On his third day in Michigan, Hurley Trout walked into a restaurant near the farmhouse and showed Hans Vorhauer's picture to one of the waitresses.

"That's Norton," she said, explaining that he was a regular customer and everybody called him Norton because he resembled the character portrayed by Art Carney in *The Honeymooners*. She told Trout they even stocked his favorite liqueur.

"What do you know about him?" Trout asked her.

"Not much," she said, "just what he told us. He's an artist and takes courses at the community college."

"Have you ever seen this man before?" Trout asked, showing her Bobby's picture.

"Yeah, I've seen him," she said without hesitation. "He came in here a couple of times during the summer. He was extremely unfriendly and he was with a real dirtball."

Tom Rapone called headquarters. He told Bob Leschoron this case was too important to be handled through the normal channels. How about a task force?

Leschoron is not your typical bureaucrat. His nickname, "Big Buck," was derived from his two avid passions in life: hunting deer and hunting fugitives. With twenty years on the streets of New York City, he'd tracked down some of the country's highest-profile skip artists. The movie *Dog Day Afternoon* was about one case he'd helped crack. His experience in law enforcement made it easy for him to identify with the problems and logistics of the cop on the beat.

He was especially proud of the fact he'd become the first "gun-toter" to be promoted this far within the Marshals Service.

He told Rapone he'd see what he could do.

CHAPTER
31

In Philadelphia, the Federal Building is a concrete and glass skyscraper at Sixth and Market streets, just two blocks from Independence Hall and the Liberty Bell, and the Marshals Office takes up a large portion of the second floor. Dark blue carpeting runs from wall to wall and neon lights provide constant illumination from above. Filing cabinets and computer equipment occupy most of the wall space. There are private offices for chief deputies, large bullpens where deputies work in teams, small conference rooms where interviews are held, and a cellblock. Fugitives make the marshals' world turn and captures keep their blood flowing.

Here, on the beautiful Indian summer day that was September 24, 1986, a Wednesday, the U.S. Marshals Fugitive Task Force met for the first time, almost three years after Bobby Nauss's escape from Graterford Prison.

"We brought in Paul Schneider," Tom Rapone would explain later, "and some of the original guys from the Liz Lande homicide investigation—George Ellis and Bill Davis." Plus officers from the Upper Darby and Springfield police departments; the Philadelphia Police Department, Sheriff's Office, and Warrant Squad; the Pennsylvania State Police and Attorney General's Office; the New Jersey State

Police Fugitive and Intelligence Units; and the Gloucester
and Cape May County Prosecutor's Offices in New Jersey.
In addition, personnel from the FBI, DEA, ATF, and the
U.S. Attorney's Office would be available as needed. Not to
forget the deputy marshals themselves and Frank Bender,
who unveiled his latest creation; a life-size full-color bust of
thirty-four-year-old Bobby Nauss, with short hair and clean-
shaven.

The group's mandate was to arrest motorcycle gang fugitives who had escaped from jail. Tom Rapone's initial list
contained the names of three fugitives—Richard "Wes"
Hamilton, a Warlock who'd escaped from Delaware County
Prison eight years earlier, the only escape during Rapone's
tenure as warden; Sandy Basile, the wife of a Warlock and a
murderess who'd escaped a year earlier; and Bobby Nauss.
But Tom Rapone's focus was single-minded. He wanted
Bobby Nauss. Unless the others led him to Nauss, they could
go to hell.

"During the time Nauss was a vice president with the
Warlocks," Rapone told the task force officers, "four young
girls from Delaware County were raped, murdered, and
dumped in the Tinicum swamps. Several sources close to
Nauss have said he's responsible for the deaths of all four
girls, but they're afraid to testify against him."

Rapone told them about Liz Lande, about Catherine Ingram. About the drugs. The arrests and convictions. The escape.

"Out of fear," Rapone theorized, "Bobby Nauss hit the
bricks running after his escape. He knows he's wanted, he
knows he's in for murder, and he knows the cops aren't
going to ask a lot of questions if they confront him.

"He had to change his appearance the best he could. He's
got the issue of the tattoos. Most likely he'll be wearing long
sleeves, but it's also possible he's changed their configura-
tion. In my opinion, Bobby Nauss will try to blend into the
mainstream. He'll clean up his act and adopt a yuppie image

and lifestyle. He'll change his name and he'll find a love-starved woman and settle down."

The investigators spent the rest of the first week setting up files, examining existing files, and familiarizing themselves with current and proposed surveillance locations. The following Monday, Tom Rapone appointed Hurley Trout and Paul Schneider as the lead investigators. They then discussed strategy with the group.

Trout spoke first. He mentioned the reported sightings of Bobby Nauss in the vicinity of Hans Vorhauer's meth lab in Yale, Michigan, and said the Marshals Office in Detroit was conducting a collateral investigation in an attempt to pinpoint Nauss in their area. In addition, wanted posters were printed and sent to the Canadian Border Police, the Detroit and Philadelphia Airport Police, and the Detroit Crime Stoppers Organization.

When Paul Schneider took the floor, he discussed possible links to Bobby. He first identified three women—Cindy Lougee, Marijane Dolhancryk, and Cookie Nauss. Supposedly, Lougee had conspired in the escape, was one of Bobby's lovers, and was operating a drug house. Marijane Dolhancryk was from Darby. She married and divorced one Warlock, married another, and was rumored to have been another one of Bobby's lovers. She, in fact, was his last visitor at Graterford prior to the escape. Cookie Nauss was Bobby's wife—make that ex-wife. She'd divorced Bobby in Atlantic City, New Jersey, during the previous summer and was currently living at the Jersey shore with her new husband, Sammy Golding.

Schneider told them Bobby and Cookie's son, thirteen-year-old Tommy, lived with Bobby's parents. Although Bobby had always expressed a great deal of love for his son, his own father's health was not good. Therefore, Bobby would probably avoid contact with the boy. However, he might try to contact his brothers and sisters.

Finally, he mentioned Bobby's closest associates with the

Warlocks. Steve DeMarco and Bobby Marconi were in
prison, but Tony "Mudbone" Merkle and Rick Martinson
were still on the streets. Martinson was supposedly cooking
meth with Chris "Chopper" Rigler somewhere up in the
Pocono Mountains. It was a distinct possibility that Bobby
was cooking and trafficking meth in concert with them, and
it was a foregone conclusion that both Martinson and Rigler
knew where Bobby was hiding.

The course of action, as Paul Schneider explained it, was
to continue the surveillances of Cindy Lougee's home, German Mike's Bar, and the meth lab on Marshall Road in
Upper Darby; to establish new surveillances on as many of
the aforementioned players as possible; to subpoena phone
records; to arrest known Warlocks at every opportunity; to
continue to look for the missing pieces of the escape; and to
squeeze existing informants and cultivate new ones. And this
last objective was the key to breaking most cases: finding
someone who was in some sort of bind and was willing to
leak information for money or legal concessions.

On Friday, October 3, 1986, one of the investigators called
Tom Rapone from New Jersey and said he'd just gleaned
some information from a confidential informant (CI).

"Twice last summer," the investigator told Rapone, "my
CI said he saw Bobby and Cookie together at Bally's Casino
in Atlantic City. And he said he saw them another time, in
August, at the Tri-State Mall."

The Tri-State Mall is situated on I-95 close to where
Bobby and Cookie used to live in Aston before he was arrested.

Wouldn't it be a bitch, Rapone mused, if Cookie's new
husband, this Sammy what's-his-name, is really Nauss.

Marmora is an hour east of Philadelphia. Ten miles south
of Atlantic City, it's just off Exit 25 of the Garden State
Parkway. Two miles from the Atlantic Ocean.

"Doesn't look like anybody's home," Hurley Trout said as he drove an unmarked car slowly past 209 Seaside Avenue the following morning. This was the house Sammy and Cookie Golding were renting for $600 per month. From there, Trout drove up to Avalon, one of the small seaside towns that line the long, narrow barrier islands along the Jersey shore.

Sammy Golding was in his mid-thirties, an informant told Hurley Trout, five-eight to five-ten, well-built. He wore a Fu Manchu mustache and a goatee and he had lots of tattoos. He was the kind of guy who paid for everything with $100 bills. His wife, Cookie, had just had a baby.

At 6 the next morning, a van was parked on Seaside Avenue, half a block from the Golding residence. A Ford camper sat on the opposite side of the street, half a block south. Task force officers were inside both vehicles—hiding. And waiting.

When Sammy Golding walked out the front door, Frank Bender looked at his wristwatch. It was 7:30. Golding was wearing jeans and a denim jacket and he got into a yellow El Camino and drove away. As the El Camino passed the van, Bender tried to photograph Sammy Golding, but he never got a clear shot.

Golding drove south along the Garden State Parkway with both law enforcement vehicles in pursuit and maintaining a sufficient cushion to avoid being seen. At Exit 11, Sammy Golding took Route 663 north until he arrived at a construction site a few miles up the road. When he turned into the construction site, the investigators kept going straight and returned to Philadelphia.

Two days later, at 3:30 P.M., the government camper returned to the construction site and found a parking spot close to Sammy Golding's yellow El Camino. Frank Bender was riding shotgun, armed with a camera.

At quitting time, the construction workers rushed out en masse. Sammy Golding was walking straight toward the camper. Frank Bender couldn't have asked for better conditions. The sun was shining directly on Golding's face. The lighting was perfect for photographic purposes and the sun glare prevented Golding from seeing Bender.

That was the good news. The bad news was: Sammy Golding was a remarkable look-alike, but he was not Bobby Nauss.

The Sammy Golding incident was symptomatic of the way the investigation would unfold. Rarely would a week pass without five to ten reported sightings of Bobby Nauss in the tristate area. Each one was investigated and a pattern quickly developed: There were a surprising number of people who resembled Bobby Nauss.

By now, wanted kits were ready. They contained reward posters; Frank Bender's latest sketches of Bobby Nauss in a variety of hairstyles, colors, and combinations of facial hair; and the pertinent information about the case. Hurley Trout sent the kits to Marshals Offices in all fifty states, foreign territories, and the District of Columbia.

He sent investigators to the Delaware County Courthouse. At the Recorder of Deeds Office, information was obtained regarding real estate holdings of known Warlocks and surveillances were soon established at those locations. A search for outstanding warrants on known Warlocks produced one on Tony "Mudbone" Merkle.

Paul Schneider then made a few phone calls and heard that Merkle was living in a trailer at a marina in Tinicum Township with a white female named Cathy. He sent a pair of investigators to Tinicum to search the boatyards.

The investigators found three trailers, but all three were vacant.

At the same time, several teams of investigators were making contacts with Bobby's parents, brothers, and sisters. One team pulled into the Veteran's Stadium parking lot in South Philadelphia and entered the Phillies' offices to interview Vinnie Nauss. A University of Miami graduate, he worked in the team's public relations department.

Visibly upset, Vinnie Nauss told the officers it irritated him that they had the audacity to enter his place of employment.

"I last saw my brother at Graterford Prison on the Christmas Eve before he escaped," he said hotly, "and I haven't seen or heard from him since."

Look, he told them, he traveled all over the country with the Phillies. If Bobby wanted to contact him, it was easy. But not once had Bobby called him. And besides that, he lived next door to his parents in an apartment attached to the house. He saw family members every day. Not once had anyone mentioned a single contact with Bobby. His father was a sick man and the recent publicity about Hans Vorhauer's capture had not helped his condition one bit.

"Why can't you just leave us alone?"

Hurley Trout and Paul Schneider were brainstorming at the Marshals Office on October 15, 1986, when a biker walked through the door. He said he'd placed an anonymous phone call to Graterford Prison a few months back about the Nauss-Vorhauer escape.

Trout and Schneider looked at each other. Could this guy be on the level?

They asked him a few key questions to test his authenticity. When he answered all of them correctly, they took him into an interrogation room and asked him how he acquired the information.

"I overheard a phone conversation at Cindy Lougee's house," he began. "Cindy said they went to her mother's business—her and her boyfriend at the time—and rented a truck."

"Who was her boyfriend?"

"His name's Frank, and I think his last name's Brute—something like that. A couple of prisoners, including the one that's living with her now, put those guys in the furniture."

"The guy living with her now," Hurley Trout asked, "do you know what he looks like?"

"Yeah."

Trout placed a mug shot on the table in front of him. "Is that the guy?"

"Yeah, but his hair ain't like that."

"How about this?" Trout said, placing a surveillance photo he'd recently taken outside Cindy Lougee's house.

"Yeah, that's him."

"What's his name?"

"I'm pretty sure it's almost like Nauss. News—or something like that. His nickname's Jocko."

"Did Nauss pay her? Did the club front the money?"

"The money wasn't sent directly to her. It was sent to her mother's business. I'm pretty sure she said he was sending it in money orders or however they send it out of prison."

"Is she a meth user?"

"Oh, yeah. Heavy."

"Where's she getting her meth?"

"From Nauss and from somebody else."

"When was the last time you saw him?"

"Me? I never seen him."

"Think about the escape itself."

"Jocko and a few prisoners put them in furniture and the guard on duty was bribed so they could load them inside the truck."

"That's all it sounded like? One guard?"

"That's all she ever mentioned. I know his name, but I can't think of it. But I know he's retired."

"How do you know he's retired?"

"Cindy was talking one day about the statue [sic] of limitations running out and she said, 'Now the guard's retired, there's nothing to worry about.' "

"Now when they got to Cindy's house in the truck, what happened? How did they split?"

"Just left on foot."

"And that was it? No contact with him again?"

"A couple of times, she went down to Uncle Charlie's and he was down there. And I know he called once and she met him at the Burger King in Norristown."

Hurley Trout called Graterford Prison and requested an update on Robert Hart's employment status. He wasn't surprised to hear that Hart had retired.

Trout next sent two investigators to Graterford to examine the disbursement files of prisoners who'd been incarcerated prior to Bobby Nauss's jailbreak. It was tedious work and it took several days to complete, but a pattern was evident: From late in 1982 through most of 1983, more than a dozen prisoners had sent checks and money orders to Adrian Mailers. The amounts ranged from forty to ninety dollars and totaled several thousand dollars. Some had been enclosed in Christmas cards, others had contained short notes such as the following:

February 1, 1983
Dear Louise,
   As this letter leaves me in good health, I hope you and yours are doing well also.
   Please find enclosed, one (1) check for fifty dollars.

The note was signed by one of the prisoners.

Mail covers were soon issued for the home and business of Louise Parness.

On October 21, 1986, Paul Schneider and George Ellis made the scenic drive through the rolling hills of central Pennsylvania. The colorful autumn foliage was spectacular, but a commune with nature was not their intent. Their destination was Huntingdon Prison and their goal was finding out what Hans Vorhauer knew about Bobby's whereabouts.

Vorhauer refused to talk.

In an attempt to elicit his cooperation, they showed him a

copy of his wife's arrest warrant and mentioned that her court appearance was rapidly approaching. Perhaps if—

"Go fuck yourself," he told them.

The investigators spent several weeks trying to locate Frank Brute. They kept running combinations and permutations of letters through the crime and BMV computers and drawing blanks. Finally, on October 28, someone ran the letters b-o-r-u-t-a and hit a winner.

Frank Boruta had a criminal record in Pennsylvania and New Jersey and an outstanding warrant existed for his arrest in Montgomery County, Pennsylvania.

Hurley Trout assigned three officers to find him.

Tom Rapone called Bob Leschoron on November 1, 1986, to say he wanted Bobby Nauss elevated to Top-Fifteen status.

Similar to the FBI's list of Ten Most Wanted criminals, the Marshals Service has a Fifteen Most Wanted program. Into this category go the elite of the Class-One violators. Cases are selected for Top Fifteen based on three criteria: complexity, high visibility, and the likelihood of making a capture.

At the state and local level, Bobby Nauss was a convicted rapist and murderer who'd been sentenced to spend the rest of his life plus forty years in jail, but federally he carried only a three-year drug rap. He was small potatoes around marshals headquarters. Furthermore, he'd committed his crimes during an era when media attention was not even close to what it is today. There was no cable TV, no CNN to make Bobby Nauss a household name in the fashion of a Jeffrey Dahmer or an Amy Fisher.

And that's exactly what Bob Leschoron told Tom Rapone.

"This fucking guy's a cold-blooded killer," Rapone yelled into the phone in a voice charged with passion. "Let me tell you, it's important to go after Bobby Nauss for a lot of reasons. The fact he was able to escape from a maximum-security prison—and remain escaped—attacks the goddamn basics of the system. After you spend all that time and money investigating and putting him in jail, it's important—*IMPORTANT*—to keep him there. He committed a heinous crime and he was convicted and he lost his appeals. The system is responsible for catching him and prosecuting him and putting him in jail. It has to be upheld.

"And if we don't go after him, nobody will. The son of a bitch will skate."

"Tommy," Leschoron told him, "I'll make the presentation. But don't hold your breath."

Later that same day, another tip came in from New Jersey.

According to a CI, Bobby Nauss had been holed up in the mountains of Virginia at a biker hideout known as "Uncle Tom's Cabin." However, Hans Vorhauer's capture had spooked him and he'd moved in with Chopper Rigler in the Pocono Mountains of northeast Pennsylvania.

Two days later, on November 3, 1986, Tom Rapone sent a contingent of twelve investigators into the Poconos near Scranton. They set up a command post at Arrowhead Lake in a rented ski lodge. There were sleeping quarters; a two-way radio base station; electronic surveillance devices; an arsenal of handguns, shotguns, and rifles; and dossiers on Bobby Nauss and Chopper Rigler.

Rigler was thirty-eight years old and a former chapter president in the Warlocks. Short, squatty, and redheaded, his arrests included narcotics violations and possessing stolen property. A year earlier, he'd purchased the Enterprise Tackle Shop for $80,000. It was a combination bait and tackle shop and an automobile radiator shop. In addition, he'd built a home in a development known as Mountain Top Estates at the dead end of Hawk Lane.

On Thursday, November 4, two of the investigators drove to Rigler's radiator shop. A mechanic came out and greeted them. He was in his mid-thirties, about five feet eight inches

tall, with dark hair and eyes, a mustache, and goatee. He resembled Frank Bender's latest sketches of Bobby Nauss and
said his name was Bob.

"We're doing some camping," one of the deputies said,
"but the damn radiator's been overheating. Got time to look
at it?"

"I'm pretty busy right now," the mechanic said, "but I can
take a look at it tomorrow morning. How's ten-thirty?"

"Sounds good," the deputy replied.

As soon as they returned to the ski lodge, one of the
deputies phoned Tom Rapone.

At 4 the next morning, Rapone, Paul Schneider, and
George Ellis started the three-hour drive to Arrowhead Lake.

At 9:30, Tom Rapone was giving last-minute instructions.
Because they'd personally dealt with Bobby Nauss in the
past, Rapone, Schneider, and Ellis would ride in the back of
the camper, out of sight. The two investigators who'd made
the initial contact with the mechanic would ride up front.
Everyone else would deploy themselves in strategic positions
as close to the radiator shop as possible without being seen.

"If the identification proves positive," Rapone said, "we
move. Remember, he's a murderer. He's armed and he's
dangerous. He's probably carrying a nine-millimeter. Be
careful. After we take him into custody, we secure the building, then conduct a search and seizure.

"Any questions?

"Let's go."

They arrived at the radiator shop at 10:30.

The mechanic came out, opened the hood, and carefully
unscrewed the radiator cap.

"Thermostat still acting up?" he asked as he worked.

"Not really," the deputy replied. "I just wanted to make
sure before I drove home."

Inside the camper, Rapone, Schneider, and Ellis were
jockeying for position, getting good looks at the mechanic.
And they reached a consensus: He was close enough to be a
twin brother, but he wasn't Bobby Nauss.

* * *

On November 13, 1986, Bob Leschoron called Tom Rapone.

"Good news," he said. "Nauss just went Top Fifteen."

Rapone smiled. The Marshals Service was offering a $4,000 reward for information leading to Bobby's arrest. Coupled with $1,000 being offered by the Pennsylvania Crime Stoppers, that brought the bounty on Bobby's head to $5,000.

A year passed with little progress being made.

The investigators kept busy logging and cross-indexing phone numbers they were obtaining on a daily basis from pen registers they'd installed on the telephones of most of the suspected key players. (A pen register is also called a DNR, which stands for "dialed number recorder.")

The work was tedious and boring. It did nothing to point to Bobby's whereabouts, but it did define a multistate meth distribution ring that was previously unknown.

CHAPTER
32

The Late Show Starring Joan Rivers debuted during the fall of 1986 on a new television network. Calling itself Fox, it began broadcasting on only seven independent "O & O" (owned and operated) cable television stations.

In 1987 Fox added a few more shows. One was *Married . . . with Children*, which aired Sundays during prime time. It was an immediate hit.

With the new network gaining the acceptance of the viewing public, Fox CEO Barry Diller hired thirty-one-year-old Stephen Chao to develop new ideas, shoot pilots, and try them out. Chao, a Harvard MBA, had a résumé that included the *National Enquirer* and Rupert Murdoch among his previous employers. His instructions from Diller were to concentrate on low-budget, low-risk shows.

At the National Association of Television Programming Executives' Convention in New Orleans in October 1987 Chao was reunited with Jim Platt, his successor at Rupert Murdoch's News Corporation of America. Over a couple of drinks, Chao started picking his old buddy's brain.

On a trip to Europe, Platt told Chao, he'd seen a television show that reenacted crimes in a cooperative effort with police agencies, in an attempt to apprehend criminals. Maybe, Platt suggested to Chao, you could do the same thing at Fox.

On January 6, 1988, Frank Boruta was arrested inside an auto body shop in Philadelphia. He offered no resistance. Afterward, Hurley Trout spoke to him in an interrogation room at the Montgomery County Prison.

"I want you to tell me what you know about the jailbreak," Trout said.

"I don't know nuthin'," Boruta said.

"That's bullshit," Trout told him. "I already know about you and Cindy Lougee and the U-Haul truck. Maybe I should call you Mr. Thompson. So don't fuck with me."

"Cindy tricked me," Boruta said. "She told me we were going to pick up furniture—I swear—that's all I thought it was. I didn't know about no escape."

The rest came easy.

"When we got back to Cindy's, I heard banging inside the truck. I opened the door and near shit my pants. These two guys I never seen before jumped out of the truck. It wasn't until I heard about it on TV that I knew who they were."

"Where'd they go?"

"They just walked away and I never seen them again."

Hurley Trout and Bill Davis knocked on Cindy Lougee's door three days later. She let them in. Jocko Nuss, who'd been sitting in the living room, ran upstairs as soon as he saw the investigators.

In an attempt to shake her, Trout said that most likely she was going to be arrested for her complicity in Bobby Nauss's escape. What did she have to say for herself?

Before she could answer, Jocko Nuss came back downstairs. He told her he'd just called her lawyer and she wasn't to answer any questions or make any statements.

As soon as Trout and Davis left, she picked up the phone. While other investigators listened to her conversation via a wiretap, she discussed Bobby Nauss and the escape with a friend.

Hurley Trout and Bill Davis tried a different approach the next day. In an office at the Montgomery County Prison, they convinced Frank Boruta to call Cindy Lougee while they listened on another line.

The call precipitated a three-way shouting match between Boruta, Cindy Lougee, and Jocko Nuss. It ended with Jocko Nuss screaming at Lougee, "Hang up! Hang up!"

Seconds later, Cindy Lougee was back on the phone.

"I'm going to get even with that fucking Frank Boruta," she told a friend. "I'll get somebody to give him a hotshot of meth and I'll plant that fucker right next to Jimmy Hoffa."

A few days later, Hurley Trout obtained a court order for the temporary release of Frank Boruta, who then directed Trout to a Gulf gas station at the corner of Ridge Avenue and Walnut Lane in Philadelphia. He said they'd rented the U-Haul there. But Trout didn't see one U-Haul truck or trailer on the premises.

The station owner's wife told Trout they'd stopped renting U-Hauls recently. She'd sent all the old records to U-Haul's headquarters in Phoenix, Arizona.

Frank Boruta then submitted to a polygraph. The results indicated that, basically, he was telling the truth. His only deceptions seemed to be in the areas regarding advance knowledge of the escape and whether or not he'd been paid.

Subsequently, U-Haul mailed a photostat of a rental agreement to the Marshals Office. It was dated November 17, 1983, the date of Bobby's escape from Graterford. Cindy Lougee's name and address appeared at the top and her signature was affixed to the bottom. The agreement indicated the truck had been driven a total of forty-six miles and the charges amounted to $37.85.

Before he finished, Hurley Trout developed additional informants who were able to refine the escape two steps further. Another female accomplice picked up Bobby and Hans Vorhauer after they walked away from Cindy Lougee's house. She then drove them to a rendezvous with Rick Martinson and Mudbone Merkle, who drove the two fugitives to a safe-house in Bucks County, a few miles north of the city.

But that's as far as the investigators ever got.

Frank Boruta, Jocko Nuss, Cindy Lougee, and Robert Hart were all subpoenaed to appear before a grand jury investigating the escape. Nuss, Lougee, and Hart invoked the Fifth Amendment.

Tom Rapone paced the floor of his office, sipping a cup of coffee. Thanks to mass mailings of reward posters and the elevation of the case to the Top Fifteen, reported sightings of Bobby Nauss were now coming in from coast to coast—Fort Lauderdale, Mobile, Knoxville, Sacramento, Des Moines.

Literally hundreds of leads were pouring in and every one—no matter how capricious or nebulous—had to be, and was, verified. But Rapone held firm in the belief that the solution to this mystery would come from someone in Bobby's family, a member of the Warlocks, or someone on the fringe of the motorcycle gang. So he stuck to the fundamentals.

"Nauss and Cookie had a love-hate relationship," he would say later, "but they were tight. And pussy usually does these guys in—just look at Vorhauer."

Through mail covers, he knew Cookie Golding was sending letters to a friend in Las Vegas, Nevada. Through a pen register on Cookie's phone line, he knew she was placing calls to a Warlock who lived in Tucson, Arizona. So he sent surveillance teams to both cities.

They came back empty-handed.

Through another mail cover, Tom Rapone learned that Cookie had been invited to Karen Nauss's wedding. She was Bobby's second-youngest sister and the ceremony was scheduled to be held at BVM church in Darby.

Dressed as bartenders and waiters, deputy marshals mixed

drinks and served tables at the reception after the wedding. Disguised as honeymooners, a male and female deputy boarded a USAir flight with the newlyweds and flew to Ix- tapa, Mexico.

But no Bobby.

"We surveilled his family," Tom Rapone explained. "We did wires, we did taps, we did mail covers. After a while, I was convinced he was not communicating with his son or his father. There was a chance he contacted one of his brothers, but no one else.

"Nauss had cut his dealings with Cookie.

"That tells you something about the man. He comes from a good family, a secure family, and he just cuts it.

"But I felt all along that Nauss had the support of a certain hard-core element of Warlocks—Rick Martinson, Tony Merkle, Rigler, maybe one or two others. You can hang those guys by their teeth, skin them alive, but they won't tell anybody a thing."

America's Most Wanted premiered on Sunday, February 7, 1988, on a shoestring and a prayer. No one at Fox had any idea if the premise of the program would work or not.

One of the last decisions facing the producers had been the choice of a host. They considered actor Treat Williams and Virginia politician Chuck Robb. In the end, they selected John Walsh, an unknown whose only claim to fame had re- sulted from the personal tragedy of having his six-year-old son kidnapped and decapitated. A TV movie had been filmed and he'd become an advocate for missing children. To the producers, Walsh came across as honest and sincere, some- one with whom viewers could easily identify.

Incredibly, the hotlines started ringing shortly after the first show ended. Dozens of callers were claiming they'd seen or knew the whereabouts of the fugitive who'd just been profiled.

The capture was made the next day in Staten Island, New York. The show worked. Now, could it hook the viewers?

Phone calls went out to the FBI and the Marshals Service. Did they have any high-profile fugitives?

Bob Leschoron suggested Bobby Nauss.

"Being the father of a murdered child," John Walsh would say later, "I thought, *This guy's a real coward.* I'm abhorred by [sic] anyone who hurts children and I don't get this hurting women. I mean, what kind of nut case are you if you make love to your girlfriend one minute and murder her the next?

"I'm not a vigilante and I'm not some right-wing hanging judge, by any means. This job is tough—not my choice of jobs, believe me.

"Ever been to a crime scene? Ever seen women split wide open? Little kids dead?

"You'd never forget it. It would make you puke. And then you'd dream about it for three or four more years. Then you're enraged. You say why? *Why?* Who could do this shit?

"But I knew one thing: The son of a bitch was out there and it was up to people like us—the police, the prosecutors, and me—to hunt him down. We thought Bobby Nauss was a big-time scumbag and we should get him."

Since it was just the second show in the series, the format was not set. The producers were experimenting, trying to lure an audience to a new concept on a new network. As a result, Bobby's spot, Episode #2, which played on February 14, 1988, was longer than today's segments, and it was more sensational. More graphic. Critics called it inflammatory. The viewers liked it and the phone lines lit up before the show went off the air.

Hundreds of calls came in. From Woonsocket, Rhode Island; Tarrytown, New York; Aurora, Colorado; Glen Burnie, Maryland; Casper, Wyoming; Florence, South Carolina; Lexington, Kentucky; Jacksonville, Oregon; and almost everywhere in between. One call came in from Venezuela and another from Brisbane, Australia.

Thirty-six hours after the show aired, Jocko Nuss died. Syringes containing traces of methamphetamines were found on the floor in close proximity to his body, but the coroner found no fresh needle marks on his body.

Cindy Lougee ID'd the body.

His remains were cremated on February 22.

On March 25, 1987, a judge acquitted Phyllis Vorhauer of all charges of hindering the apprehension of a fugitive.

"There is no positive duty placed on a wife to inform on the whereabouts of her fugitive husband," said the judge in explaining the ruling.

Meanwhile, deputy marshals from coast to coast were spending thousands of hours verifying the leads that were coming in from *America's Most Wanted*.

But as the summer of 1988 arrived, Bobby Nauss was still at large and his whereabouts were unknown.

America's Most Wanted ran another segment on Bobby on August 8. By then, the show had become quite successful and the Fox network had expanded. Episode #27 aired on 125 affiliated stations. Once again, the phone lines went crazy and the deputies went even crazier trying to keep up with all the leads.

"We were getting as many as fifteen queries a day," Tom Rapone said.

But, if anything, the exposure Bobby was getting from *America's Most Wanted* became more of a detriment than an asset. The glut of leads turned into one false alarm, wild-goose chase, and look-alike after another. It was the boy who cried wolf. In spades.

CHAPTER
33

Lighting up a cigarette, Hurley Trout was punching numbers into a phone, sending an SOS to headquarters. After nearly two years of one dead end after another, he was burned out.

Bob Leschoron arrived in Philadelphia two days later. His posture and demeanor radiated competence and instilled confidence. His attitude left little doubt that he knew exactly what he was doing.

"Let's start at square one," he said to Trout.

They sat down and reviewed the latest intelligence reports. They drew linkage charts. They theorized. They enlisted the cooperation of the local police forces in stopping known Warlocks for vehicle checks and traffic violations. They interviewed everyone even remotely involved with the case—no matter how many times each one had been previously seen. They sat outside the Warlocks' clubhouse, copied tag numbers, and took surveillance photos. They walked the streets, squeezed informants, and they visited the homes of known Warlocks.

One chapter president was shocked when he answered his front door and saw Hurley Trout and Bob Leschoron standing on his doorstep.

"Where's Nauss?" Leschoron asked him.

"I don't know where the motherfucker is," the Warlock
barked at him, "but if I did, I'd give him to you just to get the
heat off. You fucking guys are killing us."

But the effort was wasted.

"I helped Hurley out every way I could," Leschoron explained. "I spent a couple of months, but we couldn't shake
anything loose.

"And Hurley died working this case."

Janet Doyle, born and raised in Delaware County, is an attractive redhead who first came to work at the Marshals Office during the summer of 1985. At the time, she didn't get
paid. Instead, she was serving a student internship after her
junior year at West Chester University. Criminal justice
major. She received college credits instead of money.

When her internship ended, she was hired to do part-time
secretarial work until she completed her studies. After graduation, she applied for a job with the Marshals Service and
was eventually hired. In October 1987, after thirteen weeks
at the Federal Law Enforcement Training Center in Glynco,
Georgia—"The Academy"—she was sworn and deputized.

One day during the summer of 1989, Janet Doyle found herself standing inside a hospital room. Hurley Trout had started
taking sick days in July and entered the hospital for testing.

"He looked bad," Janet Doyle would say later. "Hurley
was not a heavy guy to begin with and he'd lost a lot of
weight. He was a chain-smoker and I guess that proved to be
his downfall."

Hurley Trout died of cancer in August 1989.

Steve Quinn was vacationing on the beach in Sea Isle
City, New Jersey, when he got the news.

Quinn, who grew up in Drexel Hill, was another member of
the Bonner High connection that was involved on both sides
of this case. Shortly after he graduated from Bonner in 1975,
he found himself in Vietnam. When he came home a year

later, long-range planning was not a priority. He was young
and good-looking, loved just being alive, and was infatuated
by the Jersey shore. To him, life was simple. It boiled down to
drinking beer and chasing women. Everything else was sec-
ondary.

One summer night, he was two-thirds of a six-pack into
the drive between home and Margate, New Jersey, doing
twenty miles per hour over the speed limit when he was
stopped for speeding.

The cop cut him a break. No speeding ticket. No DUI.

Maturity didn't hit him that very second, but it wasn't far
behind. He stopped drinking, joined the Marshals Service,
and started chasing fugitives.

In 1988, he'd been assigned to apprehend a convicted
bank robber who'd escaped from federal prison. Before his
arrest, the robber had stolen more than $6 million. The fugi-
tive led Quinn on a merry cross-country chase, but he eventually got his man.

His reward, with the passing of Hurley Trout, was Bobby
Nauss. Janet Doyle was his new partner. Whereas Hurley
Trout had been an old-fashioned gumshoe, Janet Doyle was
a high-tech newcomer. Quinn was a perfect compromise of
both styles.

"Here's two filing cabinets," Tom Rapone told Janet
Doyle. "They belong to you now."

"Huh?" was her reply when she saw the mountains of
files. It took her two weeks to read through the material.

"My head was spinning just getting to know the players,"
she recalled. "At this point, Steve and I thought Bobby Nauss
was a myth. We'd never seen him. In fact, no one had seen
him in years. He was a career felon, yet there was no trail of
his crimes—no rapes, no murders that bore his trademark.

"That just didn't compute. So we honestly thought he was
dead."

"If Nauss were dead," Tom Rapone assured Steve Quinn
and Janet Doyle, "I would have heard about it from the Warlocks. They want us off their asses."

Steve Quinn worked the drug angle.

"Marty Riley, Ace Kivlin, Hans Vorhauer, and Bobby Nauss controlled the drug traffic at Graterford," one CI told him. That became a starting point.

Quinn immediately scratched Ace Kivlin's name off the list. After being paroled from Graterford, Kivlin died of a drug overdose during the previous summer. Deputies had surveilled his funeral, hoping Bobby Nauss would pay his last respects. Several mourners had shown up wearing scarves around their faces, but none of them matched Bobby's height and weight profile.

Next, Steve Quinn and Janet Doyle visited Hans Vorhauer in prison.

"I'll never forget his eyes," Janet Doyle recalled, "how he stared at us through the glass. He told us to go fuck ourselves. If that glass weren't there, I think he would have killed us if he had the chance."

With Ace Kivlin eliminated and Hans Vorhauer unwilling to cooperate, that left Marty Riley.

George Ellis began following Marty Riley at the beginning of September. It was only a matter of time, as Ellis put it, before Riley broke some sort of law.

On September 23, Marty Riley assaulted and terrorized a woman. She filed a complaint. Ellis immediately contacted Tom Rapone, and Rapone joined Ellis in making the arrest.

"Look," Tom Rapone said to Riley, "I could give a shit about busting *you*. But I do want to ask you some questions and I expect some answers."

Riley shook his head.

To him, dealing with cops was no big deal. He was going to play hardball. So George Ellis locked him up.

Two weeks later, on October 8, Marty Riley changed his mind. He agreed to sit down and talk to Rapone if a deal could be worked out. It was.

The escape? Yeah, he knew about the escape. It was supposed to come down a few months earlier. Bobby gave Jocko

Nuss $2,600 to hire two men and rent a truck. But Jocko—that asshole—he pissed the money away and set the whole thing back.

The Warlocks? Yeah, they helped Bobby pull it off. Before Bobby was sent to prison, he was a chemist. You know, a cooker. Meth. Always had connections in Canada. That's why the Warlocks needed him. Always talked about Canada. Right before the escape, Bobby said that three and a half hours after he got out of prison he'd be out of the country. In Canada.

"Look," Rapone said, "do you know where he is?"

No way. Only Rick Martinson knew.

Riley kept talking. He said Bobby suffered a hernia injury while he was at Graterford, but he kept it a secret because he didn't want it on his medical records.

"Bobby and Vorhauer were working together until you caught Vorhauer and took down the lab," Riley said, "and no way he's working in a garage or playing his guitar in a club somewhere. He's cooking meth."

At one point, Janet Doyle was convinced she was on to Bobby Nauss.

"One of the first things a Warlock does when he goes on the lam," she explained, "is he changes his name. Usually he takes another Warlock's name. Somebody he knows. Because he needs money, he commits crimes. And sometimes he gets caught."

It was on the NCIC computer that Janet Doyle started scanning for names of known Warlocks.

"I was looking for out-of-state arrests after the date of the escape," she explained.

She started with known Warlocks whose last names began with the letter A and she worked her way through the alphabet to the letter W before she hit on Joseph Wescott. Joe "Fatty" Wescott was a Warlock from Delaware County. The computer showed an armed robbery arrest in San Antonio, Texas, during 1985. The social security number matched.

Janet Doyle checked with George Ellis, who confirmed that the real Joe Wescott had been in Delaware County at the time the other Wescott was arrested in Texas.

"The next thing a Warlock does on the lam," Doyle continued, "is he gets married, settles down, and has kids."

Janet Doyle ran Fatty Wescott's social security number through the Social Security Administration in Baltimore, hoping to find a flow of income that would pinpoint his present location. What she found was a record of monthly death benefits being paid to his widow since 1986.

Again, she checked with George Ellis, who assured her that the real Wescott was still alive.

The son of a bitch IS dead, was her next thought.

Janet Doyle traced the death benefits to a widow in Colorado. In her early twenties, she said her husband had died in Orange County, California, on November 17, 1985—which just happened to be the second anniversary of Bobby's escape from prison. Was it a coincidence? Or had Bobby been celebrating and taken too many drugs?

She'd only known her husband a short while before they got married, the widow told Janet Doyle. She didn't know him very well. They had one child. He liked motorcycles and had lots of tattoos. He died from a drug overdose. And that was about it.

Janet Doyle contacted the Orange County, California, Coroner's Office and learned that this Joseph Wescott had been cremated shortly after his death. She asked the coroner to describe him. What about tattoos?

The coroner pulled his file and started reading over the phone: "Let's see, there's a swastika . . . and a naked woman . . . and the inscription BORN TO LOSE . . ."

What about the fucking parrot?

The coroner described a few more tattoos.

"Did he have a big blue parrot on his upper right arm?" Janet Doyle asked the coroner.

"A blue parrot?" the coroner said. Then he paused to read the autopsy report. "No parrot."

Shit.

Janet Doyle hung up, then she started going through her files, trying to match these tattoos with known Warlocks. It didn't take her long to find a match. She hadn't located Bobby Nauss, but she did put an end to the search for one of the fugitives on Tom Rapone's list: Richard "Wes" Hamilton.

Then came the lowest part of the investigation.

Since Wes Hamilton was dead, perhaps the speculation about Bobby was right. He, too, just might be dead.

"We arrested many, many Warlocks incidental to this investigation," Tom Rapone explained later. "On related charges. On drug charges. We violated paroles and probations and put on a full-court press. We overtly and covertly surveilled and recorded. Investigated. Interviewed. Grand-juried. A lot of people went to jail as a result of our looking for Nauss—a hell of a lot—and more will continue to go to jail as a result of our investigation.

"But after a time, everyone else thought he was dead. It was an easy out for anyone who doesn't have the resources or doesn't want to do the work.

"But there was never a doubt in my mind that Bobby was alive and well."

CHAPTER
34

It was spooky. Bobby was standing in the checkout line of a convenience store in Luna Pier, Michigan. The date was February 9, 1988. All he wanted was a pack of chewing gum. His hair was short and he was clean-shaven, dressed the way he always dressed: long pants, work boots, and a long-sleeved flannel hunting shirt. This one was yellow and black.

He picked up a *TV Guide* while he was waiting and flipped through the pages. Suddenly he was reading about himself. It was shocking. His exploits were being featured this coming Sunday night on channels 36 and 50 on a new TV show called *America's Most Wanted*.

How could this be? Were they going to show his picture? How many people would be watching? Would anyone recognize him?

He asked himself the same questions over and over all week.

Luna Pier isn't even a dot on most maps. It's just a narrow stretch of resort cottages along the western edge of Lake Erie in the bottom right-hand corner of Michigan. Population: 1,480. Situated forty miles south of Detroit and less than ten miles north of Toledo, Ohio, just off I-75, Luna Pier had been a chic retreat for A1 Capone and "Pretty Boy" Floyd during Prohibition.

The bootleggers and their flappers came to dance to the big-band sounds of Benny Goodman and Ted Weems in an open-air pavilion at the end of a long wooden pier that jutted out into the lake and, hence, gave the town its name. The pier sank during the 1950s and the gangsters all disappeared—until Bobby Nauss arrived.

Bobby selected Luna Pier for its location and serenity. He wanted to live around the water and he thought this type of quiet town would provide the perfect cloak of anonymity to conceal his secret from the rest of society. But now, because of this damned TV show, he was afraid the last five years of his life were about to go right up the chimney in smoke.

Bobby met a woman in 1984 in Dearborn, Michigan, not long after he'd escaped from Graterford. She was perfect for someone on the lam—around thirty-five, unmarried, and childless—and she owned her own home on the south side of Detroit. Her biological clock had almost run down and she was pretty much resigned to the fact she was never going to get married or have children.

She wasn't tall and she wasn't particularly attractive. Her hair was dull and she was overweight. But the adjective that best describes her is *naive*. *Trusting* is a close second. And when she met Bobby, *starry-eyed* became a third. She just couldn't believe this good-looking, virile hunk of a man could be interested in her and she was determined not to do anything that would jeopardize her chances with him.

Bobby introduced himself as Rick and said he was an orphan. He'd just moved from Delaware. A nasty divorce. He came to Michigan to get his life back together and he didn't like talking about his past.

"If I'm lucky," he told her, "I'll find the right woman and settle down and have kids."

* * *

Bobby celebrated the first anniversary of his escape by getting married in Toledo. The date was November 16, 1984. The name listed on his marriage license was Richard Ferrer, and it said he was born in South Carolina.

They moved into his new wife's home and she had two sons during their first two years of marriage: Steven and Nick.

Her husband always had money. She didn't know where it all came from—he never worked. There were the business trips from time to time. Two or three days at a clip. Real estate deals she didn't exactly understand. But they never wanted for anything. When she hinted they needed a bigger car to handle the boys, he went right out and bought her a GMC Suburban wagon. There was one time, just after Labor Day in 1986 (which coincided with Hans Vorhauer's capture), when he had more money than she'd ever seen in her life.

He dragged the whole family along on a six-hour drive some 250 miles north on I-75 to the Upper Peninsula. Just like that, he peeled off $35,000 in cash for prime beachfront campground on Lake Superior in the tiny town of Brimley, which was as close as he could get to Canada and still be in the United States. It was called Whiskey Bay Park and he titled it by using her maiden name as his own last name—she couldn't quite understand why, but it seemed to make sense when he explained it. Something about being afraid his ex-wife might get her hands on it.

When she got pregnant for the third time, he told her to quit her job. He said he'd rather have her home raising the children than working. With twenty-one years as a secretary for Wayne County, she drew a monthly pension of $1,000 per month, which became the extent of their reportable income.

They moved into a mobile home at the campground in July 1987 and put her home up for sale. There were two run-down cabins and an old cottage on the property and he began renovating them as soon as they arrived.

Their neighbors in Brimley said the Ferrers kept to themselves and that "Rick" was vague about his past.

"He said he bought old homes and fixed them up," recalled Bobby's next-door neighbor. "He'd get calls in the middle of the night and say he had to go down to Detroit right away because he was selling a house and a deal was suddenly coming through. Then he'd show up a week or so later and he'd be flush, if you know what I mean. He'd have lots of cash."

Which is also what the neighbors remember most about his wife.

"She went grocery shopping with hundred-dollar bills," recalled one neighbor, "and she did her shopping in the resort stores where the tourists shop. Where everything's overpriced. People around here shop in Sault St. Marie, but not her. And she was always buying money orders at the bank to pay her bills. They didn't even have a checking account."

The next-door neighbor's wife was struck by the way Bobby dressed.

"It would be ninety degrees and the rest of us would be running around in swimming suits trying to keep cool," she recalled, "and Rick was always in long flannel shirts. I told my husband he must have tattoos or something."

When their third son, Anthony, was born in 1988, Bobby started looking for a more suitable home for his growing family. In May, he found a duplex on a 90-by-150-foot waterfront lot at 10218 Lakewood Avenue in Luna Pier. It was listed with an actual cash value of $93,566, but they bought it at a sheriff's sale for $70,000. Bobby put down $14,000 in cash and they took out a $56,000 mortgage at the Security Bank of Monroe solely in his wife's name. As soon as they moved in, Bobby started converting it into a single-family dwelling.

Because he liked to fish, Bobby bought a twenty-seven foot Sportcraft cabin cruiser for $30,000 cash shortly after he

moved to Luna Pier. He moored his new boat at the T-Patch
Marina half a mile from the house. He maintained the boat in
spotless condition and he programmed his favorite fishing
holes into the LORAN so all he had to do was push a button
and the boat navigated itself to the best walleye banks on his
end of Lake Erie.

Bobby plotted all week to watch the new TV show in private. He decided his best bet was to take the portable into the
garage on Sunday night. Then at the last minute, his wife
took the kids out for a treat and he was left at home alone.
He sat down in the living room and turned on the TV. The
date was February 14. Valentine's Day.

It was pretty hairy in the months that followed. Every time
he heard a strange noise at night or a knock on the door or a
ringing telephone, Bobby jumped. When he finally started to
get over it and relax a little, *America's Most Wanted* ran another episode about him, in August. All over again, he was
on pins and needles.

A year and a half later, on April 23, 1990, Tom Rapone resigned from the Marshals Service. With him went his passion and obsession to catch Bobby Nauss.

If Bobby were ever apprehended, it would be strictly business.

When Bobby heard that Tom Rapone had quit, he started
breathing easy once again. *America's Most Wanted* had
helped capture more than a hundred fugitives in its first two
years on the air, but Bobby Nauss was not one of them.

John LeBlanc had known Rick Ferrer for two years, ever
since Bobby started docking his boat at T-Patch Marina.
"Chief"—as LeBlanc was called because he was a full-
blooded Chippewa—docked his own twenty-seven-footer at
T-Patch. Bobby impressed him as a quiet, caring father who

was protective of his children. Chief, a retired steelworker, never questioned Bobby's source of income—even though he knew Bobby spent most of his time fishing and didn't hold down a regular job.

"He told everybody that he owns rental homes," Chief LeBlanc recalled, "about six or seven older homes in Detroit—repossessed, I suppose."

In addition, he figured Bobby was a Vietnam veteran who was collecting a disability pension.

"He always complained about his back," Chief LeBlanc continued. "He walked horrible sometimes, like his back was all twisted out of shape."

Chief's wife, Joan, was an LPN and she knew Bobby took prescription muscle relaxers for his back pain.

"But I don't think he even drank," Joan recalled, "and he rarely talked about his family. What little he did say was about the one boy's bad arm. His oldest son developed a condition in his upper arm bone about three years ago and he was concerned about it. They'd had the boy to the Mayo Clinic several times and the University of Michigan in Ann Arbor."

"He always chewed gum," Chief picked up the narrative, "and he never wore a short-sleeve shirt. Plaid flannel shirts in the winter, lighter weight long-sleeve shirts in the summer. I never seen the guy's arms.

"But this guy was beautiful. This guy was nothing but perfect. Ask anyone around and they'll tell you the same thing. I never heard anybody say an ugly word toward him and I never heard him say an ugly word toward anybody else."

The weekend after Tom Rapone left the Marshals Service, Bobby helped Chief LeBlanc add a wooden deck onto his home in nearby LaSalle.

Chief's wife watched the men work. She was impressed by Bobby's methodical work habits. When her husband went into the house to get everyone refreshments, she asked Bobby a question.

"Was your father a carpenter?"

"No."

"Is your father alive?"

"No," Bobby said, "my father was killed in a car accident. My mother, too."

Joan LeBlanc apologized for prying.

Bobby's two oldest sons were starting school in the fall so he asked Joan about the local school system.

"You could do better if you put your boys in parochial school," she replied.

"I'm a little worried," Bobby said. "I don't want them to be exposed to drugs or get involved with hoodlums or mixed up with misfits. You know, a bunch of eight-balls."

When September rolled around, Bobby sent his two sons to the public school. Steven went to kindergarten, Nick to preschool.

Bobby was now thirty-eight years old. He'd been out of Graterford for nearly seven years, married for nearly six. He had three sons, a waterfront home, a boat, and a resort campground—although he'd recently started partitioning the acreage and selling off lots at $5,000 per lot. It had just gotten to be too much work. It wasn't fun anymore and it kept him away from fishing, away from his boat, and away from the marina, which had become the center of his life.

Also, Bobby was looking to trade up to a bigger boat.

"He came down here all the time," a Toledo boat dealer said. "I took him out on the water two or three times since Labor Day. He had his eye on a thirty-foot Black Watch."

On October 22, Bobby drove to Toledo to make a deal.

"He brought me a certified bank check for ninety-five hundred dollars as a down payment," the boat dealer recalled, "and he was willing to pay fifty-seven thousand.

"But I didn't take it. The boat was worth more."

CHAPTER
35

During the nearly seven years that Bobby was at large, thousands of leads were investigated. The Marshals Office in Philadelphia had two filing cabinets and five cardboard cartons full of files.

Out of all that, there was not one positive sighting.

The investigation was stagnant. The task force still existed, but most of the investigators were devoting their time to cases they felt they had a better chance of solving. If Bobby was still alive—and that was a big if as far as the deputies were concerned—it looked as though he was buried so deep in the biker underground, he was lost forever.

On October 30, 1990, at about the same time that an oral surgeon was extracting two wisdom teeth from Janet Doyle's mouth in Philadelphia, the *America's Most Wanted* hotline rang in Washington, D.C. Bobby Nauss's name hadn't been mentioned on the air in more than two years, yet here was a caller with a tip about him.

"He's living with a woman named Toni Ruark," the female caller said.

The lead went from *America's Most Wanted* to Marshals Headquarters in Arlington, Virginia, to the Marshals Office in Grand Rapids, Michigan.

Two deputies from Grand Rapids failed to locate any Toni
Ruark at the address the anonymous caller had given to the
hotline operator at *America's Most Wanted*. But they did ob-
tain a forwarding address.

Grand Rapids called Detroit shortly after 1:30 P.M.

Bobby Nauss may be currently residing in your district,
was the word given to Ken Briggs. It was one chief deputy
passing the buck to another.

Ken Briggs, who'd spent twenty years with the Marshals
Service, liked to get personally involved with Top Fifteens.
He treated the lead as if it were the first one he'd gotten on
Bobby Nauss instead of the hundredth. The Marshals Office
in Detroit had its own file of look-alikes, follow-ups, and
collateral leads on Bobby. Four inches thick.

Briggs dispatched two deputies to follow up the new lead.
He gave them the address and told them to set up on the
house and look for activity.

"Just another look-alike," one of the deputies said on his
way out the door.

"Humor me," Briggs shot back.

It takes thirty-five to forty minutes to drive from Detroit to
Luna Pier. While the deputies were in transit, Ken Briggs ran
a background check on 10218 Lakewood Avenue, the forwarding address Grand Rapids had given him on Toni
Ruark. He soon established that the telephone and utilities
were being billed to a Toni Ferrer at P.O. Box 430 in Brimley.

At 2:30 P.M., the deputies checked in with Briggs.

"There's three small white boys and one small white girl
playing in the front yard," one of the deputies told Briggs.
"There was also a white female, approximately forty years of
age, but she just went inside."

"Vehicles?"

One of the deputies looked across the street. It was the day
before Halloween and dozens of tiny pumpkins were hanging from a tree in the front yard. A huge ghost cutout looked
out of one of the front windows. In the horseshoe driveway

were a small fishing boat and trailer, a car, and a black and gray GMC Suburban.

"Two."

"Give."

"Michigan . . . 0-1-4 . . . N-L-T. Michigan . . . "

The vehicles came back registered to Richard Ferrer.

"I did a driving history on Richard Ferrer," Ken Briggs explained later. "When I found out he'd gotten a hell of a lot of tickets recently in Pennsylvania, I said, *Something's fucked up*."

This Richard Ferrer, if he lived in Luna Pier, what the hell was he doing getting all those tickets in Philly?

Ken Briggs ordered a CCH (criminal history) on Richard Ferrer. It showed he'd served time in Graterford. Briggs then ordered Bobby's CCH. When it came through, Briggs set the two criminal histories side by side and compared them: Richard Ferrer and Bobby Nauss did time together at Graterford.

Briggs called Graterford Prison.

"When I found out they were once cellmates," he explained, "I knew I had him."

Ken Briggs phoned the Marshals Office in Philadelphia and requested a visual check on Richard Ferrer to determine that he was, in fact, physically present in Philadelphia. Then Briggs—along with three more deputies, two of them females—drove directly to the state police barracks in Erie, Michigan, which was close to Luna Pier.

Before they left, Ken Briggs instructed the deputies, from this point on, nobody could be trusted. Not the state troopers. Not the local cops. Nobody. If this turned out to be a go, he'd personally brief any outside law enforcement personnel that might be needed.

"And one more thing: No radio transmission until further notice. The son of a bitch might be listening."

Steve Quinn sent two deputies to the real Richard Ferrer's home in Philadelphia. Then he phoned Janet Doyle at home.

Full of painkillers from her oral surgery, she was groggy
when she answered the phone.

"I think we just made Nauss," Quinn told her.

"Right," she said sarcastically. "Tell me another one."

"Seriously," Quinn said. "We're about eighty percent sure.
You better come in."

In no condition to drive, Janet Doyle called a friend and
arranged a ride into the office.

At 4:05 p.m., a man and a woman knocked on Bobby's
front door. The two deputies, sitting in an unmarked Chevy
Lumina, watched intently from across the street. The door
opened and a white male—clean-shaven with short, dark hair
and wearing light green work pants and a green and black
plaid shirt—allowed the couple to enter.

Ten minutes later, the couple came back out.

Because of the radio silence, the deputies were on their
own. They took a chance, drove halfway down the block,
and approached the couple. Who were they? And what were
they doing?

He was running for the Monroe County Board of Commis-
sioners, the man explained, and he was doing some door-to-
door campaigning for the upcoming election. The woman
was his wife.

One of the deputies showed them a photo spread.

"Do you know this man?"

"It's Rick Ferrer," the politician said. "We just left his
house."

The deputies asked them what they knew about him.

"He moved here with his wife and kids two years ago,"
the husband said. "They seem like nice people. I even sold
him my car last summer."

"Rick's quiet," said the wife, "and easy to get along with."

"Sir," one of the deputies told the politician, "it's *very* important that neither you nor your wife say anything about this
to anyone. Is that understood?"

He said he and his wife could be trusted.

On one hand, the deputies felt confident that they'd confirmed the first sighting of Bobby Nauss. On the other hand,
they might have jeopardized the surveillance. If the couple
warned Bobby, if a neighbor called Bobby and innocently
mentioned seeing two strangers stopping people on the
street and asking questions, if Bobby had glanced out the
window and seen them himself, he could be spooked into
flight.

At 4:50 p.m., Bobby, Toni, and their three sons left the
house. The boys were all wound up, talking about the costumes they were going to wear the following night when
they went trick-or-treating. Everyone got into the GMC Suburban and they drove away.

The deputies followed at a safe distance. When the GMC
turned into the T-Patch Marina a few minutes later, the
deputies kept going.

It was five o'clock.

Growing up in Darby, Bobby used to call this Mischief
Night and he'd go out and soap people's windows and throw
eggs at passing cars. In Michigan, they call it Devil's Night.
To a boater, the night before Halloween means the seasons
are changing. Fall is on its way out and winter is on its way
in. It's getting cold and it's time to winterize the fleet.

In fact, Bobby had spent most of the past two weeks helping friends get their boats out of the water for the winter.
That was what was bringing him to the marina at that very
moment. Helping a buddy put his boat away.

He told Toni it would take about an hour.

At 5:35, two deputies knocked on Richard Ferrer's door in
Philadelphia.

At 5:50, Ken Briggs' office phoned him at the Erie state
police barracks.

"Richard Ferrer is, in fact, in Philadelphia."

*   *   *

At 6 P.M., Ken Briggs arrived at the Luna Pier Police Station with five deputy marshals and four state troopers.

The officer on duty was overwhelmed. He had no idea what was going on, but figured the guy in the shirt and tie was in charge.

Briggs told him he was conducting a surveillance in Luna Pier because he'd received a tip that a man going by the name of Richard Ferrer was suspected of being a prison escapee from Pennsylvania. That's all Briggs told him.

Bobby's home was situated on a fingerlike peninsula at the southern tip of Luna Pier, surrounded by Lake Erie and inland waterways. Bobby's street, Lakewood Avenue, turned into a dead end just seventy feet past his house. There was only one way in or out. By land.

Ken Briggs stationed two unmarked cars at the dead end.

Briggs' Astrovan, a state police car, and a Luna Pier police car were sitting in a parking lot at the western edge of town, out of sight, between Luna Pier and I-75. It was the only road out of town.

At 6:45, the Ferrers' GMC left the marina. When it passed the parking lot where Briggs was hiding, it made a right turn toward home. Briggs pulled out. The state troopers fell in after him, followed by the Luna Pier PD.

A short while later, the GMC made another right, onto Lakewood Avenue. When it crossed Fifteenth Street, Briggs broke radio silence.

"He drove right into our net," Briggs explained later. One of the state troopers pulled around Briggs and flashed his warning lights. That was the signal for the deputies at the far end of Lakewood Avenue to make their move. "We converged on him in the middle of the block."

"Uh-oh, Daddy," one of Bobby's sons said from the backseat of the GMC, "we're not wearing our seat belts."

Marshals learn firsthand how heart-wrenching it is for a

wife and children to see their husband and father arrested. Whenever possible, they try to avoid going in like gang-busters and dragging the fugitive off in handcuffs in front of his family. They also learn firsthand how dangerous a felony vehicle stop can be. In this case, they were dealing with a Top-Fifteen fugitive, an escaped murderer. As Ken Briggs would admit later, Bobby Nauss "was the most dangerous fugitive I'd ever encountered in my twenty years with the service, and I wasn't taking any chances."

When the GMC stopped, everyone went in together with their guns drawn. They dragged Bobby out of the driver's seat, threw him on the ground, and patted him down. They cuffed him, stood him up, and rolled up his left sleeve to look at his tattoos.

Meanwhile, Bobby was denying everything.

"That was when his wife went ballistic," Briggs recalled.

"What are you doing to my husband?" she screamed hys-terically. "What's going on? This is some sort of mistake! He hasn't done anything wrong!"

Toni Ferrer was crying out loud.

The female deputy marshals and a female state trooper had their hands full trying to calm her down and looking after the children at the same time.

"Take his shirt off," Ken Briggs said, and a deputy pulled off Bobby's shirt. As soon as Briggs saw the big blue parrot on Bobby's right bicep, he knew for sure he had his man.

"I assure you," Ken Briggs said to Toni Ferrer at that point, "I'm going to relate a story to you in a little while. When I'm done, you won't have any doubt in your mind that this is no mistake."

But Toni Ferrer never heard a word Briggs said.

She was busy telling herself, *This isn't happening to me. My kids aren't really going through this.*

By then, neighbors were coming out of their homes to see what the commotion was all about.

* * *

Bobby Nauss, Top-Fifteen fugitive, on the lam for seven years, was seated and cuffed in the backseat of a cop car speeding toward the state police barracks to be fingerprinted.

"He was well versed on what to say," Ken Briggs recalled, "and what not to say. He was being very cold about the whole thing, denying who he was."

Briggs spun around to face him.

"What about your wife? What about your kids?"

Bobby didn't admit who he was until after his fingerprints confirmed his identity. He still refused to give Ken Briggs any information, other than saying his wife knew nothing about the whole thing.

Briggs spent an hour with her and came away with that same impression. So he released Toni Ferrer.

She consented to a search of their home and allowed deputies to accompany her. The search failed to find any weapons, drugs, or large sums of money. But they found a scrap of paper in a bedroom drawer that listed Richard Ferrer's family tree. In addition, Bobby had a complete set of identification in Ferrer's name.

When Briggs examined the evidence later that night, he remarked, "He probably knew more about Ferrer's family than you and I know about our own brothers and sisters."

CHAPTER
36

Shocked. That word best described Toni Ferrer's frame of mind.

Stunned disbelief. That was the emotional climate around Luna Pier.

The Monroe *Evening News* said it all: KILLER FUGITIVE LED DOUBLE LIFE. A picture of a dejected-looking Bobby Nauss, both sleeves rolled up to his shoulders to reveal his telltale blue parrot tattoo, was beneath the headline, page one, top right.

"Is he a brutal murderer, rapist, one-time member of a vicious motorcycle gang, and a drug dealer?" the story asked in its opening line. "Or is he a loving father and husband, friendly neighbor, and avid outdoorsman?"

A group of mothers stood at the school bus stop the morning after Bobby's capture. Toni Ferrer's neighbors. They talked among themselves the way people do when they witness a catastrophe and can't believe what they just saw. A reporter walked up and introduced himself. Everybody nodded.

As he was about to start asking questions, Toni Ferrer came out of her front door. Her eyes were red. Her two older boys, wearing Halloween costumes, were running to keep up with her. As far as she was concerned, her children had endured a good dose of grief the night before and they weren't going to miss out on the school parties they'd been anticipating all week.

She walked up to one of her neighbors and they hugged.

"I had no idea," Toni said, and she started crying on her friend's shoulder.

The school bus arrived shortly and picked up the children. Toni Ferrer was headed home when the reporter stopped her. He tried to tactfully ask her what it was like to live with an escaped murderer for all these years.

"He never treated me bad," Toni said, but she couldn't go on. She couldn't stop crying. "I'm sorry, but I've been through a very traumatic experience and I really can't talk about it now."

She walked away.

"Toni's an excellent mom," one of the mothers said after Toni Ferrer entered her home. "She's very protective of her children.

"And I could see it in her eyes just now. She didn't know anything about it."

Another mother volunteered more information.

"He never talked about his past," she said. "He was nice. Nice to his wife. Nice to his baby-sitter. Nice to his kids. If he was mean or something, you'd be able to tell. And they are really good kids.

"All I know is, I feel for Toni very much. I hope she can get through it without too many scars. I feel for the kids, too."

"I woke up at quarter to four this morning," Chief LeBlanc told another reporter. "I know he's going to be thrown into this little-bitty place. But after he's lived the kind of life he's lived around here, this guy ought to be turned loose. Free.

"Is there a possibility they didn't get the right guy?"

Most Luna Pier residents were asking the same question.

Media people were all over town and they found most residents willing to speak out.

"He didn't look like a bad guy," said a neighbor who lived a few doors away, "and he wasn't hiding by any means. If I was in my yard mowing the lawn and he drove by, he'd stop and talk. We both liked hunting and fishing, so he'd ask me about that."

A woman who lived just a few doors down from the Ferrers had witnessed the arrest.

"I kidded my husband," she told a reporter, "that we'd probably see them on *America's Most Wanted*." It turned out to be no joke. John Walsh would announce the show's one hundred and twenty-third capture on the show's next telecast.

"This is a small town where just about everybody knows everybody else," the neighbor continued. "You wouldn't think someone on the run would want to hide here. But I think they've got their facts wrong. He was a great man who never said an unkind word. Ever. I think they've got the wrong man."

Another neighbor said the man he knew as Rick Ferrer lived a "Joe Citizen" life.

A police officer admitted being introduced to Bobby just days before the arrest. They shook hands. At the time, the police officer told Bobby he must have really been a model citizen because he'd never met him.

The mayor of Luna Pier was also taken in by Bobby.

"It's definitely a shock," the mayor said. "The man I knew is certainly not the person I've been reading about. I could have given him the key to the city."

Sentiments ran strongest at T-Patch Marina.

"He was a good friend to a lot of people," the marina's owner said. "If it was a windy day and a guy needed help getting his boat out of the water, he was the first to volunteer to help.

"Just last week he took a bunch of retirees out fishing. It was totally unplanned. They were just sitting around kibitzing and he said, 'Let's go.' That's the kind of guy he was and I wish they never caught him."

The owner's son agreed with his father. He called Rick Ferrer a great guy and suggested that maybe he suffered from multiple personalities.

"Or else," he said, "they have the wrong guy."

But the friend who seemed to take it the hardest was Chief LeBlanc.

"Jesus," he said, "I wish I could have met ten thousand more like him. That cat was really nice. I'd be as good to him tomorrow as I was before they picked him up. But if I could go to jail to see him, I wouldn't. It would break my heart to see him there."

Toni Ferrer was sitting outside her home on Halloween evening. Her parents had driven down from Cadillac, Michigan, to provide moral support. Anthony was asleep inside. Steven and Nick, dressed for bed in Teenage Mutant Ninja Turtle pajamas, were helping pass out candy to the trick-or-treaters who came calling.

"You don't understand what it's been like," she told a reporter, granting her one and only interview. "It's been a big shock, like something out of a movie." She stopped. Toni Ferrer was crying and it took a few moments to regain her composure.

"The man they're telling me about," she continued, "isn't the same man I married. He was a good father to my kids and he was a good husband to me. But the media and the people will draw their own conclusions.

"He's a changed man. He was a good guy. He never beat me. He never beat the kids. People do change. People make mistakes. Get in with the wrong crowd. Use drugs. And that's what makes them do things they wouldn't normally do. That was twenty years ago. He was a kid then.

"I don't know anything about his past and the media's making it sound like we moved into a mansion or something.

This is a normal family house. It looks big, but it needs a lot of work.

"But this is no drug house. There have been no drug sales here. He never used drugs the whole time I knew him and nothing like that happened here. I would never put my kids in that kind of jeopardy.

"Right now, my children are doing all right. We're sticking together and the neighbors have been great. It's been a relief to know they're supportive of us.

"If I can avoid it, I don't want to have to go back to work until the kids are a little older. I don't want to leave them alone yet. I'll have to sell the land in Brimley to make it a little easier. I have no choice. I haven't got a whole lot of money. If I can sell the place, I'll be able to manage. And I might have to sell the boat.

"It's not going to be easy. It's like waking up from a nightmare. My kids don't have a father and I don't have a husband."

CHAPTER
37

Steve Quinn and Janet Doyle escorted Bobby from Detroit to Philadelphia on November 2, 1990. The charter flight took two hours and was uneventful.

"I think he was upset," Janet Doyle said afterward, "but he wasn't extremely emotional or anything like that. He didn't cause any problems and he was very cooperative."

The plane landed at International Airport just before 1:30 P.M. Six police vehicles and twelve law enforcement officers—deputy marshals and state troopers—were waiting on the tarmac.

Shackled hand and foot, Bobby got off the plane wearing green work pants, tan boots, a plaid hunting jacket, and a baseball cap with, ironically, a hooked-fish insignia on its front. The deputies placed him inside a van and an armed convoy transported him to the federal courthouse at Sixth and Market streets.

At a 3:30 hearing, an assistant U.S. attorney dismissed the federal warrant for drug trafficking so that Bobby could be placed back within the state's jurisdiction to resume his prison sentences and to face additional charges incidental to his jailbreak.

After Steve Quinn and Janet Doyle turned Bobby over to a

detachment of sheriff's deputies and prison guards, they walked back to the Marshals Office. Standing in front of the bulletin board that displayed the Marshals' Fifteen Most Wanted fugitives, they stamped Bobby's poster with big block letters: APPREHENDED.

At 7 that evening, four prison guards delivered Bobby to a district courtroom five minutes away from Graterford Prison. A fifth guard was videotaping every step of the proceedings.

In the same attire he'd worn all day, minus the baseball cap, Bobby entered the courtroom.

Pauline Nauss's loud sobs filled the small room as soon as she saw her son for the first time in seven years. She rushed up to Bobby and embraced him.

"I love you," she said through her tears. "We all love you."

Bobby looked up, over his mother's shoulder. Standing in a group at the rear of the courtroom were eight more family members. Brothers and sisters. A nephew. His son, Tommy, by then seventeen years old and a senior at Bonner High.

Bob Nauss, Sr., was not there. Nor was Cookie. Nor Toni Ferrer.

"Are you Karen?" Bobby asked, trying to recognize siblings he hadn't seen since before he escaped in 1983. "Sharon?"

Pauline Nauss told Bobby she'd called Toni and introduced herself. She'd spoken to her new grandsons.

"I just got a letter from the boys," Bobby said. "It was like a card. One looks like Kevin and another's the spitting image of Steven." Bobby was referring to nephews.

The magistrate than entered and cut the reunion short. He bound Bobby over for trial on escape and criminal conspiracy charges.

When the forty-minute hearing ended, the magistrate allowed Bobby to spend an additional ten minutes with his family. At the end of that brief meeting, Pauline Nauss said good-bye to Bobby and used a tissue to blot tears away from her eyes as the guards led her son out of the courtroom in chains.

From there, the guards returned Bobby to Graterford to be placed under solitary confinement. A few days later, he was transferred to the state penitentiary near Pittsburgh to be closer to his family in Luna Pier while awaiting trial on his new charges.

At the time of Bobby's capture, Tom Rapone was a Delaware County commissioner.

"Sometimes it takes longer," he said, "but it's another case that was solved. The bottom line is: It's a sad, sad affair. Many people have been hurt by this whole escapade. That is really a crime itself."

Four witnesses testified against Bobby at his trial ten months later in September 1991. The trial took only fifteen minutes.

As expected, Judge Samuel Salus convicted Bobby of escaping from Graterford Prison in 1983—Bobby had earlier waived his rights to a trial by jury—but the judge found him not guilty of criminal conspiracy.

Four months later, on January 17, 1992, Bobby returned to court for sentencing. At that time, Bobby's lawyers introduced several letters from residents of Luna Pier, testimonials to Bobby's character.

"I believe that, for whatever reason," Judge Salus said to Bobby after hearing the contents of the letters, "through maturity or marrying a good woman, you've turned yourself around despite your abysmal past.

"Is there anything you would like to say?"

"My life in Michigan," Bobby told the judge in a steady voice, "was what it should have been had I left out the bad parts. I wish I could have left out the bad parts."

Judge Salus then sentenced Bobby to an additional three and a half years in prison.

EPILOGUE

The very next day, January 18, 1992, Bobby Marconi experienced chest pains while he was walking through the cemetery visiting his mother's grave. At the time, he was on a weekend furlough from Graterford Prison, where he'd been serving time for drug and weapons convictions since 1990.

I first met Bobby Marconi more than thirty years earlier, in high school. He went to Bonner and I went to Clifton Heights. At one point, we both dated the same girl. Even back then, he was considered a shady character. I'd followed his exploits through the years, but hadn't seen him for more than a decade.

Bobby Marconi died later the same day from an apparent heart attack.

It was less than a month later that I met with Steve Quinn at the Marshals Office at Sixth and Market streets.

"I'm gonna give you a little hint," he told me. "I don't think this investigation is over. I think we're finding out that Nauss was involved in a lot of shit while he was in Michigan."

A week later, on February 21, 1992, a task force of state and federal officers arrested Chopper Rigler on his twenty-

275

acre farm in Montrose, Pennsylvania, north of Scranton, near the New York state line. He was suspected of manufacturing methamphetamine on his farm, distributing same, and laundering money.

The officers found $92,000 in cash and eleven pounds of methamphetamine buried underground on the premises.

They arrested seven other individuals—three of them former Warlocks—in the same sweep. The arrests culminated a three-year investigation.

Thirteen days later, on March 5, 1992, I phoned Tom Rapone in Boston, where he is now the public safety secretary for the state of Massachusetts.

"Rick Martinson," Rapone told me, "who is still the behind-the-scenes president of the club—I believe, I truly believe—he knew where Bobby was the whole time, and I believe Nauss ran dope for him. I think Nauss was still running dope out of Michigan—using a woman in Ohio as an intermediary—into Pennsylvania, in concert with the Warlocks the whole time.

"About a year and a half before Nauss was arrested, we were on a wiretap up in the Pocono Mountains. That afternoon, we picked up a conversation. Unfortunately, we had the one guy on the wire who wasn't intimately familiar with the case and he didn't recognize the voice.

"Reviewing the recording, we believed that Nauss made the call and was coming in to meet Martinson and Rigler. We were there in force. We'd been there a couple of weeks and we believed Nauss was on his way to meet them for lunch at the Pine Hollow Golf Course. But when we finally hit, he wasn't there.

"There are three guys that I believe knew where Nauss was the whole time—Martinson, Rigler, and Tony Merkle, maybe one or two others—but they would die before they admitted it."

*   *   *

Three weeks later, on March 27, 1992, DEA agents arrested Rick Martinson at a public telephone booth in the town of New Tripoli, sixteen miles northwest of Allentown, Pennsylvania.

Later, at Martinson's home, the agents conducted a search and seizure operation. In an aviary that was attached to the house, they found an extensive collection of exotic birds—some of them valued as high as $15,000 per bird—which Martinson was believed to be breeding and selling.

In addition, they found financial records that indicated Martinson had nearly $600,000 in money-market accounts in twenty-five financial institutions and they seized $100,000 in gold coins and silver ingots and $100,000 in cash. They also seized more than eleven acres of real estate worth more than $1 million and learned that Martinson also owned forty acres of property in rural West Virginia.

The agents found fifteen aliases, sixteen social security cards, records of five rented mailboxes at locations in the United States and Canada, and several machine guns.

At the time of the arrest, the authorities described Martinson as an enforcer for the Warlocks and a supplier of falsified identification cards.

Although only eleven ounces of meth were found in a storage locker belonging to Martinson, intelligence information gathered during the course of the investigation led the federal agents to believe that Rigler, Martinson, and Bobby Nauss—who they believed was operating a meth lab he'd constructed in Wisconsin shortly after Hans Vorhauer's capture in 1986—collectively manufactured approximately a hundred pounds of meth twice a year.

Six weeks later, on May 10, 1992, Mother's Day, Tony "Mudbone" Merkle played a game of Russian roulette and lost. He died from a single, self-inflicted wound to the head.

* * *

I was talking to Janet Doyle six weeks later. The date was June 25, 1992.

"It's not over," she said to me. "There's no doubt in my mind. I'm sure Steve [Quinn] told you that Rick Martinson just got arrested. The thing is, I said to Steve from the very beginning, I said, 'Martinson is behind Nauss's escape.' Nobody believed me, but I guarantee you, when all this is over, you're going to find out I'm right.

"Steve and I were joking around the other day. When Nauss was arrested in Michigan, they found a Pennsylvania driver's license in Nauss's possession in the name of Richard Ferrer, but it had Martinson's picture on it. It was dated 1986. When we found out, I said, 'See, didn't I tell you? If they had no contact, how would Nauss have gotten the driver's license with Martinson's picture on it?'

"And then the U.S. Attorney's Office—through search warrants when they just arrested Martinson—found a poem his live-in girlfriend had written to Nauss, a joke-type poem mentioning money and how lucky he was that he lasted six years.

"So there's no doubt in my mind that Nauss was working with Martinson the whole time he was out. We're going to find out so much in the next year, by the time the book comes out, you're going to have to write a sequel.

"What went on between Martinson and Nauss was unbelievable."

I received a phone call from Bobby Nauss's lawyer near the end of April 1992. I was expecting the call.

I'd spent a couple of days in Luna Pier, getting the feel of the community, talking to the police, talking to some of Bobby's friends at the marina, reading letters he'd written from prison after his arrest—pipe dreams about appeals and getting out of jail—and I'd left my phone number on purpose, hoping to precipitate a meeting with Bobby.

The lawyer advised me that Bobby was against the publication of this book and refused to speak to me.

*   *   *

I first met Bobby Nauss in 1971. I hung out at the same bars, attended some of the same parties, saw him and his Warlock buddies in action. Once, I had to commando-crawl out of a saloon to avoid being hit by stray bullets when a disturbance suddenly broke out. More than once, I felt a lump of cowardice knotting up in the pit of my stomach as I watched Warlocks, suddenly and for no apparent reason, gang up on some innocent bystander and stomp him senseless, afraid to intervene because I knew, if I did, I'd be the next victim.

They were dangerous people.

From what I've been able to observe through the years, Bobby Nauss is a pathological liar.

He lied to his parents; he lied to his brothers and sisters; he lied to Cookie; he lied to Tommy; he lied to the police; he lied to the judges; he lied to the juries; he lied to the psychiatrists and psychologists; he lied to Toni Ruark; he lied to Steven, Nick, and Anthony; he lied to Chief LeBlanc; he lied to Luna Pier— and he lied to himself.

He lived a lie.

If Bobby Nauss says he's sorry, he means he's sorry he got caught.

Bobby Nauss was a thief, a drug trafficker, a rapist, and a murderer.

If he didn't kill one or some or all of the girls whose cases remain unsolved, he knows who did. Debbie Delozier's mother died a couple of years ago. She went to her grave never knowing who killed her daughter, never seeing justice served. I don't know where Denise Seaman's mother is today, but I bet she'd like to know who killed her daughter. See that person punished.

"Being that it's unsolved," Mary Ann Lees' mother told a reporter in 1992, "it's never behind you."

"I would hope," Layne Spicer's mother told the same reporter, "that they might be more mature by now and come forward."

But that probably won't happen.

* * *

"Martinson and Nauss possess the information on all of the unsolved murders," Tom Rapone told me in his office in Boston in April 1992. "If not factual, they have hearsay that law enforcement does not have.

"But they won't be solved."

Frank Hazel, a Delaware County judge for the past thirteen years, shares the same view. But he takes a more philosophical outlook toward the unsolved Marsh Murders.

"Those who have committed the murders have been punished," is the way he put it to me. "They are no longer among us."

The last time I spoke with Assistant U.S. Attorney Carl Lunkenheimer, at the end of August 1993, he advised me that Chris "Chopper" Rigler had been sentenced to twenty years in December 1992 and that Rick Martinson had pleaded guilty in January 1993 and received a ten-year sentence.

Bobby Nauss is currently serving a life sentence at the Western State Correctional Institute near Pittsburgh for murdering Liz Lande in the middle of a December night in 1971 shortly after making love to her. After that sentence expires, there are other sentences remaining to be served.

According to Assistant U.S. Attorney Carl Lunkenheimer, Bobby Nauss is actively pursuing appeals on several of his convictions.